DATE DUE

JAN 2 7 2015		
MAR 1 8 2015		
JUL 0 6 2015		
NOV 0 2 2015 MAR 2 9 2016		
		ıre Sensitive

D1042565

Ashes
of Twilight

Kassy Tayler

St. Martin's Griffin ⚞ New York

ASHES OF TWILIGHT. Copyright © 2012 by Cindy Holby. All rights reserved. Printed in the United States of America. For information, address St. Martin's Press, 175 Fifth Avenue, New York, N.Y. 10010.

www.stmartins.com

ISBN 978-0-312-64178-8 (hardcover)
ISBN 978-1-250-01824-3 (e-book)

First Edition: November 2012

10 9 8 7 6 5 4 3 2 1

In memory of Oliver Ray Hodge and
Robin Rae Hodge

Acknowledgments

◆

Writing a book is a long and sometimes difficult journey. It always helps when you have someone who understands the process. And I am so blessed to have several someones. My wonderful agent, Roberta Brown, who believes in me and is always there no matter what the time or circumstance. My adorable editor, Holly Blanck, who immediately saw the potential for this story. My writing posse, the werearmadillos, who are always there to share the ups and the downs and the craziness that is the world of publishing. I love all of you more than dark chocolate and peanut butter combined.

And of course, my husband, who keeps asking me if he can retire yet. Maybe someday soon, my love.

· Ashes of Twilight ·

· 1 ·

The Bible teaches us that the heavens and earth were made by the one true God. I have heard these things all of my life but I dare not ask the questions that the lessons have created in my mind. I am certain I know quite a bit about the earth, as I spend most of my waking moments within its clanking iron bowels. The heavens, however, are a mystery to me as my world is hollow and my sky is made of glass. As I lie on my back and stare up at the thick dome that covers my world, I still cannot help but wonder why?

Our history is taught in two stages. There is the before time, when man lived on the surface and roamed at will. He built great cities and sailed the oceans and conquered kingdoms. Then there is the after time, when man created the great glass dome to protect all he knew from the mighty comet that came in 1878 and burned up the sky. It is the one hundred and ninety-eighth year since the world became the dome, and I spend all of my waking moments trying to find a way to leave it.

Staring at the dome will not give me a way out. I do it to justify my wanting to escape. I am desperately seeking a sign that the earth has returned to what it was before the comet came. I need to know for certain that I will not be burned to a crisp if and when I do find a way out. Occasionally, in the morning light, I see a shadow cross over, but the glass is too thick for it to be defined. I never see the flames that are rumored to be out there, and I often wonder if the flames are just an excuse, given by the royals, who run our society, to keep us within.

"Hey now, get on wit ya." I recognize the voice and know that it holds no threat, even though his words are harsh. "If the filchers find the likes of you up here they'll be throwing you in the fires for certain."

I am not supposed to be on the rooftops, and to be caught would be costly. Max is okay though. It is his job to clean this part of the dome from the constant buildup of ash and smoke. The rooftops, many stories above the smoke-shrouded streets below, are home to the gardens that supply the vegetables we need to survive. The gardens are placed there so they can soak up the meager light that shines through the thick glass, and also benefit from the condensation that builds up beneath the dome and falls back down like the rain that was said to fall upon the earth from the sky.

I'm in no hurry to go. Instead, I stand, stretch, and walk to the edge of the building. Below me, in all directions, the city lies, just now coming awake with the morning light. To my left is where the royals live, and as usual my eyes go there first. From my vantage point above, their tall and skinny houses look like miniature palaces with their small, neatly manicured lawns and fences along the sidewalks that are even now being scrubbed clean. I've never been in their part of the city. It is forbidden for workers like me to go to that side of the dome.

Lucy, who is a shiner like me, has been there many times. She works for a laundry and is often sent to pick up bundles and make deliveries. She's told us about it, me and my friend Peggy, about the lawns painted a bright green so they will look like grass and the trees made of copper. They are too far beneath the light to grow real trees and grass so they pretend it's as it was in the before time. I've never seen grass but I know the trees on top of the building. I've felt the bark and touched the leaves. I can't imagine one made of metal. It has to be cold and rigid. It can't sigh and sway with the wind from the fans.

To the right is the industry. The foundry and the stockyards, the butchers and tanners, all lie under a haze of smoke. Cattle, pigs, and sheep live their entire lives in small pens. Every bit of breeding is controlled and every part of the creature is used when their lives are done. Linking the two sides are the smaller businesses. The weavers, cobblers, laundries, and bakeries, all small businesses run by descendants of those who were chosen to serve the royals. We all work to preserve the bloodlines and way of life for the royals, so that only the best of humanity will continue. The best as was chosen all those years ago by people who have long since been gone.

The small businesses are housed on the street level, and above them are the homes of the workers, all living in as little space as possible so that the royals may continue on with their way of life as if nothing for them has ever changed. They walk their dogs on their pristine sidewalks and have their parties and the finest our world has to offer, while the rest of us survive on what's left.

One long thoroughfare, called the promenade, goes from the royals' side to the other. In the center of the dome the promenade splits around a huge fountain with statues around it, a tribute to the creators of our world. This is where we go for news and the representatives of each union meet with the city officials. The tallest buildings look over the fountain and the small businesses. They house the government of our world along with the great library and the museum, all places I'm not allowed to go but am expected to work my entire life to preserve. These are the rooftops I haunt every morning to watch the light come and wonder why.

The scientists who designed the dome all those years ago were the greatest minds of the time. Unfortunately they are long gone and we have become victims of a sedentary government who will look no further than the dome that surrounds them. They are caught up in the here and now with no plans for our future. All they care about is the rules and law that they hand down to us, without any thought as to how it impacts our lives.

Max is right in his warning to me. I do not belong on the rooftop, and if I am caught I will be punished. The filchers do not care about rhyme or reason; they only care about the reward. They use any infraction, even those imagined, as a means to their end. Shiners, like me, are their favorite quarry.

"You going to stay up here all day?" Max asks.

"I'm going." I stand on my tiptoes and kiss him on the cheek. He rolls his eyes at me before going to work with his long-handled mop. I hear the squeaking of gears and pulleys that are attached to the huge iron girders that crisscross the glass. Men, riding the baskets that will take them to the uppermost part of the dome, call out to one another in greeting. Day has come to my world and it is time for me to sleep.

"I reckon I'll see you in the morning," Max calls out.

"You will."

"Be careful down there, gel."

"I always am." I put my goggles over my eyes to protect them from the tainted air below. I could take the myriad of staircases attached to the side of the building, but instead I head to the downspout. It is faster, and there is no chance of me running into a filcher on the way.

"Wren!" Max comes to where I'm propped against the building, my hands on the downspout and my feet braced. An angry sparrow swoops around my head and scolds me for being so close to its nest. "The filchers are hungry. People have been disappearing, most of them young and pretty like you. There's plenty of rumors afoot. All of them bad. Stay below where it's safe."

My heart pounds at his words. No one wants to mess with the filchers. They roam about the underside of the dome, a law within themselves. The bluecoats, our word for the security force in our society, turn a blind eye to their activities because they are useful to them. They do their dirty work for reward, and act as bounty hunters when someone is wanted for an infraction.

There are two sets of laws within our society. Laws for the royals, who because of their pure blood are held in the highest esteem, and laws for the rest of us, those who were chosen to serve. The laws are not the same, as we are not considered the same.

Max looks at me, his eyes expectant. He cannot see mine through the goggles I wear. I have no choice but to lie. "I will." I descend into the smoke-filled air and hope that no one is waiting below to take me in for trespassing.

The penalty for trespassing is service. My grandfather has warned me against it many times. My mother was caught when she wasn't much older than me. He does not want me to suffer the same fate as her and lose what little bit of freedom I have as a shiner. I only dare go as far as the middle of the dome, where the buildings are the tallest.

The streets, like the city, have come to life since I came above. I take the same path to the lift that I take every day. I pass the same people on the way to their tasks and the same vendors pushing their carts onto the street. Nothing has changed for the royals since the world became a dome, so nothing has changed for those of us chosen to serve. There is no way to aspire to anything above what you've been born to. Occasionally some escape it, especially a girl, if she's pretty enough and smart enough to catch the eye of someone who can offer her more without catching the attention of the filchers.

As I have.

I see a filcher as I turn in to the alley that will lead me to the coal tippler. I duck under one of the heavy fans that keep the air circulating beneath the dome. The noise is deafening, but luckily for me, my senses are keen from the years spent living underground, and I turn to see him come out of the deep shadows cast by the tall buildings. He wears the leather mask that disguises his face yet identifies him as one to fear. It gives him the look of a monster without features while his eyes remain hidden beneath small goggles.

What does the mask hide? I never want to be close enough to find out. I run and he takes off after me. My mind races with my feet as I dash onto a busy street. How long have they been following me? Why are they chasing me? Max's warning echoes the pounding of my feet. People scatter as I charge down the street. No one wants to challenge the filchers. Ahead, I see another one, waiting at the corner beneath the fan. Does he think I will stop?

I don't. I put my arms out and shove him away as I run by. He crashes into a stack of wooden crates. The fan is so loud that there is no noise, yet I know he is screaming at me to stop. A cat dashes ahead of me, scared at the sudden loss of his shelter. His ears are laid back as he races ahead and jumps into a window well.

The back of my neck feels as if someone is waiting above me with an ax, ready to swing and chop off my head. Fear grips at my heart and gives it a vicious squeeze. It is hard to run through the heavy, smoke-filled air. My lungs labor as I try to suck in my breath beneath the kerchief that covers my mouth and nose. I duck into an alleyway that I know will lead me to safety if I am fast enough, and lucky enough, to reach the shiners who work the coal lift.

I can hear the filchers now, calling out to me, and cursing me, as if that will make me stop. Is this what befell the other girls that Max said had disappeared? Were they foolish enough to stop or had they run into a trap? Will another filcher or even two of them be waiting at the end of the alley to take me down?

I force myself to run harder and faster. I will not stop until I am safe. I burst from the alley into a street that is wide enough for the coal wagons to pass. I hear the clank of a steam engine and the blast of a horn. I just miss being hit by the big cart that hauls the coal to the furnaces as I dash across the street and to the safety of the lift. I stop before it and bend over with my hands on my knees, trying to suck in air.

"What happened to you?"

I look up and see Alex, a shiner who is just a few years older than me. I look back at the alley. No one is there, no one has followed. Could I have just imagined it? I don't want to say anything to Alex because I don't want to have to stay below. I want to see the light come to the dome. I think I would die without it.

"Just trying to get back before Grandfather misses me," I say when I finally catch my breath. "What are you doing above?"

"Walked Lucy to work." We step into the lift and both of us push our goggles up on our heads. My forehead is damp with sweat so I take off my kerchief and wipe it away. Alex drops his around his neck and I can't help but admire the lean look of his handsome jaw. He has no idea what kind of effect he has on me, I hope. As soon as we descend, the sweet damp smell of earth surrounds us and the burning in my lungs disappears. "There've been stories about filchers taking girls. I worry about her," Alex says. "You should be careful too," he adds.

I study Alex as we drop into the earth. A lantern hangs above our heads and sways back and forth as we descend. I can clearly see the details of his face without it as our eyes have adapted over time to the constant darkness that surrounds us. Even though we don't need the light, I would truly miss the warmth of the lantern glow if it were gone. There's nothing lonelier, or more frightening, than being below, in the mines, without a light.

I have to admit that I've always had a thing for Alex. It started when I was young. When I was little I was treated as an outsider in our village by the other children, as my father came from above. Children can be cruel, especially when they are mimicking the things they hear their parents say when they think they are asleep.

Thankfully, Alex recognized my solitude and made an effort to include me. He was the one who taught me how to swim when I was little, and later how to catch the glowfish that live in the underground pools. Even though I longed for him, I always sensed that for Alex, there is only Lucy. I know it is right that they are together, as he is the handsomest of the young men of my generation, with his thick, golden brown hair and piercing blue eyes, while Lucy has lovely alabaster skin and black hair, and eyes that are as dark as the mines.

I think I am much plainer than Lucy, with regular brown hair that refuses to be tamed and my ordinary brown eyes behind the shine. I am often told by those who knew her that I look like my mother. They even say how beautiful she was and how tragic that she came to such an end. I would not know, as she died when I was born and there are no images of her for me to see. My grandfather says I looked like a little brown bird when I was born, and thus my name, Wren, after the tiny birds that live below with us.

"You love Lucy," I say. "It's right that you worry."

"I would die if anything happened to her," Alex says. It doesn't surprise me that he admits it. Alex has always been passionate about everything, from making sure I wasn't lonely when I was a child to saving the weakest baby bird that falls from its nest. Everything he does, he does completely, including loving Lucy. Sometimes I watch him look at her and it is as if he could not breathe without her.

What would it be like to feel that way? To love someone more than your own life? I don't think I will ever know, as there are only so many young men to choose from and none beyond Alex have stirred any feelings in me, and he was nothing more than a foolish young girl's dream.

"It must be hard to find time together," I say. "Since your shifts are opposite."

"That's why I walk her to work and walk her home. It's the only time we can really talk." Alex grins, a flash of white in the ever-deepening darkness around us. "We're second in line for marriage. After Peggy and Adam."

"That's great," I say. Because Alex always included me, the other children finally accepted me and I found a true friend in Peggy. I already knew Peggy and Adam were first in line as it's all she's talked about since Adam asked her to be his wife. The only problem is our people cannot start a new household until a place becomes available. Our city below the earth is small with limited places to live. When someone dies and frees up a home, only then can we marry. Since our life span is not that long because of the disease that eats our lungs, there is always the potential of a house opening up soon. But to Peggy every moment she has to wait to be with Adam seems like an eternity.

"Things would be so much better if we didn't have to wait," Alex goes on. "If we could marry when we choose instead of waiting for a house, or if we could live where we wanted to or work at the jobs we chose, instead of having those things chosen for us."

"They would," I agree, "but that's not the way things are."

"Don't you wish things were different, Wren?"

I shrug. I could tell him that I do. That every morning when I leave my world and seek the rooftops I dream of the world outside, of things I've only heard about and never seen, but to tell him these things would be too personal, as if I went ahead and admitted to him that I've secretly loved him all these years. "This is our world," I say. "It's the only one we've got. It's either this or the flames outside."

Alex studies me carefully. His blue eyes search my face and I can't help but wonder what it is he's looking for.

"I heard that James wants to put your name on the list with his," he finally says. There's a spark in his eyes and I think he's teasing me, and as his words sink in, I suddenly feel as I did when the filchers were chasing me. As if I'm about to stumble into a trap.

"That's the first I've heard of it," I manage to choke out. I look out of the lift, at the dark packed earth that forms the walls of the chute. We are almost done with our descent. I am glad, as this is a conversation I do not want to have.

Alex taps a finger on my forehead as the lift settles to a stop. "Then you must be blind," he says with a quick grin. "To so many things."

I shake my head, denying it, even though I fear it might be true. I follow Alex off the lift and walk right into my grandfather. He is with the leader of our council, Jasper, who walks past Alex and me as if we don't exist. He doesn't look happy, nor does my grandfather. I have a feeling that his unhappiness isn't entirely my fault; still, I fear that my escape may have been short-lived after all.

"Where have you been, Wren?"

There is no sense in lying. I cannot deny where I've been. But it is not as if he's told me not to go. I look into his face, wrinkled with time and the deep creases around his eyes colored with coal. My grandfather is the oldest of the shiners. Most of us die from black lung by the time we reach fifty years of age. There is no cure for it, and those who have it slowly and painfully suffocate because their lungs shrivel up and die inside of them. For some strange reason my grandfather has so far been spared this dreadful disease, for which I am most grateful. Without him I would be an orphan as my grandmother died when I was young and my mother never revealed my father's name. Not that it matters who he is. If he had wanted me my mother would have stayed above with him.

"Above," I say, sparing him the details, as he would not understand.

"Wishing for things that will never be." He shakes his head. "Stay below, Wren. Where it's safe." He steps into the lift.

"Wait! Where are you going?"

"I'm going to tell them once again why we're running out of coal." His voice is weary and he pushes the button on the lift. The gears shift with a hiss of steam and I watch as he disappears from sight.

It is getting harder and harder for the fans to clear the air. Some days are better than others. I noticed when I was above that today was one of the worst. The government blames it on the quality of the coal, which means it is the shiners' fault. How it is our fault that the coal is running out is a mystery to me. Exploratory tunnels have been dug, spreading out in all directions like a giant spiderweb. None have yielded anything so far. Without coal we cannot survive. Coal creates the steam that powers the engines that keep the fans going that circulate the air and keep us from boiling beneath the dome. An underground river serves as a source of water and a coolant for our air. The engines are constantly going, their noise strumming through the dome and reminding all of us of the precariousness of our world. If one thing fails, the rest will follow suit and the world within will end, toppled as easily as a strand of standing dominoes.

I believe with all my heart that it would be a good thing to happen. It would force us to move, to look elsewhere, and to hopefully leave the dome. But what I believe is not to be spoken out loud.

· 2 ·

"Wake up." I open my eyes to find Peggy staring down at me. "We're going to the pit." Her green eyes dance with excitement; still, a chill runs down my spine. The pit is dangerous, but I can't help but want to go. I roll from my bed and run a brush through my hair. I rinse out my mouth as Peggy hands me my clothes. She is impatient, and her excitement rubs off on me as I quickly dress in my work clothes. I have no idea how long we'll be at the pit.

I scoop up some cheese and dried apple and wrap a chunk of bread around it for my meal. I eat as I follow Peggy out of the home I share with my grandfather and down the long series of steps carved into the cave wall.

The original plans of the dome had a designated area aboveground for the miners to live. Dormitories were built around the entrance to the mine. It is my belief that those who designed our world never took into consideration that the miners would want their own lives. That they would want to marry and have children. Considering the years we've been beneath the dome, they would have to know that the only way for the world to continue was for more workers to be born. I can only assume they did not think that providing a community for my kind was important. Our world was designed to give the royals the best chance of survival. Everyone else was brought in to supplement their existence.

Long before I was born a large cavern was discovered. The cavern is shaped much like our dome, but is much smaller in scale. It was formed by an underground river, the same river that is our source of water. At some point in history, long before the dome came into existence, the water changed its course. A small stream still runs through the cavern. It is a source of fresh water and more important, fresh air. We use it as a power source. The rush of the water turns a large paddle wheel, which in turn generates light. This is where we live. As far as I know, no one from above has set foot here. As the coal is delivered above by a steam-powered lift, there is no reason for any of the governing class to come down. As long as we do our jobs and do not cause trouble they leave us alone.

Our homes are small and ramshackle, constructed from stone and wood salvaged from condemned buildings above. Some are on the floor of the cavern and others are set upon the many ledges that surround it. Steps are carved into the stone walls and rope bridges connect some of the more impassable ledges. Networks of lines crisscross the ceiling and are hung with lights. Small birds, mostly wrens and a few bright finches, are trapped below with us. They flit about from line to line, their small, sharp, and shiny eyes watchful for any morsel of food. We are kind to the birds. I believe it is because they are a lot like us, wanting to soar but forever trapped and imprisoned.

The place where I live with my grandfather is small; one room notched into the cavern halfway up the cliff face. There is a stacked stone wall across the front with an opening for a window and a door. Carved steps take us down to our ground level. Cats of all ages, sizes, and colors lounge along the steps and in windowsills. We are as kind to the cats as we are to the birds. The cats keep the vermin at bay. A few shiners keep dogs, but they are mostly small. I've always wished for one, but my grandfather says they are just another mouth to feed and an unwanted expense. We all keep goats for milk and cheese. They are kept penned on the other side of the stream.

Adam, Peggy's intended, waits for us at the bottom of the steps. His eyes light up as they always do when he and Peggy are together. He grins at both of us as we come down.

"You have news?" I ask. I look expectantly between the two of them. If a house had opened up I think I would know, but something could have happened while I slept.

"Adam has been chosen for council." Peggy steps beside Adam and puts her arm around his waist. Adam drops his around her shoulder and their heads tilt instinctively toward each other. I do not envy them their happiness; just like Alex and Lucy, they seem made for each other. Still, it makes me feel lonelier, as if I am intruding on a private conversation. Like Alex, Peggy is one of the few who accepted me and did not hold the circumstances of my birth against me.

"Congratulations." My smile is genuine at Adam's good fortune. Being a member of council, which is our ruling group, is a great honor and will give Adam and Peggy many privileges in their lives together. A better choice of house is one, plus they will always work days and have more time off from their shifts. Wives and husbands get to share in the privileges equally.

"Let's go," Adam says. "The others are already there."

We leave for the pit that lies deep in the earth beneath the dome. My grandfather worked with the crew that discovered it during my first year in the mines. It is so deep that light cannot penetrate it.

Many shiners have dropped torches into it but the glow disappears as the flames fall into the darkness. As a rule, we are forbidden to go there. Still, at times, the youth of our community venture forth, just because it is forbidden and dangerous. Like most young people, we crave excitement, and sneaking off to the pit gives us an alternative to the everyday drudgery of our lives.

There are times when a great wind screams upward from the chasm. It is so powerful that it will knock you from your feet. Some of the young men make a game when the wind comes. One will tie a rope around his waist and two more hold it secure while the one wearing it leans over the abyss. The wind picks him up and he floats upward with his arms extended as if he is a bird. Whoever is flying usually screams his head off and we who watch shriek along with him. As the three of us wiggle through the broken section of the barricade that was supposed to keep us away from the pit, I see that Alex is the one who is going to fly tonight.

There is much celebration with our arrival. Everyone comes to congratulate Adam by shaking his hand and slapping him on the back. The girls give him hugs and then hug Peggy as well. News travels fast in our world, passed along from mouth to ear as we travel through the caverns. Adam's smile is wide and Peggy hangs on to his arm with obvious pride.

I step away. This is not about me; it's about them. Peggy's brother, James, joins me as I move close to the cavern wall. The pit frightens me in a way I cannot explain, so I stay far away from the edge. It is not the height; I have no problem climbing to the roof of the highest building in the dome. Nor is it the darkness. I think it's the unknown that terrifies me the most.

"Great news about Adam," James says. I feel a prickle of discomfort. He is standing so close that I want to lean away. He blocks me from the others. The wall is behind me, the pit to the right and the group to the left. There is no place for me to turn. I feel trapped.

"Yes. I'm very happy for them." How is it that he and Peggy have eyes the exact same color green, yet they seem so different? Peggy's eyes have a spark in them, an innate happiness that shines from the inside. James's seem calculating when he looks at me, as if he's counting my worth. Is it just my imagination? It must be. Everyone loves James, young and old alike. I think back on the words Alex said this morning. James has put us on the list. Would he dare to do so without consulting me? As I look at him I think yes.

"You want to fly tonight, Wren?"

A lock of my hair is twisted in the button of my jacket. James pulls it loose and his fingers brush against my breasts. A shiver crawls down my spine.

Am I being unrealistic about things? Am I wishing for something that doesn't exist? Do I just imagine how things are between Peggy and Adam, or Lucy and Alex? Perhaps it's because I haven't tried. I have never taken the risk. James likes me, Peggy says so and now Alex. What do I have to lose? I give James a small smile of encouragement. "No, I'm happy to watch. Are you going to fly?"

"I might."

He stares down at me, at my mouth, and I lick my lips without thought. It gives me a feeling of power, knowing that he wants me. I decide that tonight I will try to spend time with him, that maybe I will let him kiss me. I look beyond him at the group gathered around Alex and see some of the other girls watching us. They envy me. I smile at James. "Good luck."

James grins and walks back to the group that has moved to the pit. Peggy comes back to join me and smiles broadly. Her happiness is evident and overflowing. She's always hoped that I will like James so we will be sisters. She takes my hand and we step closer to the pit.

Alex is the first to fly tonight. I imagine that he must be scared, yet he glances over at me and tilts his head in the direction of James, who is coiling one end of the rope. All I can do is shrug. I have no idea what to think about anything at the moment.

The wind suddenly screams up from the pit and sets everyone into motion. The rope is quickly looped around Alex's waist. Adam tests it and nods his head. James loops the end around his own waist for stability and another one of the young men, Peter, does the same. Alex looks around and finally spots Lucy.

If I were her, I'd be right beside him, scared for his safety and praying that nothing goes wrong. But Lucy just laughs as Alex leaps out over the pit. He falls and my stomach jumps into my throat until the wind currents catch him and he floats upward with his arms spread.

Alex yells as he soars, a sound full of fear and bravery combined. I imagine that it's the same sound the warriors of old made in battle. It sends chills down my spine and I can't help but scream along with Peggy and the other girls although I stay a safe distance from the pit. Lucy is across from me. She has this strange look on her face, as if she were daring Alex to fly higher and farther and invite death to look him in the face. I am suddenly frightened as I watch her watch him, as if some madness has come over both of them. I look at Alex. His face is contorted and strange and I get the sense that he has passed over into another realm of consciousness. It frightens me even more. One little slip when the wind stops and he could fall into the darkness and be gone forever.

Just as suddenly as the wind starts, it is gone. James's and Peter's hold on the rope tightens and they pull Alex back and up to safety. I suck in air. I did not even realize I'd been holding my breath until

Alex is once more standing on his feet. I taste the salt the wind always brings. Where does it come from, this great wind that blows up from the middle of the earth? Why does it make me think that there is something more out there, something beyond flames and destruction?

Everyone laughs and gathers around Alex to congratulate him on being brave enough to fly. James stands by the pit and looks down into it. I know he's waiting to see if there will be more wind tonight. We never know when it will come, or how long it will last, it just comes and brings a wild recklessness that infects us all.

Alex steps up to the edge next to James. "There are other ways to fly," he says.

Even though he's talking to James everyone quiets and we all watch him, wondering what he'll say next.

"All we need is the courage to do it," Alex continues.

I keep my eyes on him. I realize I can't not look at him. I have this feeling inside, one of dread and excitement mixed together, as if what I'm about to hear will change me forever.

"I believe there is a world out there, outside the dome," Alex says, and his voice carries to all of us gathered around. "I believe there is a way out and all we have to do is find it."

We all stare at him. There are some murmurs in the group, feelings of doubt, surprise, and the inevitable wait to see if it's some kind of joke, yet no one challenges him. I can't help but think . . . no, hope . . . *What if it's true?* What if all my yearning and dreaming for a world outside is more than a dream? What if it truly exists and the flames are a lie?

"If you want to join me," Alex continues. "If you seek a better life, a life where we can be what we want to be and do what we want to do. If you want a life in a world that's real, not a mockery of what once was, then join me. Be a seeker."

A shiver runs down my spine as I stand there, totally captivated by everything Alex has said. For one moment I turn my eyes to Lucy. The look on her face is one of shock. Had Alex not told her how he felt?

"What do you want us to do?" Adam asks. Adam is always sensible and steady. He'll be a good husband to Peggy. The fact that he's willing to join Alex in his venture speaks volumes, especially since he's just been elected to council.

"Let's meet when we can talk more," Alex says. "In the morning when the shift is over. I'll find a place and send word." He picks up a piece of coal and goes to the wall where he draws two curves and joins them together with a slash. "Let this be the sign," he says. "A bird in flight." Smiles and nods of agreement run through the group.

"Night shift starts soon," someone says, and just like that, the excitement is over and we all start to move on in small groups, some of us to work and some of us back to our homes for meals and sleep. As usual, I fall in step with Peggy.

"What do you think?" she asks with a huge smile. "What if Alex is right and there is a real world out there?"

"I don't know," I say honestly. "Wouldn't it be amazing if it was?" I consider it for a moment, of leaving the dome, but that's as far as my mind will go, because the threat of the flames drives me back. "What about the stories?" I ask. "Of those who tried to go out and were burned."

"Maybe that's all they are," Peggy says. "Maybe it's something the ruling council of the dome made up to keep us inside."

"But why?"

Peggy shrugs. "Maybe that's something we can figure out at the seeker meeting." She grabs my arm. "Did I tell you that Mother traded for a piece of silk? It's enough to make a shirt." She goes on, telling me of the latest plans for her and Adam's life together. Our way is lit by lamps, all powered by the waterwheel in our cavern. They are much better than the oil lamps originally used, and much safer, because there is always the threat of a methane gas buildup in the mines.

What were twenty of us dwindles down to ten. Alex and Lucy are in front of Peggy and me, Adam and James behind. I can't help but watch Lucy and Alex. Lucy seems angry and Alex sad.

Peggy notices it also and grabs my arm so that we slow down and give them more space. "I wonder if she's mad at him about this seeker thing," she says. "I think it's exciting, don't you?"

I don't tell her that I don't know what to think. That I need time to think. That the prospect is at once exciting and scary. So I say nothing. The group ahead of Alex and Lucy moves on so now we are down to six. Lucy and Alex turn off into a small tunnel and now we are four, Adam, James, Peggy, and me.

Adam comes up behind Peggy and puts his arms around her waist. She shrieks and giggles as he drags her into another side tunnel and leaves me alone with James, who falls into step with me. I can't help but think that it was a plan on their part so that James and I will be alone.

We walk in silence. I really don't know what to say to James. It is strange, as I've known him my entire life. He's always been there for as long as I can remember. He is just a year older than Peggy, and when we were small he looked upon both of us as pests that had to be tolerated. It is only recently, in the past year or so, that he has looked at me differently. I could feel his eyes upon me, watching me, especially when I am about our underground village.

"What do you think of Alex's plan?" he asks finally as we wind our way upward to the central part of the mine, from where all the tunnels spin off in innumerable directions.

"I think it's going to be more about questions than answers,"

I reply. I try to come up with something else to say, something interesting, but my mind draws a blank. The only other thing I know to talk about is my job, and James already knows all about that. My trips above are something I don't want to share with him.

And yet it's the very thing he mentions. "I've noticed you go above every morning." He takes my arm to stop me. "Do you see someone up there?"

"No." I look at where he holds on to me. His touch is firm and possessive. I search his face. We are close to a lamp and stand within the warmth of its glow. "There is no one to see."

He looks at me intently and I know he is waiting. For the first time in my life, I feel as if I have to explain myself and I don't want to. What I do above is private; it's my own time with my own thoughts, dreams, and desires. To tell James would be to share an integral part of me. I don't want to share with him. I feel as if he'll hold some power over me if I tell him.

"I've put our names on the list," he says.

I am shocked at his boldness. I did not really believe he would have the audacity to do so without telling me. "You should have asked me first."

"Wren . . ." James shakes his head and laughs. "I haven't. I just wanted to see what you'd say."

"What do you expect me to say?"

He shrugs. "Everyone thinks we should be together." He takes both my wrists into his hands. I look down at them, at how his fingers wrap all the way around my arms, like manacles. It's a strange thought and a stranger sensation. A chill rattles my bones.

You haven't given him a chance . . .

"Come on, Wren," he says as he moves his hands up my arms and onto my shoulders. He squeezes them and leans in. "We belong together."

He touches his lips to mine. I am hesitant but I allow it. It's a strange sensation. His mouth is moist and I fight the urge to lean back away from his touch and wipe my lips clean. I really don't know what I'm supposed to do.

Relax . . . I let his lips lead mine. Shouldn't I feel something? There's nothing there but a strange curiosity, as if I'm outside my body watching the two of us from above. I've watched Peggy and Adam enough to know that they really enjoy kissing. I move my lips in the same manner as James and wait to feel something. Anything.

Suddenly James pushes me against the wall. He presses his body against mine and I gasp in shock. His tongue darts into my mouth and I feel something hard pressing against the juncture of my thighs. I feel trapped and I try to break away, but he has my arms locked between us. His tongue is in my throat and I gag. I am tempted to bite down on his tongue, but instead I wrench my head to the side. He buries his head in my neck and bites the tender skin at my nape.

"Stop." I free an arm and push against his chest. "No!" I push again and raise my knee into his groin.

Before I can land a blow he jumps back. "What's wrong with you?" His face twists in anger.

"You were hurting me." I wipe my hand across my mouth and touch the raw place on my neck. The skin isn't broken but I know I'll have a bruise. Something else I'll have to keep from my grandfather.

"Come on, Wren. It's just love play."

"It's not play if I don't love you."

"There's no one else for you but me." He grabs my arm and I immediately jerk it away.

"Stop. I don't want this."

He pushes me against the wall once more and traps me with his arms. He stands far enough away that he'll have time to jump back if I try to kick him. "Yes, you do." His eyes narrow as he looks at me. "You're just playing."

"I'm not playing, James. Let me go."

"You should be grateful I want you. My parents certainly don't approve. They don't mind Peggy being your friend but . . ." He gives me his smile, the one that immediately charms anyone who sees it. The one that always gets him what he wants. "None of the families want you. But I convinced mine that your tainted blood won't hurt their grandchildren."

I shove against his chest and he stumbles back. "What's wrong with my blood?" I'm so angry that I shake.

"Who knows who your mother slept with? A scarab? A filcher? Your father could be anyone. Anyone from up there."

Fire fills my veins. My body feels as if I'm going to erupt into flames. I slap him, hard, across the face.

His head snaps to the side with my blow and he places his hand on his cheek. His other forms into a fist. I push by him and start up the tunnel.

"You'll be sorry," he calls after me.

"I already am."

• 3 •

I am more tired than usual after my shift. I could not stop playing the scene with James over and over again in my mind. I keep asking myself the same questions as I relive each agonizing moment of the kiss. Is there something wrong with me? Do the shiner families really feel that way? Or was it something James said just to convince me that I should be with him? I feel as if what happened was entirely my fault, yet I cannot figure out what I did that was so wrong. Am I simply incapable of love? Am I destined to spend the rest of my life alone since I rejected James? The thought makes me unfit company, even for myself.

I don't want to go to the seekers' meeting, especially if James is there, so I go where my heart leads me. It's probably over with anyhow as I can't imagine Alex letting a meeting, even one that could possibly change our destinies, keep him from walking Lucy to work. As I ride the lift to the surface I can only hope that watching the light come to the dome will clear my mind and restore my spirit.

I decide to change from my usual path after yesterday's scare, in case the filchers are watching for me. I will not walk into a trap, not if I can help it. I go right instead of left and walk toward the slaughter-house. I slide my kerchief up over my mouth and nose to keep out the stench. The air inside the dome feels heavy, laden with smoke, the stench of the animal pens, and the rusty tang of fresh blood. Men, stripped down to their waists, their skin already dripping with sweat, wear heavy aprons over their bare chests as they strip the hides from the morning's butchering. One stares at me as I go by and waves a long knife. He gives me a leer and opens his mouth in a grin that re-veals brown and rotted teeth. I grimace and try not to gag as I pick up my pace and cut back toward the promenade.

I mingle in with the common folk as they move toward the cen-ter of the city. Most are on their way to work, but I spot a few women carrying market baskets and a group of children, too young to apprentice, who turn off into a school. I relax as we come close to the promenade. Here I can blend in with the others, as long as I keep my goggles on. Most everyone wears them to protect their eyes from the smoke that constantly fills the streets. Without them, the silver cast to my eyes will identify me as a shiner. As we move onward the streets widen and the crowd lightens as the people scatter into the side streets and their daily chores.

Whenever I am on the promenade I wonder about my father. Is he one of the many who stroll up and down its length during the afternoons when I am asleep after my shift in the mines? I take ev-ery opportunity I can find to go there, to hide in the shadows of the passageways and study the faces of the royals.

Why do I feel the need to prove that my father is a royal? Will it make the circumstances of my birth any different? For all I know, James could be right; my father could have been anyone. Maybe the reason why my mother didn't name him is because she didn't know who he was. She could have been raped by the filchers, for all I know.

It's happened before, plenty of times. It's something not talked about, yet in a community such as ours it's hard to keep secrets.

Yet my mother managed to keep hers. I don't know why I feel the need to know. Perhaps it is just that I need some sort of validation from him. So I study the royals as they walk their endless circles with their tiny dogs, as they wear their fancy silks and satins that have been carefully tended and passed down from generation to generation. I wonder what his name is and the circumstances that brought about my birth. I don't dare to show myself, yet I can't help but think, if he were by happenstance to see me, would he recognize me? I have been told by many that I look like my mother. Would that be enough proof to claim me as his?

Today I spare no thought for the man who sired me. As I come close to the center fountain I see Alex and Lucy standing on a street corner arguing. I was right; Alex didn't waste time at his meeting. When it was time for Lucy to go to work he left with her.

It is obvious to all around them that they are arguing about something. They stand, facing each other, their bodies rigid with anger, while the tide of workers hurrying to their jobs parts around them. They are oblivious to the dark and curious looks that turn their way. I take shelter behind a street vendor's cart. I don't want them to see me, or maybe it's just that I don't want them to know I see them. I feel as if the pain and hurt that surrounds them will somehow contaminate me. What happened to Alex's high spirits and certainty from the night before? He seemed capable of anything after he flew; he was certainly capable of making everyone believe what he wanted them to believe.

Except for Lucy, it seems.

"Move on." The vendor eyes me, sizing up my clothes and the contents of my pockets in one sharp glance. His cart holds hot chips, steaming within their paper and dripping with oil. My stomach rumbles with hunger. It's been a long time since my hastily eaten meal the night before. I dig into my pocket and pull out a coin, long forgotten and covered with coal dust and lint. I rub it clean on my sleeve and hand it to him. He peers at my face in an attempt to see my eyes through the goggles. He looks over his shoulder toward Alex and Lucy, then back at me. With a grimace of disgust he hands me a paper of chips. "The likes of you should keep your business down below," he grumbles as he trundles off with his cart.

The likes of me . . . Doesn't he know that without the likes of me he would not survive? That without my people there would be no coal, and therefore no fans to keep the air cooled and circulating. When in our history did it become a bad thing to be a shiner? When was the hate born?

I step into an alley and let the bustling street hide me from Alex and Lucy, not that they would notice. I eat a chip, savoring the taste of the bacon grease in which it had been fried. I watch as Alex takes Lucy's hand and she jerks it away. Alex looks stricken. Lucy turns and walks away, leaving Alex standing all alone on the street.

Should I go to him? I want to. I want to soothe his pain, but I am unsure of my motives. Do I really want things to be fine between Alex and Lucy, or do I think that if they break up he might turn to me? What should I do? I stand there, eating my chips and trying to decide what would be the right thing. Before I can come to a resolution, Alex takes off, making my decision for me. He goes opposite of where I think he'll turn. Not after Lucy, not toward the lift, and not to me, which was what I secretly hoped. I think for an instant of following him, and then I decide not to. There will be time to talk to Alex tonight, when we are at work. Time when no one will disturb us.

Daylight now fills the dome. I've missed the coming of the light between my detour and watching Alex and Lucy. I feel empty without the dawning and drained after my exhausting shift. There's nothing for me to do now but go underground and sleep.

I'm not ready. Even though I am weary I decide to stay above, and I move in the direction of my usual place and finish off the chips as I go. My mind is full of so many things: James, Alex, Lucy, Peggy, and Adam. The things that happened last night and the things that might or might not happen in the future.

I watch for the filchers as I walk. I keep to the shadows, close to the buildings and alleyways. A bluecoat stands on the corner ahead so I cut across the street behind a steam-powered cart, laden with fruit and vegetables, on its way to the royals. I try not to stare at the bright red of the apples that are piled high in a basket. We never get fresh fruit below, only dried, and I am tempted to steal one and run. But the bluecoat, the name we use for the security force of our world due to the dark blue uniforms they wear, is too close and I dare not risk it.

I feel his eyes upon me as I turn onto the street that leads to my rooftop. I duck into the alleyway, but instead of climbing the ladders and stairs that lead to my usual perch, I go to the one right beyond it, which is the library. There are no gardens on top of this building; instead, there is a small dome, a miniature tribute to the one that shelters us.

Since there are no gardens above, there are also no steps; instead, iron rungs are bolted to the heavy brick. It's a hard climb, and it hurts my lungs, but I press on. I know the harvesters will be at work now, and they've made it plain in the past that they will not tolerate my presence during their shifts.

Finally I reach the top. I take a moment to catch my breath before I sit down against the short wall that encloses the roof, push my goggles up on my forehead, and look up at the domed sky above me. I know I can't be seen from the other rooftops as I have long considered the best places to hide when I am above. The buildings around me are all taller, but the wall and corner posts on the library roof are great for concealment.

A shadow darkens the dome. Something from the outside. I follow the lazy circles with my eyes as whatever it is hovers above our world. What could it be? A large bird perhaps? And if it is, how does it survive if the world beyond our walls is consumed with flames? I watch until the shadow fades from sight and the quietness of the world above the streets consumes me.

A shout jars me awake. I scramble to my feet and look around. Has someone noticed me? Are there filchers about? Falling asleep was a stupid, stupid mistake. I scramble to the side of the building, just in case, and will my beating heart to slow down.

"Runner!" someone shouts. I look up at the rooftop next to me. The harvester waves to someone on another building.

"There's a runner," he calls out.

A runner? Someone has tried to leave the dome? I've heard rumors of runners and stories of burned bodies shown as evidence of the hazards of going outside. But I've never seen one, nor has anyone else that I know.

Where? Where has someone tried to escape? If I can find out where, then I'd have something to bring to Alex, and maybe he would see me in a new light. There are places that are heavily guarded, places that mark you for certain death before you could even attempt to get out. Has someone found a way to get past?

Suddenly the alarm blares with a piercing blast that bores into my brain. I don't bother with the ladder, instead I lean over the side and grab on to the drainpipe. I brace my knees against it and quickly slide down to the ground where I take off at a run.

It is impossible to think. The alarms scream continually, scaring the birds from their morning rounds. They swoop and squawk angrily above my head. Dogs join in the cacophony of sound and a cat, caught in my path, arches its back and hisses at me as I pound through the alleyways. I slow down as I come to the promenade and the alarms stop.

I have to take a moment to catch my breath. The air is heavy and difficult to draw in. I had forgotten to pull my bandanna over my nose and I pay for it now with choking spasms that echo loudly off the bricks in the after-silence from the screaming steam pipes. I cover my mouth and suppress the noise as best I can. If I am caught by the filchers . . . I close my eyes and take a deep breath. The air is better here as this is the place where the royals gather. The filters are stronger and the fans more powerful. Only the best for the best of us, as it has always been.

People hurry by, tradesmen and royals, all anxious to know what caused the alarm. I cautiously peer around the corner. The need to know what is going on is greater than my fear of the filchers, who will take advantage of any opportunity to collect a bounty. There is enough of a crowd that I can blend into the group that gathers around the fountain and statues that mark the center of our world. It is not as if I am not allowed to be here, it is more that it is unwise for me to be caught here, a jeopardy that concerns me no matter where I go. I pull my goggles over my eyes and join in with the others.

A strange smell assaults my nostrils and the chips, so recently in my stomach, make an attempt to show up once more. I swallow back the bile and mingle with the others. We gather, all citizens of the dome, coming together as one whenever the alarms sound. I manage to hide in plain sight and watch as a squadron of bluecoats drops a body at the base of the fountain. A collective gasp rises from the crowd as we all look in horror at the charred flesh.

"Look, all of you!" A tall man with thick dark hair and eyes as black as coal stands on the dais around the fountain. His uniform shows that he is a bluecoat, yet it is heavily decorated with gold epaulets and a series of gold bands on the right sleeve. His right arm points downward at what once was a shiner. The tattered remnants of his clothing are all that is left to identify him. "This is what awaits those who venture outside these walls. There is nothing there, nothing but *fire* and *flame* and *destruction!*"

As he speaks I study the blackened skin. Could it be someone I know? Did someone take Alex's words to heart and attempt to leave without thinking it through? Our community is small and at some time in my life I have come into contact with every shiner. Some I know better than others. Some are friends, some are relations, most are of a like mind and spirit. I slowly move, making my way closer to where the body lies. It occurs to me that I am praying, my mouth moving over the familiar words of the Lord's Prayer without giving thought to their meaning.

He moves. Bile rises once more in my throat. How could he move? Surely he is dead. No one could survive burns such as these. I must be mistaken, so I move closer. Once again I see something, a jerk of what is left of a finger, a tightening around the slash that is his mouth, a flutter around the eyes. I look at the official and search for affirmation of the runner's death, but his words are lost to me in the nausea that clenches my gut. Everyone around me stares upward, all too shocked and sickened to look down.

As I come as close to the body as I dare, I kneel down, my eyes searching for something familiar as I realize that my prayer is that I will not recognize him. It is a moot prayer at best. If he is a shiner, then I know him. I push my goggles up on my forehead so I can see clearly.

"Alex?" I whisper the name as realization comes to me like a heavy blow. *Not Alex* . . . I am shocked to see his head turn, painfully and slowly, as if I'm dreaming the moment instead of living it.

Alex's eyes open and the whites are bright red, scorched by the fire. A tear slides forth and disappears, turned into steam by the burning heat of his charred skin. His mouth, nothing more than a deep slash in his skull, trembles as he gathers his words. He stares at me for a moment, and I see in his eyes that he knows me.

"Wren . . ." My name is nothing more than a hoarse croak. "The . . . sky . . . is blue." A deep sigh rattles his throat and mercifully, he dies.

The sky is blue . . . I look up. The official is still talking, the people are still listening. Tears stream down some of the faces. Children cling to their parents with their faces buried in the skirts of their mothers. I look beyond the official and the squad of bluecoats around him, to the ceiling of our world, far above. From here the dome is a chalky gray, bland and without definition, all of it lost in the thick air that hovers around the rooftops.

Blue . . .

Slowly I rise. My stomach heaves and I fight back the urge to puke. I need to make my escape while everyone is distracted. My back clenches as if a weapon is aimed in my direction. I cannot help but turn. If I am attacked, I want to face it. Quickly I scan the crowd. My eyes are full of tears and I have to blink them away before I find a bluecoat staring at me.

I quickly realize that he is not truly a bluecoat. The double row of brass buttons down the front of his uniform is missing. Instead he wears the red band on his arm, the one that identifies him as a cadet. He is in training and already he has reached the pinnacle of success. He is part of the squad that caught a runner. He stares at me with an intensity that burns my skin, but there is no pain; it's not even close to what Alex must have suffered.

Oh God, how he must have suffered.

The cadet's blue eyes widen in surprise. Without my goggles

he can see the shine in my eyes. I cannot help but wonder, as I return his gaze, as I wipe away the unbidden tears that stream down my face, what color blue Alex meant when he spoke of the sky. I realize now that there are many different shades of it, and the eyes of the cadet are the bluest I've ever seen.

His eyes do not waver as he touches the arm of the officer standing next to him. The bluecoat nods and I know that I am presumed guilty, as always, by association.

So I run.

◆

The city was built long before the dome was conceived. There is no rhyme or reason to the streets; they are just there, spinning away from the promenade as if made by a drunken spider. I am certain they were a cause of frustration to the engineers who designed our world, for they sought to form order in what was sure to be chaos. I consider them to be a blessing as I run because the bluecoats cannot maintain a line of sight on me long enough to conceive of a plan to capture me. I run and they chase. If the luck for either of us changes they will catch me. I know one day my luck will run out. As always I pray that today is not the day.

The streets closest to the promenade are filled with vendors' carts. They scream obscene threats at me as I dart in and out, using them and their wares as a distraction. Most have brightly colored banners attached to their carts, featuring their specialties. The banners flap wildly in the heavy breeze created by the fans. They shield me.

The bluecoats are not as kind as I am. They shove people and their storefronts aside, tipping the carts and scattering the treasures onto the bricks to be scooped up by the tiny beggars who are always present and always searching for any morsel that will keep them alive. I barely hear the shouts behind me as I run for the fan that is suspended between two buildings. The fan symbolizes a gateway between my world and the royals'. It is an unmarked boundary that keeps the royals' air cool and clear while leaving the air on the opposite side hot and sticky.

When I pass beneath it I am secure in the knowledge that the people who are tucked in the nooks and crannies of the alleyways will help me. It is not because they care for the shiners. It is because they hate the bluecoats who constantly harass them for the petty crimes they must commit to survive. When our world was made, there were no allowances given for those who managed to hide within before the dome was closed. Some went to the mines, a few managed to find work with the royals. Their descendants, called scarabs, were left to live on the edge of our society and survive the best way they can. Most of the filchers come from this part of our world, as do the beggar children. Their homes are made of bits of wood and canvas and furnished with castaway things saved from the fires. They cheer me on by beating on their pots and screaming taunts at the bluecoats.

I dare not look behind me. I know someone is close, so close I can feel him. I run, even though it is hard to breathe. My lungs labor and I hear the harsh sounds in my throat as I force my body onward. If a filcher steps in my path I am done for, as they will surely ransom me to the bluecoats. My only hope is to reach one of the secret entrances we have made to the tunnels below. I know where each and every one of them is located.

My escape is just ahead. A dilapidated building, used to store broken machinery, is in my sight. The windows are covered with bars but I know of one, in a narrow alleyway, that is loose. All I have to do is make the corner and pray that a scarab will cover my escape. I turn the corner, run to the end of the alley, and jump into the window well. The bar is stubborn and hard to move, but it won't take much to let me slip through the broken window. I pull with all my strength but I am winded from my run and my lungs scream their protest. I need time to gather myself, to put my body to the task at hand, but there is none.

A yell diverts my attention and I look up the alley. The young cadet has turned the corner. His blue eyes light on me with recognition mixed with something else. Something I do not recognize.

Desperation spurs me on. I cannot help but groan as I pry the bar open enough to slip through. Haste causes me to fall through the window and I land on my back on the stone floor. I can't breathe. The impact leaves me dazed as all the air is driven from my lungs. I imagine my lungs collapsed upon themselves, flattened, without a passage left for air to return. A shadow darkens my vision and I realize the cadet is in the well and searching the bars to find the weakened one. I don't think he can move it enough to slip through as he is bigger than me. I barely made it myself.

Finally and most gratefully, I am able to suck air into my lungs and I back away, scrambling like one of the blind crabs we hunt in the tide pools of the underground river.

"Stop!" His hands are wrapped around the bars as he peers through, trying to see me in the dim light. "You must stop."

I shouldn't answer. I want to laugh because he thinks I will obey, just because he is one of the bluecoats. I should just go on without a word and make my escape, but Alex's last words stop me. I have to know what it was he saw, in those last few moments before he burned.

"Were you there?" I stand and move back into the shadows so he cannot see my face. I wipe the tears from my eyes again. How can I still be crying? "When he got out?"

"You knew him?"

I back up another step. He is nothing but an outline, a shadow without features, yet I know his eyes are on me, just as I knew they were when we were above, when Alex died.

"He was my friend." My voice rattles. I choke on my tears and the agony of what I saw.

"If he was your friend, then you should have told him to stay inside. It isn't safe out there. Everyone knows it, yet you continually try to break out, only to die a horrible death."

"Were you there?" I ask again. "Did you see it?"

"No," he admits. "I didn't see it. Not until after."

"After he was burned?"

I hear shouts and the sound of footsteps. He is trying to delay me but I know it will take time for the bluecoats to get inside the building. The doors are barred and chained. Still, I take another step back, closer to the tunnel entrance. The bluecoats will not follow me down—to do so is certain death. Mysterious and unexplainable things happen to those who venture into the tunnels without an invitation.

Another question pops into my mind. One that needs more thought and explanation—both of which I know I will not receive from this boy. I don't know why it bothers me so much that he was not there for Alex's capture, except that I need some sort of validation for Alex's last words.

"He said the sky was blue." My foot touches the crate that hides the tunnel entrance. "How can it be, if the world out there is full of fire?"

I feel his pause as I dart behind the crate. I know this access will be shut off from below once I am through. I should go now before another bluecoat comes with tools to open the bars, but I don't. I hide in the darkness and wait for his response.

"Things are not always what they seem." His answer is slow to come and hard for me to understand.

I do not answer him. I stare into the shadow of his face in an attempt to find the meaning of his words. His hand moves between the bars and stretches out toward me, as if he wants to touch me. A shiver runs down my spine and for some strange reason I take a step forward.

Things are not always what they seem . . . I turn away. I push the lever that moves the crate aside and without a backward glance I descend into the darkness. The crate moves back into place with a solid thunk and my eyes adjust to the darkness.

I am home.

· 4 ·

"*Wren!*" My grandfather hurries to me with his eyes shining in the darkness. "I should have known you'd be in the thick of it." He grabs my arm and holds me against the tunnel wall. Three shiners pass us with their arms full of tools and odds and ends of wood on their way to seal up the hatch I just came through in the hope that it will discourage the bluecoats from following. Other shiners will guard the place for several days in case anyone is foolish enough to try.

"When are you going to learn, Wren? There's no place for you up there." My grandfather lectures me as we walk through the tunnel, his words a steady mantra I've heard a thousand times before. My grandfather's words are like smoke. They surround me and then drift away. They are the same words that he regrets not sharing with my mother when she went above. He hopes that by keeping me below he might save me in a way that he could not save her. It is a never-ending battle between us. Like my mother, I cannot stay constant in the world beneath the streets. I am forever reaching for the sky beyond the dome.

"The sky is blue." I blurt it out without thought to the consequences. They were Alex's last words. I have to share them. They are too important and his death would be for naught without them.

My grandfather stops. He takes my upper arms into his hands and turns me to face him. His skin is pale as chalk and the lines of his face are full of dirt and coal dust. "What did you say?"

"The sky is blue."

His eyes widen with shock. His grip on my arms tightens and I am afraid that he might shake me. He leans in with a need to read my meaning written plainly on his face. His eyes, the same color brown with the same exact shine as mine, search my face. "Where did you hear that?"

I close my eyes in hope that it will erase the memory of what I'd seen from my mind. It doesn't. Tears well up again, or perhaps it's just that they haven't stopped. I swallow to keep the contents of my stomach in place. The last thing I want to do is be sick in the tunnels. "From Alex." It is difficult to form the words. "He's dead."

"You saw it?"

"I saw him die."

A change comes over his face. Where before there had been worry for me, now there is something else. Something I cannot identify. He looks at me as if I am different and he's not quite sure what to make of me. "You'll have to tell it."

I am different. "I will." No, not different. Changed. As if the fire that burned Alex touched me too. Only I was lucky. I came through it unscathed. Didn't I?

I follow my grandfather down the tunnel.

◆

As we approach the entrance to the cavern that holds our village I realize the news of Alex's death arrived before me, passing from one shiner to the next, traveling faster than our passage through the tunnels. All eyes are upon me as we walk through the portal that leads to the village. Alex's mother stands at the bottom of the long ledge that leads downward, with his father close behind. Her hands twist in her apron as she stares up at me. I see hope and heartbreak intertwine across her face. Alex's father does not look up, instead he keeps his eyes downward, upon the ground, and I wonder if he's thinking Alex should be there, below us, working to bring out the coal. It's where he would be if he had not decided to make a break for the outside. No, he'd be asleep, as I should be, but no one is sleeping now. They are all waiting to hear the news from me.

What made Alex run? What was so different about today that made him think he would have a chance on his own? Did it have something to do with the seekers' meeting? Had someone challenged his belief and he felt that he had to prove there was something outside the dome besides the flames?

The sky is blue . . . How long had he been thinking about it? Was it planned? Where did he go? What part of the dome did he decide was the place to try? Did he tell anyone else his plans or was it an impetuous choice? My mind is jumbled, full of things I do not understand. I must not waver. I must be strong because everyone will want to know.

His mother's lip trembles when I reach her. Her eyes are moist with the tears she does not want. "Is it true?"

All I can do is nod. I am afraid that if I give voice to the horror of his dying, she will somehow see it. It is tragic enough that he died. The thought of his body, burned as it was, should not be her last memory of her son.

She covers her face with her hands. My grandfather places his hands on my shoulders. His quiet strength warms me. I feel I should say something more but Alex's last words are not something that she will understand at this time. Perhaps later, when the pain is not so raw. I look at his father. His body shakes and I realize he is fighting for control.

Alex's mother raises her head and looks beyond me. She lifts her arm and points. "This is your fault!" She screams the words.

I turn and see Lucy walking slowly and tentatively down the ledge, as if she is no longer sure of her welcome. Her parents break away from the crowd and hurry up to her.

They had fought, Lucy and Alex. I'd witnessed it. Was that why he ran?

"It's because of you that he tried to leave. You broke his heart. You said he wasn't good enough, that you wanted more, that you wanted a life above." Alex's mother charges up the ramp and his father follows. I want to go to them because for some strange reason I feel that I am responsible for the pain she feels. My grandfather's steady pressure keeps me in place.

Hands reach upward for Alex's mother with each step she takes. Hands that want to soothe her and take away some of her grief. She will not have it. She pushes them away and does not stop until she gets to Lucy. Lucy seems small and delicate next to the raw emotion and I see why Alex loved her. I remember the way he looked at her and the wistfulness that came over his face when he mentioned her name. With her dark-as-night hair and pale skin, her beauty is ethereal. Her lashes are long and lush and as she blinks back the tears, I see that her eyes do not shine with the same intensity as mine. She works above and the time she's spent in the light has made them fade.

Alex's mother does not care about any of these things. She strikes Lucy's cheek with her open hand and the slap of skin against skin echoes in the sudden silence of the cavern. Lucy puts her hand to her cheek, covering the large red welt left by the slap. "I'm sorry." Her eyes glitter with tears. "I didn't tell him to go."

"Sorry doesn't help him now." The words are vehement and spat out as if they are bitter and rotten to the taste. Alex's father wraps his arms around his wife and leads her away. Her sobs fill the cavern and the people shift uncomfortably as they disappear into their homes.

Once more all eyes are upon me. My grandfather nods his head and six men and women, Adam among them, break off from the group, all of them moving to a small cave across the stream. It is time for me to speak of Alex's death. So much has happened and now Lucy's words confuse me. She didn't tell him to go, yet Alex did. What went wrong between them?

The rushing water of the stream fills my ears as we cross the narrow wooden bridge. If I fall in, where would it take me? The water courses under the thick rock walls and eventually joins the mighty river belowground, but where does it go after that? Does it eventually lead to the outside? I would be dead and drowned, long before I got to wherever it goes, but my body would move onward. The Bible speaks of the seas. It is something I cannot comprehend, but I am certain the river would go there. My thoughts flow as quickly as the stream, tumbling one upon the other until one thought alone comes forefront to my mind.

Will a boy ever look at me in the same way that Alex looked at Lucy?

The sky is blue . . .

There will be questions.

Silence greets me as I walk into the meeting with my grandfather. I know all of the people gathered there. They are our elders. They have been elected to represent the shiners' dealings with the royals. But furthermore, they settle our disputes and keep shiner business private from the rest of our world. The last thing we want is the bluecoats among us. What is law above is not necessarily law below.

It is my first time in this cave that sits high on the wall opposite our home. No one is permitted to enter unless you are summoned. The series of stone steps that lead up to the entrance is always guarded to keep the curious away. The elders are seated in a circle upon a continuous bench of stone that is carved into the sides of the cave. I am not surprised to see another passageway that leads out. The most important rule for every shiner is to always have an escape route. Becoming trapped in a tunnel is a sentence for certain death. My grandfather leads me to the center of the circle, to a wellworn wooden stool, and I sit. A chill comes over me and I cross my arms in hopes that somehow it will warm me.

Is this how Alex felt? Is this why he ran? The elders' eyes condemn me and I do not know why. They look at me as if I am responsible for what happened.

"What did you see?" Jasper, who is our leader, finally speaks. I tell them what I saw, from the moment I entered the promenade until Alex's death.

"You saw him burned?" a woman, Mary, who is nearly as old as my grandfather asks.

Oh my God I saw him burned. I saw him after he'd been burned and he was still alive. I know in my heart that the horror of it will never leave me. That it will haunt my dreams for the rest of my life. "I saw him after." I am careful to keep my eyes upward and on their faces so they know I am telling the truth. "They carried him to the square after it happened."

"He was still alive?" Hans, a council member, asks.

I close my eyes. I can still see Alex's face, the skin gone, yet the pain etched upon what was left of him. I can still smell the charred flesh. I swallow and address my answer to the entire council. "Yes. He was still alive."

"How do you know that he was still alive?" Adam asks. This is his first council meeting. Little did we know last night that he would be taking an active part so soon.

"He spoke." He knew me. He knew what happened to him. He knew he was dying.

I see the doubt on their faces and hear it in the sudden rush of whispers that circles the room. All eyes return to Adam since he was the one who asked. It is up to him to continue. "What did he say?"

" 'The sky is blue.' "

"The sky is blue." Adam repeats my, no, Alex's words. His eyes dart around the room as if someone will have an answer. No one speaks so he continues, growing more secure as the elders give him leeway with his questions. "What does that mean?"

The last words spoken to me by the cadet creep into my mind. *Things are not always what they seem.* I open my mouth to share these words, but something inside me makes me stop. I look at my grandfather who sits in a position of honor at Jasper's right. He is the eldest of the elders, yet he cannot speak as he is compromised by my involvement. I am nothing more than a witness. Should I be more? I can't help but wonder about the seekers' meeting that Alex called for this morning. What was said? Who went? What did they talk about? Was it the reason Alex decided to try?

"I don't know." I keep my eyes upon Adam as I speak, as I know I have nothing to hide. "I only know what he said."

"Which path did he choose?" The question from Rosalyn, who is a few years older than Adam, comes before I finish.

I shake my head. "I don't know." I look at Adam. Did he go to the seekers' meeting? Does he know something? If he does, shouldn't he say so?

"Was it planned?" The questions come faster now, one tumbling upon another before I can give thought to my answers.

"Were others involved?"

"Did something go wrong?"

"Did someone betray him?"

"No. No. No." I want to get up. I want to run away from the endless accusations. But more important, I want answers to *my* questions. They burst forth, unbidden.

"If Alex saw the sky, then he must have been outside." The elders stop speaking as I give voice to the thing that has bothered me the most since it happened. "If the sky is blue, then what burned him? If the outside is flames, then wouldn't the sky be the same color? Wouldn't it be red like the fires? If Alex was out, then why did he come back in? If the bluecoats followed, then why did they not burn also?"

They look at me in shocked silence. Have they never thought of these things? Have they never wondered what it is like on the outside? Do they simply believe what they are told without question? If this is my future, then I do not want it. I need to know that there is something more out there, that there is a possibility of a better life for me, and if not me, then for the generations to come. There has to be more than this dome. If there isn't, then why did we survive? Surely this is not the future those in the past wanted to preserve.

Finally Jasper speaks. "Bring Lucy," he says. Hans goes to the entrance to summon Lucy. I don't know what I am supposed to do. I stay where I am and look at the stone floor. I am too confused and too frightened to do otherwise. I know now that I spoke out of turn. I have no voice here. My fears and my questions are irrelevant to the elders. Finally my grandfather comes and touches my shoulder. I follow him to his seat and sit on the floor before him to wait.

Lucy enters with her head down. Her hair hides her face; still, I know she's been crying. Is it because Alex is dead or because his mother embarrassed her? She sits on the stool and the questions begin.

"Why did Alex leave the dome?"

Lucy takes a deep breath. Her shoulders move upward and then slump downward. I watch her turn in upon herself, defeated before the battle is begun. "Because I told him I didn't love him." Her voice breaks on the words. "Because I don't want to live below for the rest of my life." She whispers as if she is afraid someone will hear her. "I don't want to be a shiner's wife."

With her confession Lucy is no longer one of us. The elders will not go so far as to banish her; still, it will be as if they have. No man worth having will have her now. As pretty as she is, she's a pariah. By rejecting Alex, who was one of the best and the brightest, she's rejected them all. The same way I rejected James. Will he tell them? Will they look at me with disgust also?

"Did he say anything about running?"

Lucy shakes her head. "He said he would find a way for us to be together on the outside. That he would show me the sun and give me the world."

I close my eyes as Lucy speaks. I can see Alex, proud, handsome, and always seeing the best in everyone and everything, including me. All he ever wanted was Lucy, and he was not good enough for her. Instead of getting angry, he tried harder to please her. So hard that he died, horribly. Was being in love with someone worth all that pain?

"You may go." Jasper speaks for the elders. They do not look at her, but I do. She rises and she walks, but it seems strange, as if her body is not sure of the commands she gives it. She is distant, vacant, like the smoke that pours from the furnaces.

She looks down at me as she passes. "I desperately wanted him to be right," she whispers. I barely hear her.

My grandfather touches my shoulder. It is time for me to go. I follow after Lucy. I need to talk to her, I want—no, I need—to know why. The guard at the entrance stops me. I recognize him as Lucy's cousin, Abner, and his action is to protect her. I stand beside him and watch as she crosses the bridge. I can tell that she is already gone.

· 5 ·

The ponies are blind. They live their entire life underground in the tunnels. It is my job to take them from their stable, deep below the earth, and harness them to the carts. The carts move the coal from where it's dug out of the earth to the shaft where it is sent above. At one time, long ago, there was talk of using steam engines to move the coal, but the shiners wouldn't have it. The ponies are steadfast and faithful. They learn the route quickly and stop and go when they are told to. I love them with a fierce passion that surprises me at times. They know my scent and recognize the sound of my voice. They greet me with soft whickers and snuff me with their soft noses, in search of the treats I always keep in my pockets.

I did not sleep much after the council. My mind was full of everything that happened, and when I finally did fall asleep my dreams were disturbing and restless. There were images of Alex, blazing fire, and the cadet with the very blue eyes that became the sky. My grandfather had to shake me awake and I stumbled from my bed, still exhausted.

Things are not always what they seem . . .

We work twelve hours on and twelve hours off. Night or day has no impact on our body clocks as it is always dark where we live and work. My shift is during the nighttime hours. It has always been so, since I reached the age of thirteen and finished my education and started contributing to our society. I like working the night shift because when it is over I can go to the rooftops and watch the light from outside fill the dome.

The questions left from Alex's death are still ever present in my mind. As I lead the string of ponies down into the mines I can't stop thinking about it. Was there something I could have done to stop it? What was he thinking?

The tunnels are long and dark, with lamps placed at the intersections of each cross tunnel. The earlier tunnels used to hold tracks for the steam carts, but the trestles and iron of the rails are long gone, foraged among the years for different projects. The earth here smells fresh and damp as these tunnels are new. The ground beneath my feet is firmly packed from a large roller that is used as the tunnels are cut. The resulting dirt and rocks from each new cut are carted by the ponies to long exhausted deposits and the tunnels are filled in. Sometimes we send the dirt above, to replenish the gardens. The dome is like a well-oiled machine, each part serves a purpose, but lately I feel as if it's about to break down because the pieces are old and weak.

The deeper I go, the further away Alex's death seems, as if I dreamed it. I touch my hand to the wall of the tunnel and feel the solidity of the hard-packed walls. I touch it to make sure that I am indeed awake, and to center myself in its solidness. The earth is the constant in my world. The one thing that will not change. The river might change its course, but the earth will always be there, only subtly shifting to fit the whims of the currents of our time.

At my first stop, Alcide, Alex's cousin, who is a year younger than me, loads the coal into the cart. His face is set and rigid and he won't look at me, as if I'm to blame for what happened. His tippler is loaded too high and chunks fall off as he tries to wrestle it into place. I go to help him and he jerks the handle away from me. I back away from the wall of his anger.

I look around at the crew. Some are pounding away at the coal deposits with their pickaxes while others toss the chunks into another tippler. None look at Alcide, but some look at me and I feel the intensity of their stares down in my bones. I don't know what to do but I must do something, so I pick up some stray chunks of coal and pitch them in the cart while Alcide dumps his load. Hans, who I saw at the council meeting earlier, jerks his head at me and I go to him.

"Leave him be," he says. "He needs to work it out on his own. He fairly worshipped the boy," he adds.

"I feel like everyone is blaming me for what happened to Alex," I confess.

"They're not," Hans says kindly. "It's just that you've seen something none of them would ever want to see. It's had to change you, Wren. Everyone is trying to figure out how."

I shake my head in denial. I don't want to feel any more different than I already do. I want things to go back to the way they were. I want to feel safe. All I feel now is alone.

Another shiner, close in age to Hans, joins us. "Sad news about Alex." His name is Miles and his story is one that keeps me cautious when I go above. He lost his wife to the filchers. They found her body by the lift where the filchers left it after they were done with her. It happened when I was quite young and it hasn't happened since, but that doesn't mean it won't happen again. "You should all stay below," he adds with a stern look. "There's nothing to be had up there, nothing to be found."

But there is. I don't bother to tell him the things that constantly drive me to go above. His anger and bitterness is buried too deep. Alcide is done with the cart so I turn the pony and with a slap on his rump, send him heading back the way I came. He'll find his way and if something happens he will wait until I find him.

I move on with the ponies to the next dig. Peter, who held Alex when he flew, is one of the workers. The coal they've dug barely covers the bottom of the cart. His movements are angry as he jerks the tippler back into place. Even though the air is cool and damp he is shirtless and he takes a kerchief from his pants pocket to wipe the sweat and coal dust from his face. What he's dumped into the cart has been hard-earned. Peter grabs the water jug that hangs from the harness of one of the ponies and takes a long drink as he leans on the tippler.

"Where do you think he went out?" he asks after he steals a look at the foreman of his crew.

"I don't know," I admit. "Didn't you talk about such things at the seekers' meeting?"

"We didn't meet," Peter says. "Because he was fighting with Lucy." He takes another drink. "And now there's no need to, as he was wrong. There's nothing out there but fire and flames, just like they say."

And a blue sky, I can't help but think.

"I heard that he didn't die right away," Peter continues. "God . . . I can't imagine the pain." He chokes on the word *pain* and at first I think it is from emotion, but it's not. His lungs are already filling with the coal dust from the backbreaking work he does every day. Finally he stops and takes another drink. He looks at me with his coal-streaked face and I realize how very young we all are. Peter barely has whiskers and his job will kill him before long. Before he has a chance to even live. "Did he say anything? Anything at all?"

I shake my head. I'm afraid if I tell Peter what Alex said that he will try too. And he will die just as horribly as Alex did. But would it be any worse than dying slowly with black lung? Shouldn't he at least have the satisfaction of knowing that he died trying instead of simply yet horribly dying? Should I tell him that Alex could have been right? But if he was right, then why did he burn?

"He was in too much pain," I say. "It was hard to understand."

I leave before Peter can ask any more questions. I hear his coughing once more as the ponies and I move on to the next stop, where the coal is just as thin as the last one. No one speaks to me here beyond a nod. Their work is too hard and they are already exhausted.

As I continue on my route I hear the ping of a hammer and voices in a side tunnel. I leave the ponies with a touch to stay put and follow the sounds. In a small cavern I find my grandfather, Adam, James, and Peggy.

"How goes it?" my grandfather asks without turning from his work. He's packing a charge into a small hole. My grandfather is responsible for blowing the tunnels to search for new coal. It's a tedious job as you have to know exactly where the other tunnels are, along with where the river runs and what is above and below you. Our tunnels spin off in more directions than spiderwebs as we dig deeper and deeper into the earth. I have this vision of the entire dome caving in on us as we continually undermine the earth it sits upon.

James and Adam are both apprentices beneath him. It takes a long time to learn the trade and my grandfather chooses the ones that he thinks have the most potential. Or the most sense, as he confided to me one time.

"It goes slow," I say. "Not much to send up today."

"There's never enough to make those above happy," my grandfather says. He nods to Adam, who steps forward to put a blasting cap and fuse into the charge. James watches Adam closely, but occasionally I can feel his eyes on me.

Peggy shouldn't be here. Her job is with the food stores that we get from above. She works with the quartermaster to make sure everyone gets their fair share and no more. Yet she cannot stay away from Adam. She needs him like the air she breathes.

"You should go, gel," my grandfather says gently. "'Tis not your place."

Peggy wants to protest but she knows if she says anything my grandfather will make sure she will stay where she belongs. If she's not doing her fair share of the work as decided by the council her family will be punished with short rations. She manages a smile to me as she leaves. She doesn't dare say anything to Adam as my grandfather stands between her and him.

Later I will tell her that it's because my grandfather is worried for her safety, nothing more. He is already responsible for James's and Adam's lives. He doesn't want to have to worry about another one.

"Jasper went above to speak with the authorities about what happened to Alex," he informs me.

"And?" I ask, hoping there will be a simple explanation for what Alex said to me.

"And nothing," he replies. "They said he went outside and was burned. The bluecoats had mercy on him and let him back in but it was too late. There was nothing they could do."

The explanation is simple, yet it doesn't answer my question.

"Move on," my grandfather says. "I don't want you near this place when we blow it."

"Yes, sir." I leave, still feeling James's eyes on me. Has he told anyone about the kiss? I think not, because he's too proud for anyone to know I rejected him. I don't want him to be angry with me; I just want him to accept the fact that for now, I don't want to be with him. I need time to think, especially after what I saw.

I know I will not find the answers I need deep within the earth. Even though the loads are light my work keeps me busy, and because I did not sleep well beforehand I am exhausted when my shift is over. I take my string of ponies back to their stable. My job is not done. They must be fed and watered before they seek their rest. Water is piped to a trough and I lead the blind ponies by pairs to drink. As the first set dips their heads to the water I realize questions are still in my mind, simmering beneath the surface and waiting to be disturbed in the same way the ponies disturb the surface of the water. I know I will find no rest until I find the answers.

◆

Instead of going to my bed I take the time to brush the coal dust off the ponies in the hope that I will become so tired that my body will demand its rest and my mind will have no choice but to shut down and let me be. The ponies enjoy the attention, each one showing its appreciation in its own way, and their quiet presence soothes me. Chickens bustle about in the stall, pecking at the odds and ends of feed that litter the floor. I give attention to my own needs before I leave the stable, washing my face, hands, and arms in the trickle of water that pours from an overhead pipe.

Most of my shift mates are gone so I have the lift to myself as I ride up to home level. I want nothing more than to crawl into my bed and sleep for a week, but something inside me that cannot be denied urges me to go above and watch the morning light fill the dome. I catch the lift that goes to the surface. The churning of gears and the hiss of steam almost lulls me to sleep as I trundle slowly upward. I watch the carved walls go by, counting in my head to two hundred, as I know, after my many trips, that that is the length of the ride.

Noise greets me when the lift settles into place. Coal clatters onto belts that carry it to the furnaces. Scarab women hang close to the belt and scoop up pieces that fall to the ground and then rush off to their hovels to feed their fires and fix the morning meal. My stomach growls with hunger. I haven't eaten much of anything lately and I have no coin for the street vendors. Maybe I will be lucky and find something left behind by the harvesters.

It is later than I thought. The dome already has the soft glow that says morning is here. I don't want to miss it so I hurry through the silent streets, going toward my favorite rooftop garden. I turn a corner and realize Lucy is ahead of me. She is carrying a bundle on her back and another one rolled beneath her arm. Where is she going? I pull my goggles down over my eyes, put my scarf over my mouth and nose, and follow her, making sure to stay within the shadows of the buildings. I don't know why I decided to follow her. Maybe it's just morbid curiosity.

Lucy walks with a purpose. I know she works for a laundry but I never really thought about where it was. The prettier girls can usually find work above. It's what my mother did when she was young. Instead of going to the mines, she went above in hopes of finding a better life. She did not find it. What she did find was a man who got her pregnant and abandoned her. She found death the day I was born. Will Lucy find a life? I do not know. I do know that Alex's death is too high a price to pay because Lucy wanted more. What made her think she deserved more than the rest of us?

Maybe it's not that she wants more, maybe it's just that she's willing to go after what she wants. The same way Alex did. At what point do you decide that what you want is worth it? When does the price become too much to pay?

I have never been in this part of the dome before. I've never had a reason to be here. The streets are busier here, as this is the trades section, where all the shops are located. Men and women are out and about, sweeping the walks in front of their storefronts. Even though I try to be inconspicuous, I receive several strange looks. I have not heard that this part of the dome is forbidden to shiners, although several different places frown upon our presence. It could be that because I am furtive they think I am up to no good. Whatever the cause of their concern, I plan to be long gone before they can act on it. I follow Lucy across the street to an alley that runs behind the shops.

I am close to the edge of the dome. The ceiling here is lower and the walls are made of concrete reinforced with iron. A large girder soars upward. It is covered with rust and birds nest in the circular openings. Lean-tos made of scrap pieces of wood use the barrier as a wall.

The parts of the barrier that are open are covered with graffiti. Drawings of flames with anti-royal sentiments painted against the backdrop. Some show an attempt at removal while others gleam with newness. It does not surprise me to see that rebellion is not limited to the shiners. The natural light from outside does not seep into the nooks and crannies created by the odd structures, so lanterns are hung every so often, casting a soft golden glow.

Doors from the line of shops open onto the alley. A long rope is strung from the girders and clothing hangs upon it. Steam rises from a long shed full of tubs. This must be the laundry where Lucy works. I duck behind a lean-to when Lucy stops at one of the doors and knocks. A little boy with a dirty face stares up at me through the cracks in his shelter. There are so many people above now that there is not enough housing for them, so some take to the streets and live from hand to mouth as best they can.

I shove my goggles up on my forehead. His eyes widen at the sight of my eyes in the dim light. I motion with a finger to my mouth for him to stay quiet and he grins mischievously at me before moving to the other side of his hovel to see what has my attention. I briefly wonder where his mother is, or if he even has one. Did whoever cares for him tell him to stay put? He stays quiet yet seems pleased for the company. I give him a smile and look onward.

Lucy stands at the door with her bundles. She does not look around. She has no reason to think anyone would follow her, and why should she? If anyone wanted revenge for Alex's death they would have taken it already. There are places in the tunnels where people can and have disappeared. The shiners have their own laws and forms of punishment. We take care of our own without outside interference.

The door opens. Lucy smiles and suddenly she is swallowed up into the arms of a young man. His hug lifts her and her laughter fills the alley. He puts her down, smiles at her, and his hand rises to caress her cheek before he lowers his mouth to kiss her. Their silhouettes fade to silver and gold in the lantern's glow. His hair shines golden where Lucy's is as dark as the world below. Light and night meet. Perhaps I didn't miss the dawn after all.

My cheeks flame as I watch. The little boy points and giggles before turning his face up to me to see my reaction. I feel as if I'm intruding on something very private; I drop down so I can't see them and they can't see me.

More questions fill my mind. How long has Lucy known the young man? How long have they been together? One realization comes to the forefront of my thoughts with the same impact as if the alarms sounded again. Alex must have found out. That's what made him run. He saw Lucy with the young man and called her out. That was when she told him, and that was why he ran. He wanted to prove to her that he was better than the other man. He wanted to win back her affection.

I steal another look and see that Lucy is gone, undoubtedly into the building with the young man. It is time for me to make my escape. I start back down the alleyway toward the promenade, my head once more spinning with all the things that have happened the day just past.

Will any of us ever see Lucy again? She has parents, brothers and sisters. Will she ever come visit them? I need someplace to think. I need to find some logic in all that has happened. Even though light fills the dome and the dawning has passed, my body turns automatically to my rooftop hideaway. My mind is so occupied that I do not concentrate on where I am going until I turn a corner and find myself face-to-face with the cadet.

"Is she your friend?" His very blue eyes shift behind me to the alleyway. There is no way he can know about Lucy. Unless . . . "Why did you follow her?"

I sputter at his question, indignant and defensive. "Why are you following me?"

"You're a shiner. You're not supposed to be up here."

I check his uniform carefully. It still shows the markings of a cadet, which means he can only observe, not act. "The law does not prohibit shiners from going above. The only place we are not permitted is Park Front." I cannot keep the sarcasm from my voice. "We wouldn't want to inconvenience the royals in any way." His sudden appearance shakes me to my core. I always thought I was being careful. I always felt as if no one would notice me as I walk the surface because I stay to the shadows, where I am most comfortable.

"You really should stay below."

His words challenge me, even though he says them without malice. For some strange reason I feel the need to contradict him at every step. "Why?"

"The filchers . . ." He looks away from me. My eyes follow the trail of his gaze. Are there filchers about? Has he betrayed me to them? I am conflicted, torn between the desire to run and the need to know why he followed me. The streets fill up, growing busy with people going about their business. No one pays attention to us, except for an occasional grunt to indicate we are blocking their way. I step closer to the building beside me, finding safety in the dim light beside it. I pull my kerchief up and place my hand on my goggles to pull them down.

"Don't," he says and moves closer to me. "Your eyes . . ." His cheeks turn red and he hastily looks away. I drop my hand and leave my goggles where they are.

"I should go," he says finally.

"Wait." Without thought I place my hand on his arm. "Why are the filchers after me?"

"The enforcers put a bounty on you. They think you know something about your friend. They think there will be others."

"I have you to thank for that. You're the one who pointed me out to the bluecoats."

"I wasn't," he explains. "I was excusing myself. I told my superior I was going to be sick and didn't want to do it in front of everyone. I used it as an excuse to talk to you. But you ran and I had no choice but to chase you."

"So because I ran the bluecoats think I had something to do with Alex's escape?"

"Bluecoats?"

"The enforcers. It's what we call you." I motion to his uniform. "Them."

"Oh." He shakes his head in understanding.

"What is it exactly that they think I know?"

"They think you know everything. About other plans for escape and about where your friend made his escape."

It doesn't make sense. "They're the ones who know where," I say. "They were the ones who caught him. Why would anyone want to escape after what happened to Alex?"

He puts his hand up. "Like I said before, things are not always what they seem."

I want to stamp my foot in frustration. I turn away, take a step, and then turn back to him. My patience is wearing thin. I am tired of him being cryptic. I want answers; no, I *need* answers to everything that has happened. "What does that mean?"

Once more he looks around. The streets are much busier now. People are hurrying around us, as if they are late. A few give us looks and I know they are marking us, a shiner and a cadet, hiding in the shadows, deep in conversation. It is not an everyday occurrence. There will be talk of it. The filchers will hear of it. They have spies everywhere.

"I can't explain it just now. If I'm late they'll want to know why. Can you meet me somewhere? Somewhere where we can talk?"

"Why?"

"I need to know if there's going to be another attempt."

"Why would I tell you if there was? Why would someone want to escape if all there is out there is fire?"

"You don't believe that, do you?" He moves closer to me. So close that I can see each and every one of his incredibly long and dark eyelashes. His eyes are upon my face, intent. The blue iris of his eye is outlined with black. It gives his eyes an unsettling depth. What does he see when he stares at mine? Does he see the shine? Can he tell that beyond the shine my eyes are brown?

"Isn't Alex proof of that?" I ask.

He looks upward. We can't see the dome from where we stand because the overhang of the roof shelters us, but I know where he's looking. It's full day now and we are surrounded by light. He keeps his eyes upward as he speaks. "If there are flames why can't we see them? Why is there night and day? Why is it cool to the touch?"

"You've touched it?" I look at him in awe. It has always been my wish to touch it, but I do not know of a place where it is reachable. Only the cleaners with their long-handled mops have any contact with it.

"I have," he says as he looks into my eyes once more. "And I wonder, after all these years, what else is out there that's left to burn?"

I study his face and his eyes in the hope that somehow I'll see the answers there, but all I see is his questions and realize that he's searching my face for the same.

"I have to go," he says. "If I'm late they'll think something is wrong. Will you meet me, Wren?"

The mention of my name frightens me. "How do you know my name?"

"They have ways of knowing everything."

"They? Who are they?" Everything he says is more confusing than before. "How do I know it's not a trap? How can I be sure that you won't turn me over to the filchers?"

"I won't." His blue eyes are intent, willing me to believe him. "You decide where and when. You pick out a place where you can see that it's not a trap."

My mind spins. I should walk away. I should never come to the surface again. I shouldn't talk to him, ever. Yet he has answers, he knows something . . .

"What's your name?" I look at his jacket and his name badge. P. Bratton.

He smiles, fleetingly, so quick that I would have missed it had I not looked up at that exact moment in hopes of finding some sort of sign to point me in the right direction.

"Pace. My name is Pace."

"The roof of the library. At dawn tomorrow."

Pace chews on his lower lip as if he's thinking. "I will be there. Tomorrow at dawn."

I step by him, anxious to be gone. I feel vulnerable, as if I am a target. My spine quivers as I am certain the filchers will be on me with my next step.

"Wren." I slide my goggles over my eyes as I turn to look at him. "Be careful."

"I always am," I reply. At the moment, though, I'm not so sure.

· 6 ·

Even though I have never flown over the pit, I can imagine what it feels like. I've felt the wind on my face as it blows upward from the center of the earth. I've stretched out my arms and felt the violent push of the force it brings. I've closed my eyes and felt my consciousness depart, as if the entire world was centered inside of me, a tiny yet brilliant dot buried someplace within my mind.

I feel the exact same way now. I could blame it on the lack of sleep as I've gone two days without. I did try to sleep after venturing out but it was impossible. My thoughts gave me no relief and I once more fell into a restless state full of dreams of Alex and flames.

My return trip to the lift set my nerves on edge as I was certain I was followed at every step. My body remained tense with the expectation of the filchers grabbing me at any minute. I hurried through the streets after I left Pace and prayed that the filchers were not watching for me. I dared not compromise another escape route. Doing so would have resulted in being called before the council, with certain punishment to follow.

Luckily my grandfather was asleep when I slipped into my bed and he was gone when I finally gave up. I must have gotten *some* sleep as I did not hear him leave. Our place is very small; just room enough for two people. Our beds are on opposite sides of our small cave and we both have curtains around them for privacy. It's hard to believe I did not hear him leave.

I finally give up on sleep and crawl wearily from my bed. I stagger to the pitcher of water waiting for me on the washstand. The water feels cool against my face and soothes the dryness that fills my eyes after my restless night. The eyes that stare back at me from the mirror over the washstand surprise me. I see the fear in them, along with the unanswered questions. I take a deep breath and look at my reflection again.

It used to bother me that I was not pretty. I've been told often enough that I am and that I look just like my mother, but I don't see it. When I was younger I would often stare into the same mirror and wonder if my eyes were the exact dark brown as hers or if her nose flared as wide as mine at the bottom. Was our hair the exact same shade of brown and did it have the same wild curls that could never be tamed? I never see pretty when I look in the mirror. I only see questions without answers. If I look just like her do I also act just like her? Is that why I constantly stare at the unseen sky above the dome and wonder what it is like beyond?

Did her eyes ever betray her fear as mine are now?

With the tragedy of the day before I've neglected my chores. The laundry basket by my bed is my grandfather's way of reminding me. With a sigh I gather everything up and make my way to the stream.

It's the middle of the day so most of the village is either at work or sleeping. It's strange that my grandfather left his bed so early. Something must have happened. Several cats follow me as I reach the bottom of our steps, each one coming forth from its perch with a yawn and a stretch, all curious to learn what I'm up to while hoping for some tidbit of food to come their way. I always set bits of food out for them to supplement their usual diet of vermin.

Toddlers play while their mothers gossip in the center of our village. I pass on through with a quick nod as I am certain I, along with Lucy and Alex, are the subjects of their talk. They grow quiet and I feel their eyes upon me as I move onward. As I near the stream I notice that Abner is once more outside the council chamber. That is why my grandfather is awake. Another council has been called. The few women around the stream watch my approach without subtlety. I kneel down by the water and separate the clothes while my mind races.

The filchers . . . It has to be about me. What else could it be? Pace said I was wanted for questioning and a reward was being offered. A sense of dread fills me as I bend to my task. If it is about me, I will know soon enough, so I go about the laundry, keeping my head down so the others will not see my face. I do not want my fear to show.

On the inside I am screaming. My hands tremble as I pick up the washboard and soap and go to work on the clothes. I wring out my grandfather's shirt and watch the trail of soap disappear beneath the wall of the cavern.

The filchers are notorious. Parents threaten their children with capture by them if they do anything wrong. They are the monster that hides beneath our beds, the bogeyman who hides in the shadows. They will sell anyone for money. Young girls and boys have been known to disappear off the streets, taken by the filchers to fulfill the more perverse fantasies of the privileged. The bluecoats offer them rewards to bring in the more violent criminals, such as murderers and rapists. The sentence is always the same, death by fire as there is no room for prison cells.

The filchers are outcasts of our society, both above and below. Most come from the scarabs. They come to adulthood desperate and strong, which they have to be to survive. There is nothing they will not do for money and will torture anyone they think may have information that will lead to their gain.

What do they want from me? They think I know something about Alex's escape attempt. They will not care that I don't know anything. The only thing that drives them is the offer of a reward.

My grandfather's pants are worn and the knees black with coal dust and dirt. I use a heavy brush on the stains. I scrub with a purpose, challenging the fabric to stay strong as I move the brush back and forth, back and forth. I clench it so hard that my hand cramps and finally I let go.

The pounding of the water and the creak of the wheel drown out my grandfather's approach. It isn't until he touches me on the shoulder that I realize he is there. I look beyond and see the members of the council staring at us from across the stream. My grandfather holds a piece of paper in his hand.

Paper is a valuable commodity in our society. Every scrap of it is collected after use, washed until it is pulp, and then re-formed again. Any time paper is used it has an impact because it is used only for the most serious of matters.

My grandfather places the paper in my hand. It trembles as I look at the banner.

WANTED FOR MURDER

CADET PACE BRATTON

REWARD OFFERED FOR INFORMATION

LAST SEEN IN THE COMPANY OF
SHINER WREN MACAVOY

ANYONE KNOWING THE LOCATION OF EITHER
SUSPECT SHOULD NOTIFY THE OFFICE OF
ENFORCEMENT

The notice includes a description and drawing of Pace. The drawing and description of me is more vague, yet there is enough there that I will be noted should I venture above.

"What have you been up to, Wren?" My grandfather's voice is sharp and I flinch at the tone.

"Nothing." I look up at him, begging him to believe me with my eyes, but he will not be swayed.

"This paper says different." He takes it from me and waves it before my face. "What about the cadet?"

What can I say? I have as many questions as my grandfather, if not more. Still he is waiting for an answer. "He is the one who saw me with Alex, when he died. That's all I know."

"It says he's a murderer." He points a finger at the words, but I do not see them. Instead I see the coal buried deep beneath his nails, a stain that will never go away no matter how hard he scrubs. "It says that he was last seen in your company."

My grandfather's anger is a tangible thing. It is fueled by fear for me and frustration that I have placed him in this predicament. The safety of all of us is at risk if the filchers decide to come below in an attempt to capture me.

"He didn't do it." The words come unbidden, from deep inside me. Why did I say it? I don't know him. I don't know anything about him. Is he capable of it, and it's just that I don't want to believe it?

To do such a thing would be a desperate measure, especially since there is no place to hide. You will eventually be found and sentenced to the fires, to be burned alive while the populace watches. My stomach turns at the thought. "Things are not always what they seem." I repeat Pace's words, more for my benefit than my grandfather's.

My grandfather studies me, his face a mixture of anger, concern, and bewilderment. I see the pain he feels and wonder if it is the same as when my mother came back from above, pregnant with me. His doubt in his ability to raise me is always there, just below the surface, wanting to take hold and draw him back to the past. He seldom speaks of my mother, and when he does, it is with self-loathing and repeated recriminations. It is always accompanied by heavy drinking, as if the liquor brings back the memories.

"Stay below, Wren. For all our sakes." It has never been my desire to cause him to feel the same pain he felt over my mother, yet there are things I cannot control.

I nod in agreement as my grandfather walks away. I can only hope my face does not betray my lies. I finish the laundry with my head down against the stares of the others who are gathered around, waiting to hear why the council meeting was called. My situation will be the main topic of discussion tonight. The theories put forth around the hearths will be only that. Like me, everyone will have questions without answers.

Thankfully, my grandfather is not at home when I return with the laundry. With a sinking feeling I realize that he has most likely gone off to drink, and I can only hope that he will be able to work his shift tonight. If only I could miss mine as well. I am not looking forward to the questions that will come as I take the ponies down into the mines. As it is with most things in my life, there is nothing I can do about it.

I hang the laundry out to dry and fix the meals for our shifts.

My stomach growls while I work and I realize that I cannot recall the last time I ate. I fix myself a quick snack of bread, butter, and dried apples. I taste nothing as I eat; my mind is centered on everything that has happened. One of the cats comes to the door and meows. His look is hopeful so I fill a bowl with the crusts of my bread and the last of the goat's milk. As I set it down outside the door I see Peggy running up the steps.

"You look horrible," she says. "Oh, I'm sorry," she immediately apologizes when I cringe at her words and she pushes a lock of my hair behind my ear. "What I meant was you look tired. Can't you sleep?"

"I slept, but not well," I confess.

"Come on," she says. "I've got something that's going to cheer you up."

I want something cheerful. I want something that will make the past few days go away, as if they never happened. I know that can't be but I'm curious, so I pick up my pail and she links her arm through mine as we walk up the ramp that takes us from the village.

· 7 ·

"We found a way to honor Alex," Peggy says when we are away from the village. "It was James's idea. We're going to continue with his dream. We're going to have a seekers' meeting. We're going to find a way to leave the dome."

James's idea. Of course it was. James, who has a way with people and can convince them to do whatever he wants, everyone but me. Will his idea to honor Alex turn into a death sentence for another one of us?

Alex was right about one thing. Seekers is a good name for us. Since the world became the dome, the royals have kept the lower classes in servitude. Change is prohibited and without change there is no reason to aspire. Man must have something to work for, beyond the everyday drudgery of existence. There has to be more to life than eating, sleeping, and work, or else why even bother?

It surprises me to think that there have not been seekers until now. What were the shiners that came before us thinking? Did they ever wish to rise above their place of servitude? I have to believe that there is a better world out there somewhere. Man was not meant to live belowground. God created the world and gifted it to man. He destroyed it once by flood and it came back to life. Could it not do the same after the fire?

Pace's words once more come back to haunt me. *Things are not always what they seem. After all this time is there anything left to burn.* And of course Alex's last words. *The sky is blue.*

Peggy and I follow the trail of the bird in flight, marked on the tunnel walls with coal at each crossing. The meeting place is deep, farther down in the oldest part of the mine than I've ever been. The walls are cold and damp and the lamps are few and far between. I hear the gay song of a canary up ahead and I pause by its tiny cage. Its feathers are bright yellow and stand out in stark relief against the monotone dimness of the tunnels. It examines me with its black bead of an eye before it resumes its song. As long as the canary sings we are safe against the buildup of the silent and deadly gases. I hope that whoever brought it down here will remember to bring it back to the main part of the mines when we are done. I cannot stand the thought of it being left to die in the darkness alone, singing to the nothingness with its last breath.

Peggy and I are the last to arrive. The soft buzz of quiet conversation fades to silence as I enter the cave and the ominous drip-drip of condensation on the walls accompanies me as we sit cross-legged on the ground. These are my peers, the ones I'd gone to school with, played with, and then, as we grew older, gone into the mines with. Even though I carry the stigma of my birth I trust these people. It is a bond we'd built when we were children. When we played by the underground river we would hold hands and venture out into the water, forming a chain of stability as the water pounded against us. If someone let go, there was the danger of being swept beneath the rocks and drowning. We learned at a young age to depend upon one another and it serves us well now when we work in the mines.

I can voice my fears here, and ask my questions without fear of recrimination. Still I am nervous because James watches me closely. There is something in his eyes, something that makes me think I will, indeed, be sorry for rejecting his kiss.

Finally the shifting of two dozen bodies stops and the buzz of conversation quiets. James looks at each one of us, and smiles mysteriously.

"I think we should start by honoring Alex," he says. "And what better way to honor him than to hear about his last moments. Wren? Will you tell us what happened?"

My stomach lurches and my hastily eaten meal threatens to come up. I swallow, hard, and shake my head. I don't like being the center of attention and I certainly don't want to talk about Alex's last moments.

"Go on," Peggy whispers in my ear. "For Alex. So we can know what he died for."

Tentatively I stand and hesitantly I begin. It does not take much imagination to know how excruciating it would have been for Alex. Death by fire has to be incredibly painful, if the screams we've heard from the public executions are any indicator. One of the reasons I have not been able to sleep is I see Alex's burned face when I close my eyes, and I still smell his burned flesh. These are details I leave out as I tell them the story as I remember it. They all look in wonder at me when I tell them Alex's last words.

"The sky is blue?" Alcide, who is Alex's cousin, asks. I realize that the council has not seen fit to share any of the details of Alex's death with the rest of them. I'm certain Adam has discussed it with Peggy and James but the rest have no idea.

"That's what he said," I say. I feel more confident now that I realize they really didn't know what exactly had happened. It's better that they know the truth than some story that will get further away from it with each telling.

"Why would he say this if it wasn't so?" someone asks.

"How can the sky be blue if the outside world is still burning?" Peter asks.

"Where did he go out?"

"How did he find a passageway?"

The questions tumble forth, each one heaping upon another like rocks in a cave-in until there are so many that they stop and everyone looks at one another and realizes that there are no answers.

"Did Alex share his plans with anyone here?" James speaks up. His look is pleasant, even charming, as it usually is. He keeps his eyes upon me as he speaks. I feel trapped under his gaze, much as I did when he kissed me. Perhaps, if I had more experience with kissing, then I could say what it was I didn't like about it. All I know is that when he kissed me, I felt as if he was smothering me. I couldn't breathe. The thought of spending the rest of my life like that is unbearable.

Alcide speaks up. "A few nights ago while we were working, Alex mentioned the main fans. They have to lead to a source of fresh air. He thought there might be a way through there."

The main fans are the most closely guarded part of the dome. Without them, the air inside would fail and we all would suffocate. We do not know how many there are, just that there is a series of them. The blades run continually so it would be impossible to pass through.

"Impossible," someone says. "He must have gone another way."

"Has anyone stopped to think that perhaps he did not actually make it out?" James speaks over the quick exchange of opinions that streak through the meeting. His eyes once more rest on me and I have to resist the urge to look away, or to leave under his heavy perusal. "That everything we've heard has been a lie?"

What is he saying? I shake my head. "But I saw him," I say. "I heard him."

James's careless shrug dismisses my words and anger surges through my body. A collective gasp ripples through the seekers and I feel all their eyes upon me. Peggy stands and pulls on my arm to stop me and I jerk away.

"Alex burned alive." I grind the words out between my clenched teeth. My jaw aches from the effort as my hands curl into fists at my sides. "There was nothing left of him but charred flesh, yet he was still alive." My voice breaks at the memory of Alex, but I am determined not to cry. I must not sound weak. " 'The sky is blue' are the last words he ever spoke. Why would I make something like that up? Why would I lie about it?"

"Why would you lie?" James pulls a paper from within his shirt and waves it before the group. "Why would she lie? Because she betrayed Alex to the bluecoats. Because she's been with one of them."

My jaw drops in shock at James's blatant lie. "No!" I have to shout to be heard above the protestations of the group. "It's not true." Peggy stands beside me. She places her hand on my arm and looks between me and James. I see the pain on her face and the decision she will need to make before this meeting is over. She will have to choose between her best friend and her brother, as James's accusations cannot, and will not, be ignored.

James reads the paper out loud. His voice cuts through the din and everyone quiets to listen to the words. " 'Wanted for murder, Cadet Pace Bratton. Last seen in the company of shiner Wren Mac-Avoy.' " Before I can protest he continues. "That's where you go every morning. To meet your lover. And to help your lover you turned in Alex because of what he said about the seekers."

"That's a lie!"

"The proof is right here, Wren." He waves the paper. "How can you deny it?"

I *could* tell them what I do. That I go to watch the sunrise. I could tell them that I just met Pace two days ago, but it's related to Alex's death and that event is already tainted with James's accusations. I could tell them that there is something beyond the facts, something else that leads to more questions, but I don't know what it is. I could say that James hates me because I rejected him when I rejected his kiss, but it would all fall on deaf ears. James's seeds of doubt, well planted, have already taken root. Nothing that I say to prove my innocence will matter because I have nothing to prove my innocence with except my word.

I look around at the faces of the people I've known my entire life. James has given them a choice. Believe him, one who truly belongs, or believe me, one who's lived among them, but always on the edge. Me, the one who spends most of her time by herself, content to keep company with my dreams. There's no choice, not really. James has always had their love and admiration. I could have too, if I'd accepted him.

Peggy drops her hand and the absence of her touch makes me feel naked. She rubs her arms as if she is chilled and looks away. An image of Lucy comes to mind, of how everyone looked at her after she admitted her betrayal of Alex, followed by her subsequent leaving.

Except I have no place to go and no one is waiting for me above.

Things are not always what they seem . . .

"I know what I saw and what I heard. It's something I will never forget." I look around the cave, at the faces I've known my entire life. I see the doubt and the betrayal they think I've committed. "I have not lied to you." There is nothing else for me to say, so I go. I stop in the tunnel when I realize I've left my lunch pail behind. I dare not go back in, the humiliation is too strong. I am tempted to listen and see what is said about me, to know if anyone will stand up for me.

James's revenge, which I could never imagine, is complete. At least Peggy still feels some compassion for me, as she comes out with my pail and leads me to a small alcove off the tunnel. Dim light pours out from the meeting place and we are nothing but shadows, grays and browns against the dark earth. It is hard to see her face but I know her so well that I realize her intent. She wants to make things better. She wants to make the hurt go away and go back to the way things were when we were children and believed the best of everything.

"You could have told me about the boy," she says. "I would have understood."

"There was nothing to tell . . ."

"I always wondered where you went." Peggy has always been single-minded. I know her well enough to let her talk it out, even though I shake with anger and disappointment. "You didn't talk to me as much once you started going topside after your shifts . . ."

I want to answer her. And tell her we grew apart because of Adam, and her engagement. Because we worked in different places. Because when we did manage to talk she was full of plans for a future beneath the ground and I was looking at the dome, wondering if there was a way out.

"I don't understand why you don't want to be with James," she continues. "You know he'll be on the council someday, which means you'll get to live in one of the nicer homes . . ."

The meeting is over. The seekers come out in small groups,

their heads together, talking about me and my betrayal. A few look our way and shush the others so I will not overhear their words. I watch for James over Peggy's shoulder. He's the last one to come out. He stops and stares at me while Peggy continues, oblivious to what's going on behind us. I think he will stop her and make her come with him, but he doesn't. He just turns and walks away.

I realize while she is speaking that in one way James is right. I may not have taken a lover in the world above, but I have looked outside my world for something more, just as Lucy did. Our motives were different, but our desires the same. My leanings, while not a conscious decision, are still made, nonetheless. I will never be the same to the shiners, and I will never look at them in the same way again.

I no longer belong. Yet I have no place else to go. I realize that Peggy has stopped talking. Her eyes are upon me, shining in the dim light, nothing more than a reflection of her hopes for me.

"You're thinking about him now, aren't you? You're planning to leave, just like Lucy." She grabs my arm. "You can't go, Wren. He's wanted for murder and the filchers will be after you. You've got to stay here. You've got to stay safe."

"I'm not going anywhere," I say. "Except to work."

"It's going to be harder now," Peggy says. "For us to be friends. I have to think of Adam, and James . . . and their futures. I ca—"

I cut her off before she can say anything else. "I understand. Don't worry about it."

She smiles brightly. "I can walk back with you."

"I'd like that."

We walk on, without conversation, back to the main tunnels, and then we part ways, me to the stables and Peggy back to the village. I keep my head down as I work with the ponies, hoping beyond hope that James's accusations have not been voiced down in the mines. It's a lot to hope for but still I do. I don't want to cause my grandfather any more pain than he's already felt. It isn't until I lead the first cart down into the mine that I realize Peggy and I were the last ones out. And we left the canary behind.

· 8 ·

The library is one of the most sacred places in the dome. Only on rare occasions are the shiners allowed to enter, and this is after we've been inspected to make sure our bodies are clean so we will not contaminate the books. We're not allowed to take them out as the royals are. Books are one of our most precious commodities. As a child I could barely contain my excitement when we were allowed to go in. I would listen with rapt attention to the stories my grandfather read to me, and later, when I was older, and able to turn the pages carefully, I would study the drawings of faraway places, all made before the comet came and burned up the world.

I want nothing more than to be in a faraway place when my shift starts and everyone I come into contact with looks at me with doubt. James's accusations, like everything else in our world, travel quickly, whispered from mouth to ear and moving into the tunnels as quickly as the water runs through our village. Whether by his choice, or happenstance, I do not see my grandfather and for that I am grateful.

I have to clear my name. The only way I can is with the truth. The only one who knows the truth is Pace. I have to meet him. I can only pray that he can avoid capture until then. He knows what happened to Alex.

The sky is blue . . .

I have to admit to myself that it's about more than just clearing my name. I need to know what it was Alex saw.

Things are not always what they seem . . . They aren't for me either.

According to the flyer the filchers are after me. Riding the lift to the surface would be a sure way to be caught, so I hurry through the older tunnels that run closer to the surface. I search for an escape hatch, one that will lead me close to the library. I did not take the time to grab a lamp and they are few and far between in this part; still I move quickly, my eyes seeing the different hues of darkness that make up the twists and turns.

The tunnels in this part of the mines have been reinforced, multiple times. The air is stale and old. There is a watery trail down the center of the tunnel that stinks of waste. That is not a good sign. I hear a drip off to the side. I don't want to think about where it comes from.

Suddenly another noise echoes through the dark quiet. A rock skittering through the water? I freeze in my tracks, every part of my body straining to hear something recognizable. Could someone be following me? Moments pass in which I feel as if my heart is going to pound through my chest. It is so loud that I can't hear anything but the beating, so I take a deep breath and will my body to calm down. If I'm this frightened in the tunnels how can I possibly hope to avoid the filchers?

I have to move. I told Pace to meet me at dawn and I know it is coming. I can feel it inside me, a pulling in my body and a craving for the soft morning light. I move onward, quietly and carefully, in case someone is following me.

It's just a rat . . . Why would anyone want to follow me? I convince myself that my imagination has run away and created threats that simply aren't there as I come to the ladder that will carry me up to dome level. The struts are old and weak and I can only pray that they hold me as I climb ever upward. If I fall I would lay forever in the darkness, waiting for someone to find me.

The rats would find me . . .

My fears are getting the best of me. I cannot allow it. To do so will compromise me when I go above. I convince myself that my imagination is once more running away as I steadily climb. Suddenly a strut breaks beneath my foot and I dangle precariously in the air for what seems like an eternity before my foot finds the next step and I hold on for dear life, too far up to go back and too frightened to go on.

Is this worth dying over? I should be home, in our little house, in the cavern below. I should be in my bed, with the covers pulled up to my chin and a cat curled up next to me. As I press my forehead against the cool dark dirt of the access tunnel I cannot help but think of all the things I'd rather be doing.

But then what will happen? Does the prospect of getting up every evening, going to the mines, coming home and going to bed, and then repeating it again and again until I die, suffocated by the death of my lungs, give meaning to my life? After James's accusations I am destined to be alone. I see my future stretching out ahead of me, dark and lonely. Shouldn't there be more to life than this? Is that what drove Alex? To show Lucy that there could be more?

My life, whatever it was, is forever changed. I can never go back to that innocence, not after James's accusations. Not after Alex's death. I have to move upward and onward. I have to go above. It's either that or die right here, lost and without hope.

I take a deep breath and climb. It's a long way but finally I see the wooden hatch above me, growing closer with every step up the ladder. The latch is rusty and it takes every bit of my strength to slide it open and push the hatch upward. I climb out and lie on the smooth dirt for a moment, taking the time to catch my breath and contemplate what I am about to do.

I am in one of the access tunnels for the subterranean part of the dome. Our hatch opens into a storage area. From here I move into the channel that holds the vents and lines that bring power to the royals. Below me are the sewers. I hear the rush of water running beneath the wooden boards that creak as I crawl on all fours toward the service entrance. I listen to make sure no one is around before I cautiously emerge in a dark alley.

My original plan had been to go to my usual spot and watch to see if Pace showed up. Now, with the warrant issued for me, I decide that I should stay to the shadows, as I am certain the filchers more than likely know my usual haunts. I pull my scarf up over the lower part of my face and loosen my hair from its band so it will fall forward and around my face. For once I am happy for the unruly curliness as it will help cover me and hopefully obscure the shine of my eyes. My goggles will identify me as a shiner for certain so I stuff them into my pants pocket.

I see no one except for a lonely cat investigating an overturned can of trash as I make my way to the library. The light is already filtering in from above and I know Max and his coworkers are more than likely already above. I realize I should not risk going to the roof of the library. If I can find a safe enough place, I can wait and watch for Pace.

I am lucky as the smoke is thick this morning. With the shortage of coal the ruling committee has had to turn the fans back at night. I think it is a stupid ruling as the fans will only have to work harder when they are turned up to disperse the gathered smoke.

But as no one has asked my opinion on such things I keep the thought to myself. Still, it won't be long until it is light and the smoke and fog will clear and I will be vulnerable. As will Pace.

I refuse to think that he has been captured. It is certainly a possibility. A full day has gone by since I saw him and so much has happened in my life. I don't want to think about what I will do if he does not appear. It has come down to this. My very life depends on what he knows. On what I hope he will tell me.

I find a spot in the alley behind the library. I fade into the shadows of a doorway that leads into a basement and keep an eye on the network of stairs that lead to the roof of the building. I do not have long to wait, as a figure appears out of the smoke and stares upward.

Is it Pace? I cannot tell. His head is covered with a hood. He is not wearing his uniform. He's dressed more like a scarab and the thought that it could be a filcher sends me back into the shadows with a gasp. He turns toward the sound and once more I feel that burning sensation and know that his eyes are upon me. The one thing I had not considered when I dropped into my hiding place was the prospect of a quick escape. I can only pray that he is alone as I dart my eyes back and forth in hopes of finding some sort of weapon.

"Wren?" He takes a step toward me.

It's Pace. Even with his face hidden in the shadow of his hood, I recognize the fall of his dark hair across his forehead, the lean angle of his jaw, and the bright blue blaze of his eyes as he takes another step.

"Shhh," I say as I climb out of my hiding place. I hear the creak of the dome washers moving their baskets above us. Footsteps sound on the street beyond but they are distorted in swirling smoke and fog. I cannot tell if it is close or far away, if it is one, or many.

He shakes his head as he comes to me. What I thought before

were shadows on his face turn out to be bruises. There is a cut over one of his eyes that fades into the slash of his brow. Dark circles show beneath his eyes and I realize that, like me, he has had no rest since Alex died.

And he is wanted for murder.

"I didn't do it," he says, as if reading my mind. "I need a place to hide. I need time to figure this out."

A thousand thoughts fall through my mind as I look at his face. It is forbidden to bring anyone below, especially a bluecoat. What will my grandfather say? What will the council say? Where will I hide him? More thoughts follow, each one piling upon the last until I fear the weight of them will crush me. With a sudden burst of clarity I realize I've already made the decision. I made it when I decided to come to the surface. The only thing I need to decide now is where to hide him.

I hold out my hand. Pace looks at it as if it's something he's never seen before. Then a look of such intense relief washes over his face and he takes it. I realize that he is shaking. I give his fingers a squeeze and he squeezes mine back.

"Thank you."

I nod. I even manage to smile. Beyond Pace I see two men walk into the alleyway. The smoke is so thick that I'm not certain if they are real or some sort of ghostly apparition. Then the fans suddenly start and they stop and look and their faces are covered with the filchers' masks. The fear must show on my face because Pace turns to see what I am staring at.

We run.

◆

I always thought I knew what fear was. Before today fear was worrying about being late for my shift. Wondering if I'd get caught and disciplined for going to the rooftops. The possibility of a cave-in down in the mines. Now I know exactly what fear is. It's the bone-chilling, sick-to-your-stomach knowledge that if you get caught you are going to die a slow and horrible death.

Pace keeps a tight hold on my hand. I don't know if it's because I'm not as fast as him, or because he's afraid I will leave him to the filchers while I slip into the tunnels. Either way, we pound through the awakening streets, Pace's speed and grip on my hand adding wings to my feet.

We round a corner. Dash into an alleyway. Cut back in a narrow gap between two buildings. Duck beneath a cart that stands tipped against a wall. My heart pounds in my chest and my ears ring with the rushing of blood through my veins. My lungs scream in agony. Pace holds my hand against his chest as he peers out of our hiding place. His grip is so tight that my fingers feel numb.

"It's just a matter of time before the alarms go off." His words are soft, yet steady. I can barely breathe from our wild run. His lungs are clearer than mine and much stronger from living above. "Are we close to one of your escape hatches?"

I start to protest—how does he know about escape hatches?—and then I realize he'd seen me use one. I need to catch my breath, to get my bearings. I have no idea where we are.

Pace looks at me, his blue eyes steady on mine. "I'm sorry you got caught up in this."

I shake my head. Now is not the time for blame or apology. We need to get below. Without him I have no way of proving the truth of Alex's death. My breathing evens out so I can speak. "Where are we?"

"We're close to Park Front. On the same street I saw you on yesterday. Further up."

Park Front. Close to where the royals live. Pace led us in the complete opposite direction of where we needed to go. There are no escape hatches in Park Front, nor in the trade section to where I followed Lucy the day before. My mind races as I try to decide our best route to below. We can't go down in the lift as the blue-coats will be watching it. And I seriously doubt the filchers will let the threat of the tunnels keep them from following us if we use one of the escape hatches. Before I can form the next thought the alarm goes off, scaring me so much that I jump with the suddenness of its scream.

"Which way?" His words are lost in the screeching noise that is amplified a thousand times over with its reverberation off the dome.

I point because I know Pace cannot hear my words. "We've got to get close to the coal lift. That's where most of the escape hatches are." It's on the opposite side of the dome. We've got a long way to go. The odds of us making it are close to impossible. Pace still has hold of my hand. For some strange reason, it reassures me, as if together we can make it. We have to make it; our very lives depend upon it.

Pace looks right and left, and then leads me out from our hiding place. He flattens against the wall when we come to the end of the gap and cautiously looks around. The alarm is still shrieking its call. Some will remain in their homes to wait to hear news of why the alarm is on. Those who are already out for the morning will go to the fountain where Alex died to hear the news. The streets will be mostly empty, until we get to scarab town. We will be easy targets if we are seen.

"Let's go," he says and we dash across the alley. We continue on, sneaking from corner to corner, place to place, Pace leading, and holding on to my hand until I feel like I'm an extension of his arm. My pulse falls into the same pattern as his, thumping slowly as he checks the next steps in our escape, then pounding as we expose ourselves to view with our mad dashes to the next hiding place. I stop thinking about the fear and the end result if we are captured. Instead I concentrate on being invisible, on willing the tradesmen, whose shops and storefronts we use as shelter, not to see us.

I am now in more familiar territory. I recognize the place where I last saw Lucy. So much has happened since then that it is hard for me to believe that it was just one morning since I followed her. Two since Alex died. Where was I three days ago? It's hard to even conceive of what was once my normal routine.

Pace stops and flattens against a wall beside a display of crockery. He inclines his head across the way and I see Lucy staring at us from a window in the building she went into the previous day. She motions for us to come. Pace looks at me questioningly and I nod my agreement. I have no reason not to trust Lucy.

With a quick look each way to make sure we're unseen, we dash across the street. Lucy opens the door and we run inside. She quickly shuts it, locks it, and checks the street. The alarms stop as Lucy leads us to the back of the building where Pace finally releases his hold on my hand. I get a vague impression as we walk through of a long counter and piles of neatly folded laundry. Baskets are stacked against the wall and thick bags with names on them hang on hooks above.

I want nothing more than to collapse into a heap on the floor. I want the past two days to go away as if they've never happened. I want to go back to being a little girl and sit on my grandfather's lap and watch the kittens chase one another around the steps to our home. I look at Pace. He throws the hood back from his face and I see that he's damp with sweat and realize that I am too. He runs his hands through his hair and the dark ends stand straight up with moisture. He looks around the room. We're in a kitchen, nicer than anything I've ever seen, with a large stove and a series of cupboards and a sink. There's even an icebox. The door and window face the alley. Lucy quickly pulls the curtains closed on both of them.

Pace takes a deep breath and looks at me. I see the worry on his face and know without him saying a word that, like me, he also wants the past two days to go away. But they can't, and they won't. He gives me a slight smile, and then he nods and turns to Lucy. "I know what the flyers say," he says. "And I want you to know that I didn't do it."

If only it were that simple.

· 9 ·

You shouldn't risk your life for us," I say to Lucy. "If they find out you've helped us . . ." My voice trails off at the prospect of what punishment awaits us now.

"Does this have anything to do with Alex?"

Before I can answer her the young man I saw her with the morning before comes into the kitchen from upstairs. "No one is following," he says.

"This is David," Lucy says simply. There is no need to say more. It is evident that they are in love. David takes Lucy's hand in his with the same look of devotion that I once envied on Alex's face. The difference is Lucy returns it. The glance between them holds the same intensity of Peggy and Adam's, and now I understand the kiss I saw between them the day before.

I know now that I never saw Lucy look at Alex the way she now looks at David. After my experience with James I can maybe understand what drove her to put Alex aside. Wishing things had turned out differently for him will not change what happened. It only makes me realize how fragile we really are.

"I am only helping you because of Lucy," David says. He stares intently at Pace and his desire to keep Lucy safe is apparent. "But I will turn you in if it means our lives."

"I know." Pace goes to the door and cautiously peers through the side of the drapes. "We should go before they get too close." I join Pace close by the door, ready to go if he says to run and praying with all my might that he won't.

"Wait." Lucy grabs my hand and takes it in hers. "I never wanted Alex to die."

I look into her dark eyes, past the fading glimmer of her shine, and see the sorrow she carries. Will it be there forever or will it eventually fade? Is it sorrow for Alex, or sorrow for the mistakes she made? It's not for me to judge her. "I know."

The smile she gives me is tearful and grateful. If not for David she would be as alone as I am. At least I have my grandfather, but that relationship could be tenuous after I take Pace below. If we make it below. At least here, Lucy will be safe, as long as no one knows she helped us.

"Are they after you because of what Alex did?" Lucy asks Pace.

Pace looks at me for a long moment, his eyes full of questions that I have no answers to. I don't know him, not really, and he doesn't know me, yet for some reason he trusts me with his life. Circumstance has thrown us together and I have to believe it's because of what Alex said. Because of what he saw.

"Yes," Pace says, "and they killed my friend, Tom, because of it. That's the murder they've accused me of. If I had not followed Wren yesterday morning I would be dead too," he continues.

He drops the drape and turns from the door. Should we stay?

Should we go? Do we have time for this? If I'm going to be taken, if I'm going to die at the hands of the filchers, then I want to know why. So I ask. "Why?"

"Because of what we saw." Pace shakes his head and shuts his eyes. Is that all he has to say? A long moment passes. A long moment where he swallows and gathers himself for the words he finally says. "The outside didn't burn your friend. They did."

My stomach revolts, acid burns its way up my throat and I swallow it back. I refuse to believe him. It cannot be. Could it? "What do you mean 'they burned him'?"

He clenches his hands into fists so tight that the smooth skin on the back of them turns ghastly white. Pace looks down at his fists and relaxes them. He stretches his fingers out and then back in. "He found a way out and they brought him back in." His voice trembles. "And then they turned the flamethrower on him." His voice drops to a whisper. "He screamed 'The sky is blue' over and over again until all he could do was scream in pain."

They burned him alive? On purpose? I can't take it anymore. My stomach wins the battle and I run to the sink. It's hard to believe there is anything inside me to come up, but it does with a vengeance. Behind me I hear Lucy's cries. A hand touches my back and someone hands me a cloth. It's Pace. I wipe my mouth and feel my face burn with embarrassment when I finally raise my head.

"I did the same," he says quietly. Does he think it will make me feel better? My throat is raw. All I can do is nod in agreement. Behind Pace, Lucy weeps while David consoles her.

"Tom and I were there. They're afraid that we would tell someone so they killed him. They planned to kill both of us, but I was late, because of you. Tom must have realized what they were going to do because he fought them. I came in and he told me to run so I did. I left him there to die." He squeezes his eyes shut once more and when he finally opens them they are wet with unshed tears. "They framed me for his murder. They think you must know something, either from your friend or from me, which is why they want you too."

I listen to his words but for some reason they won't sink in. My mind races as something else, something important, pounds its way through my mind.

"Alex got out."

"Yes." Pace agrees with me, but doesn't share my sudden excitement.

"Where? How?"

"I don't know."

"But it must be close to where you were."

"It doesn't matter. You could never get there. It's too closely guarded. They will kill you."

A shout interrupts us. David leaps to his feet and runs to the front of the house. Pace follows him. Lucy takes my hand as I follow as well.

"Tell his parents he made it out." Her eyes are moist with the tears she's shed. Tears of regret or sadness, I cannot say. "That he knew the way."

"Will that change anything?"

"Not for Alex." She looks at me with hope and smiles tremulously. "But maybe for them."

"I will." I squeeze her hand. *If we make it . . .* I don't say the rest to her.

"They're searching the houses now." Pace returns. "Someone must have seen us come this way."

"Can we go out the back?" I ask.

"No, they'll be watching the alleys," David says. "This way." David leads us to a door beneath the staircase. When he opens it all

I see is a closet, but he slides a trunk aside and there is a hatch, much like the ones we use to hide our access tunnels from the above-world. "This leads to the sewers," he explains. "Lucy said you have tunnels that connect."

"We do." I give Lucy a quick hug. "Thank you."

"Tell my parents I'm fine," she says. "And happy with David," she adds.

I nod and give her a slight smile as I drop into the darkness. I feel the walls around me, nothing more than a narrow chute of hard-packed dirt. I brace myself to land with bent knees and pray that I will find solid ground beneath me instead of the runoff from the royals' sewer. Gratefully, I land on packed earth. I look up at the square of dim light some ten feet above me and see Pace's face is full of fear as he looks down at me.

"Come on," I whisper loudly.

He disappears, and then nothing more than a heartbeat passes before I see his feet dangling above.

"Just let go."

He does and falls straight down with his arms stretched above his head as if he might change his mind and grab on to something. There's nothing there, nothing but a free fall through darkness. David closed the hatch as soon as Pace let go and the sound of the trunk moving back into place fills the darkness. I move to give Pace room to land and he does, heavily, at my feet before he scrambles up and stands beside me.

"Ow!" I hear the clang and look up. Pipes are directly overhead and Pace has hit his head on them.

"Shhh." I step away from Pace to give my eyes a moment to adjust to the complete darkness that engulfs us. I hear the skittering of rats and the trickle of water. The smell is horrendous so I pull my kerchief up over my mouth and nose. It's not much help but it's better than breathing the straight fumes. I must get my bearings if I'm to get us to safety. I also feel the need to move, just in case they find our escape route. I see pipes overhead, nothing more than lines that crisscross above like spiderwebs. We're in another access tunnel, much like the one I came up through.

"Wren?" Pace's voice is tight and his breathing quick and shallow. He can't see me in the utter blackness that surrounds us. All I can see is contrast, darker where the walls are and lighter where it's open. It doesn't take me long to see that we're going to have to crawl to get out. The place where we landed shouldn't be here. How many people have used it in the past to escape just as we have? Is David a part of something like our seekers or has this been here longer than he's been alive? The closely packed dirt is like a lot of our older tunnels. Why is it here?

"He should have given us a lamp." I touch his arm and he grabs on to my hand and squeezes it so tight that I try to jerk away from the pain.

"Sorry," he chokes out.

"Are you afraid of the dark?"

"I'm afraid of being enclosed," he admits with a shaky voice.

I have to laugh. "Like living in a dome?" I can see the planes of his face now, the darkness that is his eyes and hair and the lightness of his cheeks and nose. He takes a deep breath.

"More like being underground, I think." His voice is steadier now and his grip on my hand solid.

"Good thing you weren't born a shiner."

"Aren't you afraid of anything?"

I don't even have to think about it. "I am. Falling." Falling into the pit and not knowing what's below me, not knowing if I'll land.

And knowing that I'll have to land somewhere eventually. What if the fall doesn't kill me? What if I'm there, dying, alone in the dark like the canary, trapped and abandoned in its cage? *Falling* . . .

I tug on his hand. "Let's go."

"Where? I can't see anything."

"I can."

"How?"

I turn to look at him. I know what my eyes look like in the dark, as I've seen others just like them my entire life. They glow like a cat's and are the same color as polished brass. Now, in the total blackness, they just shine, like beacons.

"That's why they call you shiners." Pace states the obvious but I don't mind. Talking will help to take his mind off his fear. I only hope he can keep it at bay for a good long while because it's going to get a lot worse, if what I see before us is any indication.

"And we call you bluecoats."

"Not me. Not anymore."

"Let's go." I tug on his hand and he follows me, slowly.

"Do you know where to go?"

"Do you hear the water?"

"Yes."

"It runs downward and that's the direction we need to go in, to go below."

"Below?" He stops and jerks on my hand.

"It's the only place you can hide."

"I know but . . ."

"But what? You didn't think it would be dark? Or closed in? Dirty? Smelly?" I drop his hand and step far enough away that he can't reach out and touch me. "I don't have to help you, you know. I can just walk away and leave you here."

"If not for you and your friend I wouldn't be in this mess." I hear the panic in his voice, but I also hear that he's thinking clearly. He didn't ask to be a part of this. For that matter, neither did I. One reckless decision by Alex has put both our lives at risk.

But he got out . . .

I purposely don't look at him so he can't see my eyes. I feel him standing close by, so very still, as if he's afraid that if he moves, the entire dome will come crashing down on top of us. Maybe if he knows what to expect he can prepare for it. I can't help him if he panics on me. I can well understand his fear of being closed in. I have my own fear that sometimes wakes me shivering in my bed. He's going to have to face his fear if he wants to survive. "We're going to have to crawl through a tunnel," I say. "We have to get down to the sewer level. After that it's just a matter of finding a hatch to go below."

"Is it like this below?"

"No. It's bigger. Like the dome almost."

"Except it's dark."

"We have light."

He doesn't speak for a moment. What if he does stay here? Will it make any difference to me? Will it mean my life or my death? "You can come with me, or you can face the fires. Which is it?"

"I'm ready." I catch a movement out of the corner of my eye. He's stepped closer, lured by the sound of my voice. He may be frightened but he's thinking things through. He's in control of himself.

I take his hand once more and lead him forward. "First up is a tunnel. You'll have to crawl. We're following the water so we're going to get wet." I place his hand on the wall above the tunnel. "I'm going in," I say. "Just feel your way down to the opening."

I drop down to my hands and knees and crawl forward. The water trickles between my hands but it's hard to keep my knees out of it. To my eyes, the water gleams like a strip of silver. To Pace it's nothing more than a sensation. I'm no more than five feet in when the walls of the tunnel fill my ears with their dense quiet. The trickle of the water is nothing compared to the pounding of my heart in my chest and the roar of the blood in my veins. I feel Pace behind me as he scrambles to keep up with me, afraid that I will abandon him here in a place worse than the one we left. It's too narrow to turn around.

What if we can't get through? There's no guarantee that this tunnel is big enough for our bodies. All it is required to do is carry water that is nothing more than condensation off the pipes. We must move on. To go back and go above is certain death for both of us.

Alex got out . . . What did he see? *The sky is blue* . . . But what does it look like? The pictures I saw years ago in books have nothing more than emptiness where the sky is supposed to be. What else did he see?

The tunnel gets smaller as we move downward. My shoulders drag against the sides and my neck cramps from holding my head down. Pace isn't following as closely as he was when we started. I hear him straining behind me.

"I can't move," he says after a long moment.

"Hang on."

"I'm not going anywhere," he says.

I grin and shake my head. If it's tight for me it has to be worse for Pace. Not only is he much taller than me, but he's also broader. I don't want to because of the water but I have no choice. I drop down to my belly and wiggle onward. My clothes are quickly soaked and I shiver with cold but I'm able to make it through without too much trouble. The tunnel widens out and the smell of the sewer is strong, so strong that I gag.

"We're almost through." I turn around and face Pace so he can see my eyes. "You're going to have to crawl." He looks at me, his face ghastly white against the blackness of the dirt that surrounds him.

"I won't fit." His voice is hollow and distant, lost in the heavy weight of the tunnel.

"You've got to." I try to sound encouraging and to keep the frustration from my voice. If not for him I'd be below by now. I'd be safe. "There's no place else to go."

There's no going back . . . Everything is changed now. If I could just go back to the way life was a few days ago. To the night that Alex flew. What could I change? What could I have done to make Lucy choose Alex and me choose James and for all of us to live out our lives as they were intended?

Alex got out . . . I hear Pace struggling through the tunnel. Good. He's trying. I'm able to stand, not straight, but straight enough, and I creep down to where it opens into the sewers. It's raw with the smell and I gag once more. The wide pipes that are supposed to carry it to the septic ponds are broken and some of it has spilled out onto the ground. It's not surprising, as they are over two hundred years old. Why haven't they been repaired? The pipes are wide and tall and the tunnels carrying them are big enough for us to stand and move easily. The thought of walking through the waste . . .

"Wren?" Pace's voice trembles. "I'm stuck."

I crawl back into the small tunnel. He's wedged in tight. "Can you move anything?"

He rolls his shoulders, gasps, and manages to get his left arm out from under his chest. He stretches his hand out and tries to get a handhold in the dirt. "Wren?"

He's terrified. I can see it on his face. What am I doing here? If not for Pace I'd be gone. I should go on, leave him. Just like I left the canary stuck in his cage.

"I'm here." I crawl as close as I can get and grab his hand. He squeezes mine so tight that it goes numb. His breath comes in gasps. He's so very afraid. "I'm going to get you out." I put my other hand over his and run my thumb under his palm to break his hold. "You've got to let go of my hand so I can dig."

"It will all come down." He twists his head around in an effort to see. "We'll be buried alive."

I gently touch his cheek. It's so cold. "Trust me." He leans into my hand. "This is what I do."

He stares at me, trying desperately to see me in the darkness. The whites of his eyes surround the deep blue that is nothing more than black holes in the darkness. "I don't want to die," he whispers.

"I don't want to either. I'm going to do my best to make sure that doesn't happen."

Pace nods against my hand and takes a deep breath. I place my hands on the dirt around his shoulders. It's packed so tight. I dig in with my nails and scratch against it. A small chunk comes out and I pitch it behind me. "Can you slide any? Even an inch will help."

He shifts a bit. "Not really."

"Hold your breath and try again."

He does but doesn't move much. I try to dig again but the dirt is so hard and I don't have any tools. There's not much I can do. Pace realizes it. I can tell by the way he's breathing. If he panics and tries to wrench free I'm afraid he'll hurt himself, or worse. What can I do? I can't get help, it will take too long, and if I leave him he'll be terrified. Besides, there's no one that will help. I can't ask my grandfather. He'd turn Pace in if he thought it would save me.

I could go now and leave him. Take care of myself. Disappear into the mines and never go to the surface again. But he'd die here, trapped and alone, like the canary. I wouldn't wish that on anyone. I don't want to spend the rest of my life thinking about his body, decomposing here as he's eaten by the rats until there's nothing left but bones.

Pace is the only one who knows where Alex got out.

"I'm going to pull you out."

"You can't."

"I will."

I grab his forearm with both hands. He clasps his hand around my wrist. I back up as far as I can, spread my legs and brace them against the wall. I lean back and pull with all my strength.

Pace yelps in pain.

"Are you hurt?"

He grits his teeth. "Keep going."

I slide back a few inches, brace my legs and pull again. He moves forward. He twists a bit and pulls his right arm out.

"Again," he gasps.

I slide back and do it again. I pull on his arm until I'm laying flat on my back. He grabs my thigh and pulls until he's lying on my legs.

"I'm free." His voice sounds weak, as if he's fighting back tears. I backpedal out of the tunnel and he slowly follows, using only his right arm to pull himself forward. I wait at the tunnel entrance and help him to his feet when he reaches it. He leans wearily against the dirt wall and wipes his face across his shoulder. "I take it this is the sewers?"

"Yes."

"The smell gave it away."

I have to laugh. This has to have been one of the scariest experiences of his life and he's able to make a joke. I see the bright flash of his teeth in the darkness as he quickly smiles.

"I'm going to need some help with my shoulder," he says when my laughter fades away. "It came out of its joint."

I take a good look at him. His left arm is hanging at a funny angle. "I did that?" I ask.

"You're stronger than you look."

Stronger than I ever thought. I pulled his arm out of joint. How could he stand the pain? How could I do that? Words weren't enough. "I'm so sorry."

"Just put it back," he says. "This isn't the first time it's happened."

"What do I do?"

"Pull it straight out and then shove it in and up until you hear it pop."

I gingerly pick up his arm. I can feel the muscles clenched beneath the fabric of his jacket. He winces. "I'm not sure if I can."

"You have to."

"But it will hurt."

"It hurts now." He puts his right hand on top of mine. "Just do it, quickly. Once it's done I'll be fine."

I nod, take a deep breath, and shove with all my might. I hear a pop and he grabs my shoulder as he grunts in pain. His lowers his head and the strain of him gritting his teeth shows on his jaw. I hang on to him, just in case he passes out, but thankfully he doesn't. He raises his head and nods.

"Better now," he says weakly. "I hope there are no more tunnels like that."

"We should be okay from here," I say. "Ready?" I take his hand once more and lead him along the pipes. I can only hope that we find a way out before they decide to search underground. I have no way of knowing how long we've been running or what we're liable to run into. All I can do is pray.

· 10 ·

*D*o you ever wonder where this all goes to?" I ask when we
come to a joint in the pipes. I go left, in the direction of
the mines. One benefit of being a shiner is that we are born with
some sort of internal compass that helps us survive life underground.
The way is narrow because of the pipes so Pace follows me, trust-
ing in my eyes to get us to safety. He keeps a tight hold on the back
of my jacket so we won't be separated.

"I know where it goes," he says. "I've been there. It's not a place
you want to visit, believe me." Even though we speak quietly our
voices seem to fill the space and echo off the pipes.

"Why were you there?"

"It's the first shift you work as a cadet. Guarding the septic. The
smell is horrible. I puked the first time I was down there."

"Why do they have guards there?"

"They use prisoners to handle the waste. They have to walk in it
and shovel it out. My squad leader says it makes them grateful for
the fires when it comes time for execution."

I see Alex's face once more and a shiver runs down my spine. "I don't think anyone would be grateful for that."

"They drug them before execution. So they won't fight so much."

"Alex wasn't drugged."

"No. He wasn't."

"Do you know where he went out?"

"No. I have an idea . . ."

I start to say something but he interrupts me. "Don't even think about it. They'll roast you just like they did your friend."

"Don't say that." A shiver runs down my spine at the memory of Alex's charred body.

"Say what? Roast? It's what they did to him. I'll never forget it."

Neither will I. I don't want to remember Alex like that. I want to remember him as he was the night before he died, when he flew, with his face full of life and wonder. "Did he say anything else?"

"No. Just 'the sky is blue.'"

"Doesn't that make you wonder? About the outside? About why we can't go out? About what it's li—"

A sharp ping stops us in our tracks and I drop into a crouch with Pace following on my heels. "Can you see anything?" I feel his breath on my ear as he speaks. His chest is against my back and I have to fight the temptation to just lean back so he will put his arms around me and make me feel safe. I want to turn it all over to someone else. I don't want to be brave or strong. I just want to go home and have things back the way they were. If that will only make this horror go away.

I look around, my eyes straining to see something, anything, and hoping beyond hope that I don't.

"It could be a rat," Pace whispers.

"Shhh." I turn to look past him. I finally see something behind us. A faint light back the way we came. "Someone's coming."

"From above or below?"

"Either way, it's bad." I take his hand. "Let's go."

We creep forward, staying low and using the pipes as cover. I know it's all up to me. Pace can't see anything. My eyes strain desperately to see what's ahead of us. We need to find another junction. Whoever is behind us could be looking for us, or it could just be maintenance for the pipes. Considering the shape the pipes are in, my guess is that it's someone searching for us.

Finally I see an opening. It's on the opposite side of the pipes. My internal compass, as natural to me as breathing, tells me this will take me to the hatch I used this morning. I stop and look behind me. Pace does too. The light is closer. I'm sure he can see it too.

"There," I whisper. Pace looks but I know he can't see anything. "We've got to go under the pipes."

"Will I fit?"

"I hope so." If he gets stuck again we'll be caught for certain. I put his hand on the pipe and then I slide under. It feels like mud and I don't even want to think about what I just dragged my body through. "Come on." Pace drops to the ground. I take his sleeve to guide him through.

The light is closer. It flashes over the ceiling and the top of the pipe. Pace sees it too and quickly slips through.

"Stop!" a voice yells. The light is close enough that Pace can see the opening. We run for it.

"How many are there?" Pace whispers. The pipe is smaller here. I'm certain we're where we need to be.

"One. Maybe two?"

"We need a weapon."

"You're going to fight?" I ask incredulously.

"Better now than later when there's more."

What he says makes sense. As we run I look around for something

Pace can use. Surely with the pipes in such bad shape there should be something lying about. There is. I trip over a piece of wood and fly forward before I land on my hands and knees. Miraculously Pace stops before he falls on me. I flail around with my hands, desperately searching until I find the piece of wood. It's stout. It must be from one of the supports for the pipes. I shove it into his hands.

"Find us a place to hide," he whispers. We can hear them now, two voices raised with excitement. I look behind us and see the light scan across the entrance. I look around once more, desperate for someplace to conceal us. Then I realize just a few steps behind us is where the support came from. The pipe has fallen and is crooked to the left.

"Here." I pull Pace to the pipe. He feels around with his hand and then nods. He settles into place with a firm hold on the piece of wood.

"Run ahead. Give them something to chase. Then come back on the other side."

His plan makes sense. They're in the tunnel now. I take off and swat at the pipe when I'm well beyond Pace's hiding place. I'm rewarded with a resounding thump. I hear a shout and the light flashes across my back. They find me; my shadow stretches before me like a giant, as large as my fear.

The tunnel curves and there's a ladder against the wall. An access port to the tunnels above. I could go on, climb it, and leave Pace to his fate. But his words about the executions haunt me. I wouldn't condemn anyone to the fires, and if he's caught that will be the result. The two who are chasing me flash the light around. They lost me! I skid to a stop, slide under the pipe, and run back toward Pace.

I hear a thump and a shout. The light now shines on the ceiling. Pace has struck. I hear the sounds of blows landing. How can he fight with his injured shoulder? My heart pounds in my chest as I get closer. I reach the place where the pipe has fallen, brace my foot on a joint, and scramble up the side. One bluecoat lies on the ground, facedown. The other has Pace against the tunnel wall. He pulls his fist back to punch and Pace jerks his head aside so the blow lands on the hard-packed dirt.

I jump and land on the bluecoat's back. He stumbles and we land against the pipe. It knocks the air from me. Lights swirl before my eyes and my head swims. My stomach wobbles against my spine. I can't let go. I won't let go.

Pace swings at the bluecoat's knees with the piece of wood. The bluecoat drops to the ground with a yelp. I let go and stagger back as Pace swings at the side of his head. He drops like a stone.

We stand there for a moment, staring at each other while both of us pant from the exertion. Blood trickles from a cut on Pace's lip and his right eye is starting to swell. We're both covered with dirt, sweat, and other stuff that I don't want to think about.

"Are they dead?" I finally ask.

"Does it matter?" Pace picks up the lamp.

Does it? A choice between us and them and them winning would have meant our death.

"No."

"Are we close?"

"Yes. I found the way out."

He steps aside so I can lead the way. I can't help but wonder, as we quickly run to the curve and the ladder, if my name will be on another wanted poster come tomorrow.

◆

Finally, we finished the long descent into the mines down the same ladder I'd climbed just this morning. I had my doubts at the time as to whether it would hold Pace's weight. My legs wobble as I drop wearily to the ground and I step back to allow Pace room to dismount. He'd stuffed the lamp in his shirt during the climb and he reaches for it when he's on solid ground.

"Don't. Someone might see it."

"But you said there was light down here."

"There is. It's just a long way between them. We don't use them in this part of the mines. No one can know you're here."

He sighs wearily and I can't help but agree with him. Now the problem is where do I hide him? And then what do I tell my grandfather when I show up covered with shite?

"Where are we, exactly?"

"Close to the library on the surface. In the oldest parts of the mine."

"Close to the library?" His voice is indignant.

"You're the one who led us in the wrong direction," I snap. I'm tired and I'm worried and I want nothing more than to scrub my body clean before crawling into my bed and sleeping forever.

"Sorry."

He doesn't really sound that sorry and I'm once more tempted to stomp off and leave him on his own. At least here he won't have to worry about being caught by the bluecoats, or worse, the filchers. If he's found then the council will know I'm the one who brought him down and then I'll be in worse trouble. As if it could get any worse.

"Come on," I say and take off, not really caring if he follows me or not.

"Ow."

I hear him trip and keep going.

"Wren."

I ignore him.

"Wren!"

I stop.

"I can't see. Either wait for me or I'm turning on the lamp."

I take a deep breath and look at Pace. He stands beneath one of the supports with his hand on the beam. In the other is the lamp and he's poised, ready to turn it on if I don't answer him. His eyes are lost beneath his hair and his face grim yet resolute. His clothes and face are streaked with blood, dirt, and shite. He's a fighter—the darkness can't hide it, nor will he let it beat him. I have to admire him for it.

We're not so different, I realize, in spite of us coming from completely different worlds. We both saw our friends murdered for nothing more than circumstance and now we've both become victims. We have no one to depend on and nowhere to turn but to each other.

I go to him. Pace senses me before him and straightens his spine as I put my hand on the lamp. I pull his hand between us and turn on the lamp so he can see my face. We both blink against the sudden brightness. I wait until he looks at me to speak. I see the terror in his eyes, but I also see the determination.

"I'm sorry," I say. "Sorry for everything that's happened to you. I'm going to find a place for you to hide, someplace safe, and then I have to go home before my grandfather comes looking for me. Can you live with that? Can you be patient until I work things out?"

"I will."

His voice is nothing more than a whisper. I turn off the lamp and take it in one hand and his hand in the other before I turn.

"Wren, wait."

I turn back to him. He raises his free hand and feels his way tentatively up my arm until he's grasping my shoulder.

"I'm sorry too. Sorry that you got sucked into my mess." He pulls me to him and wraps his arms around me. He bends his head close to mine as he embraces me. For some strange reason, I feel safe and secure. The terror that held me in its grip all day fades away and I'm filled with a warmth that starts on the inside and flows outward. "Thank you for saving my life many times over today."

"You saved mine too." Tears come to my eyes and I quickly blink them away. It's because I'm tired and I've been so scared. Now is not the time to give in and be weak.

"We've got to stick together if we're going to survive this."

"I know."

He lets go of me, and I suddenly feel strange and awkward. I don't know where to turn or what to do.

"Do you think maybe you can find someplace with running water?" he says jokingly. "I could really use a bath."

His words inspire me. "I know just the place." Once more I take his hand. I know exactly where to hide him.

◆

"You mentioned a grandfather?" Pace asks. We've been descending, following the tunnels that wind their way deeper into the oldest parts of the mine. We walk side by side and hand in hand. His grip is not desperate now, just steady. We've gained a lot of trust in each other the past few hours. Our destination is close to where the seekers met and James betrayed me. It seems like it happened a lifetime ago. I'm puzzled by the fact that all the lamps are dark. They are few and far between in this part but they were lit when I went up this morning. Why are they dark now?

"Yes, I live with my grandfather." Our voices disappear into the darkness as we walk. "My mother died when I was born and my grandmother soon after."

"Your father?" He's making conversation to hold back the darkness. I don't blame him. How scary it would be to feel as if you were blind, especially in a place you've never been before. My eyes strain ahead, hoping to catch sight of the next lamp.

I shake my head but realize he can't see me. "I don't know him. He's from above. She never told anyone who he was."

"My father died before I was born," he says. "I never knew him either. It's always just been me and my mother. I'm worried about her. About what they'll do to her."

I'm glad he can't see the horror on my face. The filchers will stop at nothing to get what they want, and if they think his mother is the key to catching Pace then they'll use her. It has to be frustrating to him, the not knowing, and not having any way to get word to her. There's nothing I can do to help his worry, instead I keep him talking. "How old are you?"

"Eighteen."

"Two years older than me."

"Only if you're sixteen."

I laugh. He's funny, in a dry sort of way that really tickles me. What would he have been like if he'd been born into my world instead of above? Would he have the same fears or different ones? Would he have the same sense of humor? Would we have grown naturally together instead of fate throwing us together?

"I hear water running."

"It's part of the river."

"The one that services the dome? Won't there be guards there?"

"No, not this part of it. There are many places where it goes beneath and then comes up again. It also splits into many channels before it comes back again. Part of it runs through our village. We have to be careful when tunneling because it could flood the mines, so we have it mapped out."

"That's how your kind has survived underground for so many years."

"My kind?" Is that how he sees me? Another dirty shiner?

"Independent. Self-sufficient. I've always envied your way of life. It's like you thumb your nose at the royals."

I'd never thought of us that way. I like it. We have been thumbing our noses at the royals all these years. Having our own way of life instead of what they dictated for us when they built the dome. Pride fills me, but I know it's not all independence or self-sufficiency.

"We still have to work for them. And we're not self-sufficient. We can't grow vegetables or fruit. We need the world above as much as you need what we provide."

"And the royals reap the rewards."

I have no response to that. It's strange that I've never thought of those above resenting their way of life also, except for the scarabs. Of course they would, but everyone else? The butchers and bakers, the street cleaners and harvesters, the shopkeepers and teachers and bluecoats? Why wouldn't they resent it? They were all sentenced to the same thing as the shiners. Service to the royals for each and every generation.

The noise of the water is louder now. My skin itches with the need to wash and I would love to burn my clothes, but as I don't own many, I'll have to scrub them clean and hope I don't have to explain how they got so nasty.

"I didn't realize how thirsty I am until now," Pace says.

"Me too. And hungry. I can't remember the last time I ate."

"Me either."

"Watch your head." I put his hand on an overhang. We just have to duck through a short tunnel, no more than three feet long and four feet high, to get to the small cavern that the river has carved out. "It will only take a few seconds to get through."

Pace doesn't complain, he just quietly follows me into the cavern. I believe he's as anxious as I am for water.

"Can I turn on the lamp?"

"Not here. There are no guarantees that someone won't come by. This part of the mine is old and the coal is exhausted but we still use the tunnels. People even come here and swim sometimes."

"It seems like there are miles and miles of them."

"There are. And some of them go really deep. We run out of coal in one place and have to dig until we find more. We use the rock we dig out of new ones to fill up old ones. The old ones we keep because they lead to the water and to our escape hatches around the dome."

"Are there a lot of escape hatches?"

"Not enough."

I see the flash of his grin in the darkness.

"Feel like washing up?"

"Yes. Wait, I can see something."

"Glow fish." The water here is gentle. At one time long ago there was a cave-in, so the water bubbles up from beneath and forms a pool before doing the same on the opposite side. There's a lot of life in the pool, crabs and plankton and the fat fish that glow like white orbs floating beneath the surface. The floor is sandy instead of the hard-packed dirt of the tunnels and the water is shallow enough that you can walk across to the other side.

I sit down on a rock and pull off my boots and Pace does the same. He's much quicker than me, shucking out of his clothes until he's down to his shorts. He wades into the water until it's ankle deep.

"It doesn't drop off, does it?"

"No." I look at him, furtively, as I slide out of my pants. He's straight and he's strong, with well-defined muscles in his back, arms, and legs. He's a good six inches taller than me too. "It shouldn't be more than waist deep on you." I'm glad he can't see me. My face flames with my concept of where the water should hit him.

"Good." He walks out until he's thigh deep and lowers himself with a sigh. "I can't swim." He goes under and then comes back up. He shakes the water off and pushes his hair back from his face.

I'm down to my undershorts and the sleeveless shirt I wear beneath my work clothes. I gather up my clothes to carry to the opposite bank. A good scrubbing with some sand should get a lot of the filth and most of the smell off until I can get back home to wash them out. I drop my clothes in the sand and wade back out. The glow fish, scared by Pace's splashing, gather close to the cave wall. They are so close together that it looks like a fire burning beneath the water and half of the pool is lit up, enough so that I know Pace has no trouble seeing anything. The water is cool against my legs but turns icy when I'm deep enough that it touches the small of my back, and I shiver. "How can you not know how to swim?" I ask as I lower my body into the water.

"Where do I have to learn? Nobody up there can swim that I know of."

"We learn to swim as soon as we learn how to walk." I sink beneath the surface and welcome the sensation of the water cleansing my panic along with the nasty smells from my body.

"Lucky," Pace says when I finally break the surface. He looks my way and then quickly back at the bank where his clothes lay in the pile where he dropped them.

I shrug. I've never thought about it much, one way or the other. Swimming is as natural to me as breathing. We learn how at an early age because there's always the risk of a child falling into the water and being swept beneath the cavern walls. Most of our play as children involved the water and seeking out pools, such as this one.

Pace has a sudden interest in his clothes. I can't help but watch as he wades to the bank to pick them up. The fabric of his shorts is transparent from the water and doesn't do much to hide the curve of his behind. Just as he turns I drop down into the water with the sudden awareness that if I can see through his, then he can see through mine, even in the darkness. Both of us have skin so pale that we practically glow like the fish. I crouch down, in water up to my chin, and wave my hand at a curious glow fish that nibbles at my toes. They are used to us now and bob happily beneath the surface as if we are here for their entertainment.

Pace wades back across. He holds his clothes in front of him so that they trail in the water. His eyes dart down at where I'm crouching and he grins. The water is so clear that it's not doing anything to disguise what I'm showing. I flick water at him as he passes by and he laughs.

"What are you doing?" I ask as he kneels in the sand.

"Using the sand to clean my clothes."

I arch an eyebrow in admiration. It was the same thing I planned to do, so I join him. There's no use pretending we can't see each other. We're long past that place. Still, I wring the water from my hair and comb it forward with my fingers over my shoulders. Pace slicks his back from his face and winces when he accidentally touches the swelling around his eye.

"You've got quite a wall-eye growing there." I can't help but wonder if he'll understand my slang for a bruise covering his eye. I stretch my jacket out flat on the shore and start scrubbing at the stains that cover it with a mix of sand and water.

He does. "Stupid yob," he says. He joins me in attacking the stains on his own clothing.

Maybe our worlds are not so different after all. "You did pretty well for facing two of them."

"I was junior champion in boxing at school."

"Oh, did you club your opponents with stout pieces of wood there too?"

In the next instant I find myself flipped over on my back and Pace lying on top of me. I don't even try to fight him. I can feel his strength covering me, from the tip of my toes all the way up to my breasts, which are squashed flat beneath his chest. I don't want to fight him. My skin tingles against his and I'm so warm where he touches me that I can't help but wonder if I'm glowing like the fish. I've never felt this way before; it's strange and scary but also kind of wonderful.

"I'm pretty good at wrestling too." His hands are on my shoulders, pinning me down. He relaxes his hold and pushes back a strand of hair that is stuck to my cheek. I wonder how I look to him, through his eyes. I feel very self-conscious as he studies my face, but it all goes away when I find myself staring into his beautiful blue eyes. His hardness presses against my thighs, much the same as I felt from James, but for some reason it doesn't bother me like it did with James. *It's because of me* . . . Knowing I have that power thrills me, and the warmth I feel explodes to a blasting heat. Just as suddenly as he flipped me on my back, Pace moves off and turns back to his clothes.

"Your eyes are amazing." He looks over his shoulder at me. "What's it like? What do you see?"

So are yours . . . so different from anything I've ever seen. "Shadows and definition. I don't see a lot of color."

"Ever?"

"Yes. I mean in the dark. In the light I see the same as you." I shake the sand off my jacket and examine the stains. "I mean I think I do. I guess there's no way of knowing as we can never see through each other's eyes."

"What color is this?" He picks up my bandanna.

"Red."

"Barely." He flips it at me and I snatch it up as if he's threatening to steal it. My bandanna is older than I am, as is most of my clothing. Some of it belonged to my grandmother, some my mother, some of it I picked up in various places. I don't think much about it. Clothing is a necessity, not a luxury. I feel fortunate to have what I have and privileged to call it my own. I put my shirt on, now relatively clean compared to the rest of my things, and go to work on my pants.

I also feel the need to prove to Pace that I can really see like him, so I start a list of things I know we've both seen. "Apples are red. Some are green. The leaves on the trees are green. Cheese is orange or yellow."

Pace nods along in agreement as he works on his pants.

"Your eyes are blue." He turns his head to look at me. In the dim light from the glow fish his eyes are dark, but I can still see the color. "Very blue." I swallow back the sudden dryness that fills my throat as he stares at my mouth. Is he going to kiss me? I want him to very much.

He turns away. "So is the sky." Pace's voice is rough and hoarse. The reason we're here, the reason why we spent most of the day running for our very lives, comes crashing back to me. Alex was murdered and I'm thinking about kissing a boy. A boy I don't even know.

"I need to hide you." I pull on my pants, not caring that I'm still wet and covered with sand. I gather up my things and splash back through the water, soaking myself up to my waist.

"Can't I stay here?" Pace asks. "Where there's light?" He follows me, smarter than I am; he carries his clothes and puts them on when we reach the opposite bank. "And water?"

"No." I jerk on my socks and work boots. "Someone might

decide to come and swim. We can't risk you being found. They'll cast us both out."

He doesn't speak as he finishes dressing. He knows what it will mean for both of us if we are cast out. He keeps a tight hold on the lamp. Neither of us speaks as we crawl through the portal that leads us back to the tunnels. It's not far to the place I think to hide him. I choose the cavern where we held the seekers' meeting last night as I know it will be left alone for a good long while. Beyond that I can't think of what to do.

"I'll never be able to find my way out of here," Pace mutters as we dash through the tunnels with me leading him by the hand once more.

"Good," I say. "Then I won't have to worry about you stumbling about and falling into a pit, or something worse."

"I can't imagine much worse."

"I can." Alex dying fills my mind once more.

"Are there pits?" We've arrived at the cavern. Pace stands behind me, blind once more, as I look up the tunnel to make sure no one is about. The stillness is oppressive. It feels as if we're the last two people in the world. Where is everyone? Even though we've been in a part of the mines that has long been deserted and doesn't usually see traffic, it seems like I should have heard or seen something of the shiners. And I still haven't seen a lamp since I came down here. It's as if everything and everyone is gone.

"Yes, there are." I don't go into detail. If his fear of falling into the unknown will keep him from wandering about, then that's one less thing I have to worry about. "In here." I lead Pace inside. "You can turn on the lamp long enough to get oriented."

I leave him for a moment and go to check the escape tunnel on the far side to make sure it's clear. To escape you have to crawl back about four feet, then there is room to stand and climb up to the next level. It will be a good place for Pace to hide if someone comes by.

"It won't come on." I've heard him messing with the lamp, continually flipping the switch that ignites the filament.

"It must have gotten damp when we were by the water." I take it from him and look but it's too small and detailed for me to make out in the darkness. "Probably a good thing, now you won't be tempted."

"Great. So I'm stuck in the dark for how long?"

"Until I can get away again. I have to check in with my grandfather, and hopefully get some sleep before my shift tonight. I don't even know how much time I've got until work. If feels like I've been gone for days."

"Yeah." Pace leans against the wall and folds his arms around his body. "Me too." He has got to be cold, as his clothes and hair are wet. I know I am.

"I'll try to bring you another lamp. And some food."

"How about a fire?"

"No fires in the mines. Ever. If you have a fire and there's a gas pocket . . ." I shiver. An explosion in the mines is our biggest fear.

"This just gets better and better."

"I'm sure the bluecoats would be happy to give you a fire."

"I'll settle for a blanket."

"You don't want much . . ."

"What? I'm the one who has to sit here in the dark and freeze."

"And I'm the one who's risking everything to keep you safe."

"At least you're doing something," he grumbles.

"Look, I know you're frustrated and I know you don't like being closed in. I can't even imagine what it would be like to feel blind and helpless . . ." My voice trails off. Maybe my words of encouragement weren't the best things to say. I can't see his face as he has his head down. I take his hand—he's shivering—and lead him to the corner away from the opening. "Sit. Try to get some sleep. I'll be back as soon as I can."

Pace puts his hands against the cave wall, turns his back to it, and slides down. "What if someone comes?" He puts his hands under his arms and huddles up in a ball.

"We'll just have to hope for now that it doesn't happen." I turn to go, then stop. "I'll whistle, like this." I demonstrate a two-note song that I've heard the canaries do. "That way you'll know it's me."

He doesn't answer. He doesn't need to. I stand in the entrance for a moment, torn between the need to go and the urge to stay. I have to go. I have this strange nagging feeling that something happened while I was gone, something much worse than ever before. I leave without another word and run back the same way I'd gone the night before.

The canary is still there. His cage hangs from a nail stuck in one of the arch supports. I stop when I see it and check to make sure he is still alive. He is. He stares at me resentfully with his black bead of an eye, condemning me for leaving him alone the night before.

"I've got a friend for you, little one." I run back to the cave where I left Pace. I hear him moving as I reach the entrance. I've forgotten to whistle.

"It's me."

He lets out his breath. "What?"

"I have something for you."

"Food? A blanket?"

"No . . ." I feel foolish. It seemed like a good idea when I came across the canary. I put the cage next to him and placed his hand on it. "It's a canary. They alert us about the gas buildup. As long as they're alive . . ." Once more I'm not sounding very encouraging or optimistic.

"I know what they're for."

"I just thought . . ."

Pace reaches out, searching. I take his hand and he squeezes mine. "Thank you."

"I'll see you in a bit."

"Yeah . . . see you."

I certainly hope so.

· 11 ·

We are never without an escape route. Every tunnel and every cavern has two ways in and two ways out so that you are never trapped. I use the one for the village, located behind the turning wheel, and hope and pray that I have not been missed. There isn't any way I can get to our home without someone seeing me, but the village is strangely deserted. No wives at their chores, no toddlers playing, no one gossiping. It's just eerily quiet. Even the birds, which sit on the lines and swoop down for crumbs, are all at rest. I feel as if I'm being watched as I quickly run up the steps that lead to my home. Cats arch their backs and hiss at my haste before slinking into hiding places, except for one that follows me in.

I eat with some guilt. I know Pace is hungry but at the moment there's nothing I can do about it. I quickly shed my clothes and scrub them clean with the water in the pail before hanging them to dry. Then I tumble into my bed, exhaustion finally catching up with me. The cat, sated on my crumbs, jumps onto the bed and curls up against me.

I don't know how long I sleep before my grandfather shakes me awake. He throws my clothes on the bed as I scrub wearily at my eyes. The cat yawns widely and meows in protest. I rub between its ears as I fight off the remnant of a dream that held me in its grip.

"Council wants to meet with you."

Pace? Was he discovered? Did he tell them I brought him into the tunnels? Did he even have to? *Don't panic* . . . I take a deep breath.

"Why?"

My grandfather sits down in the one chair we own. His goggles hang around his neck precariously. The strap is broken on one side and needs mending again, something else I've neglected lately. He always makes sure that I have what I need, even down to a better pair of goggles, yet his needs are greater as he actually digs for the coal.

He takes off his hat and runs his hand through his hair. My grandfather has beautiful hair, long, wavy, and thick. I remember when I was little it was a rich brown color, a lot like my own. Now it is streaked with silver and the lines on his face are deeply etched and stained with black.

I finish dressing and he nods me over to sit on the edge of his own neatly made bed. He takes my hands between his and I see the coal rimmed around his nails, deep in his cuticles, never gone no matter how much he scrubs at them. Will my hands look the same someday? Worn and wrinkled with twisted fingers that are forever blackened by the coal the royals demand?

"Filchers came below today, Wren." He squeezes my fingers and I feel his terror. Because of me. For me. "They were looking for you and that boy."

I can't speak. I'm shocked beyond words. Never have filchers dared to come below. I can only stare into my grandfather's eyes, the same color as my own, as he continues.

"They were killed and dropped into the pit."

More death. Because of what I saw. Because of what they think I may know. Is it worth it? Isn't Alex's death enough? What are they so afraid of?

But more important, who is the one afraid of us?

My grandfather waits patiently while I absorb the things he's told me. "Who killed them?"

"Does it matter?"

"Yes, if it was because of me, then yes."

"It was Jasper's crew that found them. They won't say who done the killing. I sent Adam and James down to work with them today."

"Was anyone hurt?" I ask, holding my breath.

"None of ours," he says, and I let out a sigh of relief. "No one's saying who done it. They say they all done it together to protect you from them above."

They killed for me. And now they want to talk to me. Grandfather hasn't mentioned Pace. Maybe they don't know he is below.

"You need to tell me the all of it, Wren. I don't want no surprises in there."

I couldn't. I couldn't tell him about Pace. I knew my grandfather. He'd trade Pace for my safety without blinking an eye. I couldn't let that happen. Pace was the only one who knew what happened to Alex. Pace was the only one who knew Alex made it outside. He might even know where and how.

"There's been talk that you've been seeing that boy from above. That he's why you're always sneaking off."

James spreading lies . . . "I wasn't." I pull my hands free and twist them in my lap. "That's not where I go."

"Where did you go then? Every morning since you were big enough to go out on your own?"

"To the rooftops." I know he won't like it. That he'll think it's nothing more than flights of fancy. That it won't put food on the table or give me a better life. He won't understand that I can't help it. That I need to see the light the same way I need to breathe. "To watch the light come into the dome."

"Every morning?"

I look my grandfather in the eyes. "Every morning."

"What about the boy?"

"He was there when they killed Alex."

"What do you mean 'when they killed Alex'?"

"He made it outside and they killed him for it."

My grandfather grabs my arms and jerks me to my feet. He shakes me, violently, until I'm afraid my head will pop off my neck from the force. His face is inches from mine and his anger so tangible that I shrink back from it.

"That's nonsense, Wren. Nonsense that will get you killed." I expected him to scream and shout, but instead he speaks quietly, which is more frightening than his shouting. His tone scares me more than his anger. "You will speak no more of this."

"But it's true." I can't keep the fear from my voice or the tears from my eyes.

He pushes me away so suddenly that I fall back onto his bed. "You're just like your mother. Never content. Always looking for something that isn't there. And look where that got her."

What it got her was me. And I'm the reason she died, during childbirth. Does my grandfather hate me for it? Is he ashamed because his granddaughter is a bastard with a father who could be anyone?

I wipe my eyes, not sure if the tears are from fear or anger. How can I know if I'm like my mother if I never knew her? All I have are his comparisons and they are always condemning. I know he doesn't believe me. He won't even listen. And if he won't listen, then surely no one else will.

"You will never speak of it. Not in there, nor to anyone, do you hear me?"

I could have died today. Been thrown in the fires and burned to a crisp before he'd even hear about it. I'm alive now because I fought to stay alive. How can he dismiss me so easily when I've had to fight for my life because of what I know? I stand and face him. I've never really noticed how short he is, just a few inches taller than me. Maybe it's because Pace seems so tall, or maybe it's just that all the men in my world are shorter than those above. Whatever the reason, I feel something different inside me, an inner strength that somehow subdues the doubt I felt before. I've never talked back to my grandfather before. But I've also never been wanted for questioning, or ran for my very life from people who wanted to kill me without a second thought.

"Shouldn't they know what they killed for?" My voice sounds strangely calm, as if it belongs to someone else. "Shouldn't they know what they are fighting for?"

"What good will it do them? What good will it do any of us to know there's an outside? We can't go there. No one can. Don't you see, Wren, you're wasting your life and throwing away your chances on things that can never be."

"Chances for what? Service to the royals for me and my children until the coal finally runs out and there's nothing left to power the fans? And then what? Sit here until we all suffocate? There's got to be something more. If there's not, then why bother?"

"It's not like that. Not at all." My grandfather turns and walks away. He stops at the washstand and leans on it with his arms braced against it as if he needs it to hold him up. He stares into the piece of mirror and I cannot help but wonder what he sees. Does he see himself as he was long ago? A young man full of hope and dreams for a better future? Or does he see what I suddenly realize? An old man, beaten down by life and so terribly afraid. When did he cease to be my hero and become everything that I didn't even know I was fighting against until now?

He looks at me through the mirror. "I was happy. Your gran and I were. All we needed were each other and this place . . . It was enough."

"Not for me . . ." I shake my head. "I want more. I want a better life. I want hope."

His shoulders sag and he sighs. There's water in the bowl, but not much since I'd washed my clothes. There is, however, enough for him to splash on his face, and he does so, taking his time to pat it dry before he turns to me. "James will still have you. He told me so today."

I shake my head. "James betrayed me to the others. I can't trust him."

"It can come if you give it time."

"No. Never." I look at my grandfather. On this one thing I will not change. I'd rather spend the rest of my life alone.

"You'll change your mind eventually."

It's as if I've never said a word.

"They're waiting on us."

"What should I do?" I may not agree with him, but he's still my grandfather. What I do affects him also. I don't want to hurt him any more than he's been. First my mother disappointed him, then me. It's a horrible legacy. One I never realized until now.

"Don't tell them about Alex getting out. It will start a war that we can't win."

My heart swells in my chest. "You believe me?"

"I believe that you believe it."

I suddenly realize that for my grandfather and me it goes both ways. He's as disappointed in me as I am in him. He had expectations for my life, just as I did. Maybe they weren't so different from each other. Maybe the results were supposed to be the same. Maybe we were both focused on different tunnels to the same destination.

Worst of all, maybe we're both wrong. And if we are, then what does that leave for us? A war we can't win? An empty life until my lungs shrivel up and die inside of me?

Lucy asked me to tell Alex's parents he got out. Would it change anything for them, knowing it? Would it change anything for any of us?

All I have to do is look inside myself for the answer. Yes, it would.

◆

The first person I see when I walk into the council chamber with my grandfather is James. He stands beside Adam, whose seat is on the end of the carved bench as he's the youngest of the elders. Jasper, who is the head, sits in the middle and Mary sits to his left. The rest take up their positions according to their rank. Hans, Frank, and Rosalyn. My grandfather takes the seat to Jasper's right, which surprises me as I thought he would not be allowed to participate since I was the one called. Seven elders watch me as I take my place on the seat in the middle of the chamber. James watches me also. Was it just last night that he betrayed me? Was it the night before that when he kissed me?

I feel like a lifetime has passed since both. One has. Alex's. More than one. The two filchers who were killed. Nearly mine and Pace's also. Too many lives sacrificed in such a short time. Is it worth it? Only if we're able to leave the dome. Only if we survive.

"Do you know why you're here?" Jasper asks.

I look at my grandfather. His expression does not change so I look back to Jasper. "Two filchers came below looking for me and you killed them."

"Why are they looking for you?"

"They think I know where Alex got out." That he got out is not in dispute. That he got out into a world that was not on fire is. I can only think of how sad it is that my grandfather thinks that it is better to live your life not knowing there is a world with a blue sky outside the dome.

"Why do they think that?" Jasper continues.

"Because he spoke to me before he died."

"What did he say?"

They already know this. Why do we have to go through it again? The first time I was called to council I was afraid. Now I find that I'm impatient. Lives are at stake and they're wasting time. I can't stop thinking about Pace. Is he safe? Is he where I left him or has he moved in an effort to find food and water? The dream that had me in its grip when my grandfather woke me suddenly comes back to me: Pace falling into the pit as he stumbled about in the tunnels in an attempt to find me.

"The sky is blue." I look once more to my grandfather. His face is immobile, as if it is carved from stone, but I see his eyes imploring me.

"We've already heard this," Mary says. "Tell us about this boy." She picks up the paper with our names and waves it before me. "What is your relationship with him?"

I can't give anything away. Pace is the only one who knows how to get out. As I look at the council, all of their eyes on me, I realize that out is the only recourse I have. Above is certain death for both of us and life below is not a kind alternative for either of us.

"He chased me the day Alex died. He's a bluecoat." *Was a blue-coat* . . .

"Lies!" James interjects.

"Silence!" Jasper shouts. "You have no say here."

"I killed to protect her." James steps out to the center of the cave. "That gives me a right to speak."

James killed them. I would not have thought him capable of it. I didn't think him capable of the horrible things he said to me either. Isn't it funny how you think you know someone and then you realize you don't. Not really.

"I didn't ask you to." I jump to my feet and face James. "Or expect you to. I can take care of myself." His hostility washes over me as if I fell in the stream and I return it, bitterly angry at his betrayal. Yet Grandfather said he asked for me. I don't understand why when his hatred is so evident.

"Enough!" Jasper holds up his hand. "When one of us is attacked we all are." He points to me. "Sit." And James. "Quiet and back to your place or you will be removed."

I sit, rebelliously. I don't want to sit. I want to go, but I know Jasper is right. Because of me the filchers came below. Because of me James has blood on his hands. Did he kill to protect me? Or just because the opportunity arose?

"Answer Mary's question," Jasper says.

"The first time I saw Pace Bratton was the day Alex died." I look directly at James as I speak. "I saw him again the next morning when I went above. He followed me. That must be when they saw us together. He tried to talk to me."

"What did he say?"

"He wanted to know about Alex. If I knew him. What he said to me." I shrug. I had not lied. I hadn't been forthcoming either. My secrets are piling up around me since I am now responsible for

Pace's life, along with my own. I can't trust James and therefore can't trust the council. I can't even trust my grandfather because he will surely forfeit Pace's life for mine.

The only person I can trust is Pace. He placed his trust in me, even though he knew he had to face his greatest fear. Or was it just the lesser of two fears? His fear of being burned alive has to be greater than his fear of being closed in. What would I chose if given a choice? To jump into the pit or burn alive? I pray I never find out.

"Why did the filchers come below?" Mary asks.

"Ask the ones who killed them," I say. "I had no knowledge of them until I was told by my grandfather."

"Elias?" Mary turns to my grandfather.

"She was in her bed sleeping," he says.

James leans down and whispers in Adam's ear. "And before that?" Adam asks.

"I swam with the glow fish." Not a lie but I tread on a very thin line. If anyone from the village saw me, then they would see that my hair was wet, along with my clothes. I could only pray that they wouldn't ask if I brought Pace below. Perhaps they didn't think that I would dare.

"What's done is done." My grandfather, thankfully, changes the subject from me. "It doesn't matter why so much as that the filchers dared to come below. There will be more. We must have a plan in place."

"A plan that will let them know that they cannot trespass," Frank says.

"You should not have disposed of the bodies." The look on Mary's face is vicious. "We could have sent them back as a warning."

"No," my grandfather says wisely. "Let them wonder and worry. If we send back dead bodies then it's a challenge. As of now it's only filchers. They are testing us." The council nods in agreement so he continues. "We should post guards. Not at the entrances but at the cross tunnels. Let any who come below *fall* into the pit. Then if the bluecoats come knocking, we can show them how dangerous it is for anyone not familiar with the tunnels. It will serve as a warning to them also."

It will also make it difficult for me to get to Pace. Difficult, but not impossible.

"Let it be done," Jasper says and the council gives their assent. "Each shift will post guards."

"But that will slow down the coal production," Rosalyn protests.

Jasper shrugs. "Let them see what they will suffer if they challenge us."

"It can go both ways," Rosalyn warns. "They control the food."

"We will make do." Jasper sounds confident. "We must conserve."

Jasper continues. "No one is to go above." His eyes are on me as he gives the ruling. "Until the boy is caught. He can't hide forever. Eventually they will find him."

A shiver runs down my spine. How long do I have before my lies catch up with me?

· 12 ·

My grandfather doesn't want to leave my side. I don't know if it's worry that there will be some backlash from someone about the filchers coming below, or just the fact that he feels as if he's neglected me lately. He makes sure I have a proper meal before my shift, packs my lunch pail, and walks me to the stables. I have no opportunity to sneak off and check on Pace.

The ponies sense my distress. They are restless and push at me with their heads as I harness them to the carts. The chickens scatter and flap their useless wings as I start the first group down the tunnel to the work site. The miners aren't much better. Their workload is heavier because part of the shift is on guard duty. The ones that speak to me are curt and the rest glare at me as if I personally invited the filchers down.

I guess in a way I did. I know in a way it is my fault that they came below, but I also have to wonder, if it had been James, Adam, or even Peggy with Alex at the end, would their hostility be as evident or even be there at all? All my life I've borne the stigma of my unknown father's blood.

How much of this have I brought on myself and how much is due to my mother's own rebellion I'll never know, as much of my mother's life is a mystery to me. All I know is that she went above, got caught trespassing where she shouldn't have, was sentenced to service, and finally came back home hugely pregnant with me. She died without naming my father. It could be any man who lives above.

Any man but Pace's father, as he died before Pace was born. For some reason that gives me a sense of relief.

I can't help thinking about Pace as I trek back and forth from the stables, into the mines, and back to the tipplers with the ponies. In my mind I go over different places to hide him, places where we can easily get by the guards. Then I alternate between panic and frustration as I wonder if he's still where I left him. He'll need blankets and someplace where he can have light and I have no way of getting either to him today. I do grab a filament from the supplies in the barn for the lamp, just in case.

Finally, after what seems like days instead of hours, my shift ends. I feel the light calling to me as I take the ponies back to the stable. My body yearns for it as if I have an unquenchable thirst. I never realized how much I craved the light until I find that it is impossible for me to see it.

I force myself to take my time with the ponies. I don't need any unwanted attention on me. I can't risk anyone following me. Their gratitude, as usual, warms me. I can't help but laugh as the white one I call Ghost blows bubbles in the trough.

I put them in their stalls and start to give them an extra portion of feed, but then I stop. Jasper's words of warning ring in my ears. We must conserve everything and that includes feed for the ponies.

I would rather go hungry than see them starve because of me. And hungry I am. I didn't eat my lunch. I saved it for Pace.

Pace . . . It's been twenty hours more or less since I left him. I've got to get to him. I leave the barn and look around. I let go a sigh of relief when I see that I am alone. The day-shift ponies have already gone down into the mines and the workers have moved on to their homes. I know guards are stationed at the lifts and all cross tunnels close to our escape hatches. I've got to get to Pace without anyone seeing me.

Luckily the two ways in and two ways out holds true for every tunnel and cave. I make my way to the oldest part of the mine by following that rule. I take the tunnels until I'm close to a cross point, then I duck into the closest cave and go out the other way.

Eventually I come out on a ledge high above the main branch of the underground river. It runs fast and hard here, tons of water rushing nearly one hundred feet below me. To fall in would be instant death either by being smashed against the rocks that have fallen from below the ledge or drowning when swept beneath the cave walls. I wasn't able to find a lantern so I'm careful, swallowing my fear and keeping my eyes on the ledge before me as I make my way down to a short tunnel that leads me close to the pool we swam in the night before.

From there I hurry on. There shouldn't be anyone in these tunnels, only stationed farther up, where we came in, and farther down, closer to our homes. The guards would have had to go by when they were dispatched to their shifts. I'm certain if Pace was discovered I would have heard about it by now, unless something happened since my shift ended. I can only hope and pray that I'll find him where I left him.

I stop outside the cavern and whistle. I hear a slight noise, a shifting of his body? "Pace?" I whisper.

"Wren?" His voice is a desperate call in the darkness.

"It's me," I whisper as I come in. He's in the same corner I left him in, curled around the canary's cage as if he's trying to draw some comfort from it. He slowly unfolds until he's sitting up. The canary flits about in its cage and pipes a curious note.

Pace's face is ghastly pale. He blinks, desperate to see something, anything. I kneel down beside him and touch his knee. He grabs my wrist and squeezes it.

"Wren?"

"Yes." His hand slides up my arm and he shifts to his knees. He's so cold that I feel his chill through my clothes. He finds my shoulder and I catch my breath as his hand moves to my cheek and around to the back of my head. His fingers move into my hair until his hand cups my head. He leans forward, so very slowly, until his forehead touches mine. He puts his other hand on my shoulder as he lets out a deep sigh.

"Am I dreaming?" His voice is the barest whisper. I see the shadow of his eyes, searching to see.

My hands creep up of their own volition and I cradle his face. "I'm sorry, I couldn't get away . . ."

He shakes his head, back and forth, saying no to something but I have no idea what it could be. Suddenly he pulls me against him, pinning my body against his so that we touch from our bent knees to our chilled cheeks. I flatten against him, feeling all the hard planes of his chest and hips and his damp clothes all the way through to my skin. His arms shake against my back. His chill fills me and I wrap my arms around his neck in an attempt to share my warmth. He buries his face against my neck and his entire body shudders.

I've never felt anything like this. It is powerful and humbling, exciting and scary. Is it just because he was frightened and lonely? Is it just because I'm here and he would act the same with anyone, or is it genuinely because it is me? I'm scared to find out.

Pace moves his head. I feel his cheek against mine, and then the ridge of his nose as it moves across my cheek. He finds my lips with his and he kisses me. His hand moves from my back to my face and he holds me, oh so very gently, as his lips move over mine. A spark of warmth ignites in our kiss. I feel it spreading through me, like air. It fills my mouth and my lungs and moves throughout my body, until I can feel it running through my veins. It's everywhere yet it's centered between us. It's nothing I've ever felt before, anticipation and a sense of rightness mixed together. This can't be happening. Can it? Am I imagining this?

Finally, regretfully, he breaks the kiss, and leans his forehead against mine once more. "I thought you'd forgotten about me." His voice is the merest whisper, impossible to hear if we hadn't been so close.

I'm strangely disappointed. What did I expect him to say? "No . . . so much has happened. I couldn't get away." I make excuses to fill the absence of his kiss. "And I had to work. I didn't want anyone to get suspicious."

"How long have I been down here?"

"Not quite a day."

"It felt like forever. I'm so cold. I can't remember what it's like to feel warm."

"I know. I'm sorry . . ." Why do I keep apologizing? I'm babbling and he's freezing and starving and scared. "I brought you some food." I offer up my pail and realize he can't see it.

"Food is good," he says when I finally place it in his lap. "How about some light?"

"There're guards posted. We can't risk it . . . unless . . ." I look at the escape route. "Which is worse? The dark or closed-in spaces?"

"Does the closed-in space have light?"

"Yes, but it will be tight."

"I need light. Just to make sure I'm alive. To make sure I'm not blind." His whisper has the same dry humor of his regular voice in spite of the chattering of his teeth.

I pick up the lamp. "Stay here until I tell you to come."

"And here I was planning a long stroll on the promenade."

I could only roll my eyes at his humor. To laugh would make too much noise. I hoist myself into the escape tunnel and crawl forward to the space where you have to stand to get out. I take off my jacket and spread it over the top of the hole, so no light can escape, then sit and replace the filament in the lamp. A few strikes of the flint and a warm glow fills the tiny space.

"Come to the light." I hold it above my head so it doesn't shine as bright in the cave. Someone would have to come in to see it.

"Thank God," I hear his whisper.

To my surprise Pace shoves the canary cage in first and follows with my lunch pail. I wasn't counting on the cage. I knew we'd be crowded but I also knew he needed the light, just for a while. It must be horrible to think you've gone blind, no matter what his humor shows. Pace crawls in after the pail with a huge smile on his face and one hand shading his eyes from the lamp.

"Put your back to the entrance so it will block the light," I instruct. He does, settling into the opening. I knew he was broad enough to cover it. He sits back with his knees up and his legs splayed. It leaves enough room for me to sit between his knees, cross-legged with the canary cage on my lap and the lamp by my side. I turn it down as low as it will go. I am fairly certain we will be safe for a while, as long as we are quiet. Sound doesn't carry far down here. There are too many nooks and crannies for it to get lost in.

His eye has turned black and blue from the fight and the cut on his forehead is healing. Thank God his injuries weren't any worse. I don't know what I would have done if he'd broken something.

"How is your shoulder?" I ask.

"Fine. Once it's back in the joint it takes care of itself."

"I didn't even think about it when you were fighting."

"Fighting for your life kind of makes the injuries unimportant."

"I still can't believe I did that."

"I'm glad you did. If not I definitely wouldn't be cold now."

"I'll try to bring you a blanket next time."

"Don't do anything that will get you in trouble."

"I'm already so far in that a blanket's not going to make much difference."

He grins. He has a beautiful smile. The kind that makes you feel it, on the inside. Like it's a gift.

Pace sticks his finger in the cage. "This is Pip," he says. "We're friends now, despite the fact that he's not covered with fur and therefore of no use in keeping me warm." He opens my lunch pail and bites into the sandwich with a happy sigh. He breaks off some crumbs and drops them in Pip's cage as he chews. "We shared our life stories while you were gone." Pace takes another bite and pokes in the pail to see what else is inside.

I cover my mouth so I don't laugh out loud. Pace sees my smile and continues. "No, really, he's quite interesting once you get to know him."

I can only shake my head and grin. What would it be like to have a normal conversation with Pace? Without the thought that we could very easily die in the next few minutes? He's so funny, without really trying, it's just the way he is. What made him so? What was he like as a boy growing up? Just him and his mother. I hope they haven't hurt his mother . . . the thought of Pace in pain is more than I can stand.

He pulls out my crock of goat's milk and sniffs it before turning it up and drinking half of it. He wipes his mouth with his thumb and finishes the sandwich in another bite. Then he carefully searches for crumbs and drops them in the cage. Pip pecks delicately at his meal with soft chirps of satisfaction.

"What's going on out there?" he asks as he starts on the crusty cake my grandfather packed in my pail. He's serious now, his blue eyes intent upon my face. I feel my color rise as he looks at me. I can't stop thinking about his kiss. Why did he kiss me?

"Filchers came below. They were killed and their bodies dropped into a bottomless pit. Now there are guards at every cross tunnel."

Pace shakes his head. He understands what that means. "What should we do?" We're sitting so close. My knees are beneath his, his ankles press closely against my hips. The only thing that separates us is Pip's cage. I've yet to decide where to go from here. Back to where he was or onward to another place. I need to figure it out soon. I've got to get back to my home and my bed before my grandfather suspects something.

"I don't know," I confess. "You can't stay here forever. We've got to find someplace where you can stay for a while. With supplies in case I can't get to you."

"Or you can just hand me over," he says quietly.

I shake my head no. I couldn't. I wouldn't. "They'll kill you."

"Am I worth the lives of your friends?" Pace picks up my hand. He does it so easily, almost without thought. I'm glad I washed them and my face before I left the stable. I run my other hand through my hair and wonder if it's full of coal dust. He turns our hands so his fingers splay through mine. He doesn't even look at them, just at me with his wonderful blue eyes that are unlike anything I've ever seen.

"You said they killed two filchers who came below and they're prepared to kill any more that come down here. How long do you think it will be before one of your friends gets hurt, or maybe killed?" He squeezes my hand. "Wren, you know they'll come with weapons the next time."

"We have weapons."

"Knives and clubs just like them. What if they bring a flame-thrower?"

I shiver at the thought of flames shooting through the tunnels, possibly hitting a pocket of gas, with the resulting explosion. It's a horrible thought. What if they find our cave and burn our homes? What could we do to stop them? But the alternative is just as bad.

I squeeze his hand. "I can't just turn you over to them."

He gives me one of his fleeting smiles. "I can't live the rest of my life hiding in the tunnels either."

"Just give me some time to figure things out. Everything has happened so fast."

"I know."

We sit, quietly, just looking at each other, and once more I wonder if he's going to kiss me until Pip lets out a peep. It startles both of us. Pip flutters up to his perch, and beyond the wispy sound of his wings I hear a pebble bouncing.

I put my finger to my mouth and turn off the lamp. We're plunged into darkness. My ears strain with the effort to hear and I silently pray that Pip will stay quiet. I hear Pace breathing, hard and fast, and I know his fear of dark, closed-in places is taking over.

I move my hand up his arm so I won't startle him and touch his face. Then I lean my forehead against his, just as we did when we kissed. "Breathe with me." I mouth the words more than say them. He nods and quiets, listening for my breath until he finds it and then echoing it with his own.

Voices sound in the tunnel. I try to identify them but they are too jumbled—two men, speaking low and fast. Has something else happened? They don't seem to be in a hurry, their footsteps sound normal as they fade off into the distance. Just to make sure, I stay as I am, quiet, leaning against Pace, breathing evenly so he won't panic. He shivers and I move my arms up around his neck to give him warmth.

"They're gone," I finally say.

"I guess turning the light back on is out of the question."

"It is."

"Can't blame me for trying."

"No. I don't blame you at all."

· 13 ·

We need to move you someplace else." He can't stop shivering. "Someplace not so close to the main paths."

Pace's teeth chatter. "I thought this was off the main paths."

"That was before they decided to post guards."

"What if they catch us moving around?"

"They won't." I stand and grab my jacket, shrug into it, and hoist myself up. "Hand me Pip first. Then the pail and the lamp." I lay prone next to the opening and stick my arms inside.

Pace moves slowly, feeling his way with his hands before standing tentatively. He picks up Pip's cage and holds it up. We repeat the action two more times as he feels with his feet for the lamp and pail and then hands them up to me.

"You're only about a foot short of the top," I whisper. "Not even that much. Just jump and feel for the sides."

"That's easy for you to say." His grumbles are lost in the hole he stands in. Pace jumps up and misses. "I can't see." He turns his face up to me. "How am I supposed to find something I can't see?"

"Hold up your hand."

"Don't pull it off."

I bury my face in my sleeve and silently laugh. My body shakes with the effort to keep quiet. The more I try, the worse it gets.

"Wren?"

I move my head enough to see him. I have to wipe the tears from my eyes before I can look. He's standing in the chute with his hand up in the air waiting on me.

"What are you doing, Wren?"

"Laughing at you."

"Pulling my hand off is funny?"

"No. The way you say it is funny."

"Can we go now?" He sighs dramatically.

I reach down and grasp his wrist. He wraps his hand around mine and I pull. Pace braces his feet against the wall and walks up with my help until he's able to leverage himself out of the hole. He comes out with one last powerful thrust and crashes into me. The top of his head hits my chin and I fall flat on my back with Pace on top of me. Lights dance before my eyes as I blink and try to catch my breath.

"I can't remember the last time I had so much fun," Pace says as he flops over on his back. "Lamp?"

"No." I rub my chin. It feels like it's shattered into a million pieces, but to my amazement it's still all in one very tender piece.

He sighs. "So where are we going?"

"To the river."

"With the glow fish?"

"No, but where we're going you should be able to use the lamp." *If we can get there* . . . I didn't want to frighten him. I was scared enough for both of us.

"Are you sure we can't turn on the lamp?"

"I'm sure."

"Let's go." I hand him the lamp, which he stuffs inside his shirt. He takes the cage and I grab my pail as he stands. I take Pace's hand and lead him forward. Once more we venture forth into the darkness.

◆

It's not easy guiding Pace through the escape tunnels. It's difficult compared to earlier when we just walked through the tunnels. We have to deal with the cage and my pail, which I can't leave behind for someone to find and get curious. So we bump and feel our way along through the narrow passages and winding turns. I can tell he's frustrated because he snaps at me several times.

"Just let me turn on the lamp."

"We can't risk it."

"You can't risk it. Maybe you'd think differently if you were the one who was completely helpless." He stops and pulls me to a stop with him.

I know I would be the same if the situation was reversed. Being helpless and dependent is not something I would ever want to be. I squeeze his hand. "Just trust me. I won't let you fall," I assure him. He follows me, but I'm not sure if it's because he trusts me or if he feels like he doesn't have a choice. Which he doesn't.

We finally arrive in the cavern with the river. We come out above the ledge as I had before, as we'd gone up when we'd left the cave I originally hid him in. The water roars below us, ominously filling the darkness.

"What is it?"

"The river."

"The sound . . . it's big. How big is this cave?"

"Big . . . mostly long and narrow. The river is below us."

"How far below?"

I take a deep breath. I don't want to lie to him. But I don't want to scare him either. "As deep as the tallest building."

"Turn on the lamp, Wren." He takes a step back. "I can feel the emptiness in front of me."

I look around to make sure no one else is there. I haven't seen or heard anyone since we left the old hiding place. People do come here occasionally, to fish, or just to tempt fate and the water. I've got to believe that everyone will be sticking close to the village now, as the threat of the filchers is very real. The light will help me to find a cavern below the ledge secure enough to hide him in.

"Don't move."

"Not planning on it." It takes a moment for me to pull the lamp from his shirt. A moment when my fingers brush against the bare and chilled skin of his chest. I've got to get him a blanket before his chill turns into a fever. I flip the switch and the soft glow doesn't do much to turn back the darkness. I hold the lamp out over the ledge and Pace lets out a gasp.

"You expected me to walk down that? In the dark?"

"Maybe it's better when you don't know what it is," I offer.

"Like outside the dome?"

I'd been concentrating on the immediate so much that I'd almost forgotten about what got us here. Almost.

"There are caves down there?"

"Lots of them. They're not big, but I think they're secluded enough that you can turn on the lamp occasionally."

"The sooner we start the sooner it will be over," Pace says. He sounds weak, even with the light. The cold is draining him. I'm so used to it, I don't think about it. I wear layers of clothing and stay warm by moving about. But he was stuck for a long time in wet clothes that robbed his body of its warmth. I would have to figure some way to get him a blanket. Or at least more clothes to wear.

I take the cage and give him the light. I lead the way down the ledge. He was right. It would have been dangerous to lead him down in the total darkness. More so when we get to the bottom, as the floor is covered with huge boulders. We pick our way through them, startling the minnows that live in the pools between the rocks when our feet slip in. Pace shines the lantern on the wall below the ledge as we make our way back.

"There," he says finally. He points to an opening about eight feet up. The lamplight gets lost in its depths, which means it should be big enough to shelter him without anyone seeing him if they happen to come down.

"Boost me up," I say. We put the cage and pail on a flat boulder. Pip chirps a questioning note as I stuff the lamp in my shirt. Pace puts his hands together and I step in them and up to the opening. I flop in on my stomach and pull the lamp out.

It ends about six feet back and when I stand my head brushes the top. I take a few steps back and to my surprise find that it curves to the right and opens into a small cave.

"Wren?" Pace calls out.

"Hang on." I go into the cave and shine the light around the walls. It's a good eight feet in diameter and ten feet high. It was probably a complete tunnel at one time as the far wall is tightly packed with rocks. I shine the light on the ceiling. It's smooth, and it's obvious to me that at one time the water coursed through here until the river cut a groove so deep that it changed course. There's nothing to indicate that there would be any danger from a cave-in.

It's the perfect hiding place for Pace.

I crawl back to the entrance. "Come on." He hands me Pip and the pail and scrambles up. He bends over against the low ceiling and with Pip in hand follows me back into the cave. He turns a slow circle before he sits wearily in the middle of the floor.

"No one should see the lamp from outside." He's tired and worn and I don't know what else I can do for him.

"It's perfect," he says. "It will make a great tomb."

I sit down beside him, so that I face him. Our knees are side by side as we prop our arms upon them. The lamp sits by his hip. The circles under his eyes are worse and his earlier good humor with the meal has been replaced with a morose futility. "This won't be forever." I hope I sound encouraging.

"Yes it will. They're not going to stop looking for me and you can't keep risking your life to protect me." He sticks the end of his finger through the bars of Pip's cage and looks at me from beneath his dark hair. "I don't even know why you're doing it."

"I'm doing it because you know where Alex got out. I'm doing it because I hate to think that his death is meaningless." I'm not sure if that's what he wanted to hear. I know that's not my only motive. I can't stand the thought of Pace dying because he happened to be in the wrong place at the wrong time. I really don't know how to tell him that. I've been so confused since he kissed me. Especially since he acts like it didn't happen. *Why did he kiss me?*

"What was he like?"

"Alex? He was always nice to me. Nice when others weren't. He always made sure I was included when we were children."

"Why were you excluded?"

His eyes are so direct. So piercing. They see things that I've never admitted to anyone, including myself. Or maybe it's just that because he's here I'm looking at myself differently. I can't look at him. I'm afraid of what he'll see, so I look at my boots and rub at one of the many scuff marks with my finger. "Because of my father." I point to the roof without looking up. "Because he wasn't a shiner."

Pace nods. "Did you love him?"

His question startles me enough that I lift my head. Was I in love with Alex? "He was with Lucy."

"I know that." He continues to play with Pip, softly whistling and waving his finger to entice him. Pip studies the finger with his dark bead of an eye. "But that doesn't mean you weren't in love with him."

I think about it. Did I love Alex? Have I ever loved anyone? My grandfather, certainly, and Peggy, who is so kind and giving. But Alex? I recall how he looked at Lucy, how Lucy looked at David. How Peggy and Adam look at each other.

"I wasn't in love with him," I confess. "I never *let* myself be in love with him because he only had eyes for Lucy."

Pace studies me for a long minute before he finally speaks. "I don't know where Alex got out."

"But you have an idea."

"Yes," he admits. "I do." He continues. "I think there's some, in the inner circle of the enforcers, who've been out. And they don't dare say anything for fear they will die too. It seems like there are two different groups of enforcers. The ones like me, who patrol the streets and keep order, and the ones who report directly to Sir Meredith."

"Who is Sir Meredith?"

"He's the one who's in charge, up there." Pace points to the ceiling of the cave. "The royal king is just a figurehead. Sir Meredith runs the dome."

"And the enforcers who report to Meredith have been out?"

"It's just a feeling I have. From different things I've heard. And I think there's something out there that they're afraid of. That makes them keep everyone inside."

"But it's not flames."

"No, not flames."

We sit quietly for a moment. I'm thinking of all the possibilities of what could be outside while Pace looks around the cave.

He picks up the lamp and moves it closer, as if it will give him some warmth. "Did you know that before they moved into the dome people used to bury their dead in the ground?"

I didn't. I never ever considered the possibility of burying people like we bury our waste. "Really?"

"Yes. They were called cemeteries. They were in churchyards and they'd put them in a wooden box and they'd dig a hole six feet deep, called a grave, and then they'd mark it with a stone."

"Instead of burning them?"

"There must have been thousands of graves out there." He shrugs. "Hundreds of thousands. Probably more than you could count." He looks up at the ceiling. "That's why I hate being in the dark. I feel like they're reaching for me. From up there. And they want to pull me in there so they won't be alone in their boxes."

I shiver. "I'd rather be burned after I'm gone. Because then at least maybe my ashes would have a chance to escape."

We are quiet again. I need to go but I don't want to. I hate the thought of leaving him.

Pace puts his head on his knees and wraps his arms around them. "I don't think I'll ever feel warm again." And then, just like when he kissed me, he surprises me by wrapping his arms around my waist and sliding over so that he's lying in my lap. "Help me be warm."

I should go. I know my grandfather will be looking for me. I need to eat, I must get some rest, but more important, I need to know what's happening in my world and the one above.

Instead I do the one thing I shouldn't do. I take off my jacket and spread it as wide as possible on the cave floor. Then I lie down and pull Pace into position next to me. I wrap my arms around him and he moves in as close as he can get. His head tucks under my chin and he threads his legs around and through mine until we're wrapped together and touching every possible way. He doesn't speak; he just huddles against me, trying his best to soak up my body heat. Finally his shivering subsides and I realize he's fallen asleep.

And then so do I.

· 14 ·

I wake up as if I've been kicked. Something jolts me from my dreams but I don't know what it is. It takes me a moment to ground myself as I don't know where I am.

Pace . . . Sometime in our sleep we moved. He lies pressed against my back with his arm around me so that I am pulled tight against him. He's warm. I can feel the heat rolling off him.

A fever? I turn slowly, easing myself around. Pace murmurs something unintelligible and tightens his grip around my waist. I stop, wait until he settles, and move once more until I'm able to place my hand on his forehead. He's warm but not burning hot. If he has a fever it's a slight one. It's a chance I don't want to take. I've got to get him some things to survive on.

How long did I sleep? I have no way of knowing. I do know I have to get back, that it's already too late and that I will be in trouble.

"Don't go." He's awake and staring at me with his beautiful blue eyes. He holds me in his arms and hooks his leg over mine to hold me in place.

"I have to go. I have to get food. I have to work. If I don't they'll come looking for me."

He stares at me another moment. A moment in which I once more wonder, no, not wonder . . . I hope that he'll kiss me again. He doesn't. He sits up and runs his hand through his hair.

"Is there any way to get news from above?" he asks as I stand and stretch from sleeping on the ground. "I'm so worried about my mother." He clenches his hands into fists. "I'm afraid . . ." He swallows and stops.

I put my hand on his shoulder and he places his over it. "I'll find out what I can," I say. "I probably can't get back until morning. But I'll try to come before my shift."

He hangs on to my hand until our arms are outstretched and then finally we let go and I make my way once more into the darkness.

◆

I hurry back the way I came, making sure to stay out of the main tunnels. I have no way of knowing what time it is or how long I slept. I can only imagine the chaos that might be happening. To play it safe I go directly to the stables. My ponies are still there, dozing in their stalls as the other shift is still out. I am so relieved that I go into Ghost's stall and put my arms around his neck. He's confused as to why I'm here so early and tosses his head about at my interruption of his nap. I rub his long nose between his shadowy eyes. I have to admit I'm hiding instead of going home. I've got to make it back without anyone seeing me and come up with a good excuse as to where I've been.

At least my grandfather can rest assured that I haven't been above. With all the guards about, there's no way I could get there.

"I've been looking for you." My heart jumps into my throat as I turn.

"Lucy?"

"This is a good place to hide," she continues as she leans against the stall door. She looks up at the loft. "Maybe sleep even? No one could find you. No one would even think to look for you up there except for me."

I'm so shocked by her appearance that I can only nod in agreement. She knows Pace is below and she's keeping the secret. She comes into the stall. Ghost snuffs at her scent. It's a new one to him.

"How is he?" Lucy asks.

I look around to make sure no one is about. There isn't. It's funny how paranoid I've become lately. I guess it comes with having secrets.

"Cold. Hungry. Scared. He hates the dark."

Lucy shivers and rubs her arms. "I know how he feels."

I give Ghost a last pat as we leave the stall. "What are you doing here?"

"News has a way of getting around above the same way it does below. There's talk about some filchers coming below and disappearing."

"It's true," I say.

"So said Poppa," Lucy says. "I went to find him after I came here." She stops by the tack room. "I brought you some things from above." She picks up a bundle. "I knew it would be hard for you to get things down here since it would all be easily missed."

I take the bundle from her. Inside are two blankets wrapped around a clean shirt, a loaf of fresh baked bread, dried strips of beef, apples, and a wedge of cheese made from cow's milk, which is a delicacy for us. "Why?" I ask.

She shrugs. "It's just some things that were left at the laundry. And the food? I just knew you'd need it."

"That still doesn't explain why."

"I'm doing it because of what they did to Alex. Because they murdered him. Because helping your friend hurts them."

I'd never heard Lucy talk this way before. It surprises me, but it shouldn't. She feels the same way I do. Why would I expect her to feel differently?

I hide the bundle behind a feed bin so I'll be able to grab it easily tomorrow morning when I go back to Pace. I rub the ears of an orange cat that sits on top of the bin. I know she'll keep the rats and mice away from it.

"I can help you," Lucy continues. "They won't question me going back and forth. I can bring news down. It's the least I can do for Alex. For his memory."

"What is the news?" I ask as we walk to the village.

"There's talk of a full assault from the bluecoats. David thinks they'll let the filchers try for it first. The reward is the biggest ever offered. Quarters in Park Front and full privileges."

"The royals will never allow it." I shake my head at the thought. Filchers living among the royals. What a bizarre joke.

"The royals aren't the ones in charge," Lucy says with authority.

"Who is?"

"Lord Meredith. He's over the enforcers."

The same man Pace mentioned. Lucy stops me before we come to the cross tunnel and guards. "There's something you need to know about Alex and the seekers."

I see the pain in her eyes. Is it the pain from Alex's death or the pain of her betrayal?

"Alex found out about the seekers from me. David started them. Alex didn't know about me and David then, but I think he suspected. He wanted to know what I found so interesting above. So I told him. I told him there were people up there who were not happy with the way things were. That they wanted things to change so that everyone could have a better life, not just the royals. And it's not just the people in service like David and his family. It's people from all factions of the dome. Even the scarabs. What they have in common is the belief that the world outside should be explored and we're being kept inside for a reason beyond the rumor of flames. That's why there was a tunnel for you to escape through. Any gathering is suspect, especially one that includes people from separate parts of the dome. That's how they gather."

"So Alex decided to start a seeker group for the shiners to compete with David?"

Lucy shook her head. "I should have told him before that I loved David. I just didn't want to hurt him. I kept pushing him away and he kept coming back." Lucy chokes back tears. "He saw us together and that's when he said he'd prove it to me. That he'd do more than just talk about it. And that's when he died."

"Did David tell the seekers about what happened to Alex?"

"Yes. And they are more determined than ever to find the place where he got out. For most of them it's all the proof they need."

"If only it were the same way down here," I say.

"I heard about what James did to you. How he's poisoned everyone against you."

"Now they'll never believe me. Pace is the only proof I have."

"But that's only if they believe him too."

"He's scared, Lucy. Scared of what they'll do to him and his mother." A shiver goes down my spine and I rub my arms against the chill. "I guess I'm scared too."

"You've got every reason to be," Lucy says. We walk through the cross tunnel. The guards, a man and a woman, watch us pass without a word. I can feel their dislike as I walk by. I can't help but wonder how long it will be before it blossoms into full hatred. How long before I am suspect in everything? I can't slip up. Not if I want Pace to live. Not if I want him to show me the way out.

"Pace said he thinks there's some in the bluecoats who've been outside."

"David says the same thing."

"It must be true."

"That's why they killed Alex, why they killed Pace's friend, and why they want to kill him and now you," Lucy says. "But it's got to be something more than just going outside. There has to be a reason why they don't want anyone out there."

There are guards at the entrance to the village cave. "Maybe it's not that they want to keep us in so much as they want to keep whatever is on the outside out," Lucy says as we approach them.

Another thing I haven't considered. Another question that needs an answer. Not knowing is the worst feeling. It's just another part of not having control over your own life.

"Pace is worried about his mother. Can you find anything out about her?"

"I'll see what I can do," Lucy says. "The one thing I've discovered up there is that people love to talk. All you have to do is stand back and listen."

My grandfather stands at the bottom of the ramp. As I expected, he's missed me.

"Where have you been?" he asks as soon as we're in earshot.

Lucy laughs. It's a pleasant sound, like water trickling over the rocks. "I found her asleep in the loft at the stables." Her lie comes so easy. Almost without effort. I'm glad for it, yet I'm filled with a sense of sadness. Things will never be the same for my grandfather and me after this. I've had to make a choice, and it breaks my heart that I couldn't choose him.

"You chose not to come home?" he asks me.

"I don't exactly feel welcome here," I say, which is not a lie. "Has anything else happened?"

"Nothing yet. The guards have made sure no one comes below that doesn't belong here," he says with a smile at Lucy. "It's good to see you, gel."

"Thank you." Lucy's smile is dazzling. "I shared what I know with my father."

"And he'll tell us at council," my grandfather returns. "Don't you be doing anything that will put you in danger. We've got enough to worry about as it is."

"It doesn't take any effort to listen," Lucy says. "A lot of people pass through the laundry. And people like to talk."

"That they do."

"You had anything to eat today?" he asks me.

"No."

"Go on . . . there's food on the table for you." His kindness and trust make me feel worse about my lies, and I have to remind myself that a life is at stake. That he wouldn't understand.

"I'll walk with you," Lucy says. Another surprise. In all my life I can't remember her ever coming to our house.

Cats come out of the nooks and crannies as we walk up the steps. I see Lucy's mother watching us. Lucy waves to her, an assurance that she'll be there soon. I see Alex's mother also, her eyes on both Lucy and me as if we were the ones who murdered Alex. I have yet to talk to her. I've yet to tell her the whole story. I don't know if it will make things better or worse so for now I leave it alone.

Lucy looks around my home while I eat. I'm starving yet I know it's much worse for Pace. My not eating won't help him at this moment and thanks to Lucy I have food to take him. Still, it will be a long time until tomorrow morning. She sits down after I slow down and take the time to chew the stew my grandfather prepared.

"Do you have a plan?" she asks.

"Beyond keeping Pace alive? No."

"Do you think there's a way out of this?"

"If so I've yet to find it," I confess. "He thinks I should turn him in so no one else will suffer."

"They'll kill him."

"Yes."

"And you too for the things they think you might know."

I nod. It's nothing I haven't already thought of. "Neither of us is worth the lives of everyone else. If they find a way below. If they bring weapons . . . I'll have to surrender him."

"Will you be able to?"

"It's not about being able to. It's about doing what I have to do."

Lucy smiles. "I've always envied you."

I nearly choke on my milk. "Me? Why?"

"You were always so independent. You went your own way and did what you wanted no matter what anyone thought."

"I was independent because everyone hated me for what my mother did. I had to be."

"No one hated you. Oh sure, some might now because of the trouble. It's just that you were different in the way you thought and acted. You didn't fall into your assigned role. You thumbed your nose at everyone."

My mouth drops open in shock.

"It's because of you that I went above to work. It's because of you that I found the courage to try for something more." Lucy reaches across the table and takes my hand. "You inspired me, Wren. I just wanted you to know that in case the worst happens."

I don't know what to say. Words fail me. Lucy stands, gives me a quick hug, and leaves. I sit in silence as she goes, dumbfounded by her words.

And then it hits me. It *is* my fault Alex is dead. Because of me Lucy chose to go above, and because of me she met David and rejected Alex.

How many more people will die because of me?

· 15 ·

As I expected, it is impossible for me to get away to see Pace before my shift. I'd left my lunch pail at the stables so my grandfather packs both our lunches in his and walks me to work.

"I know this has been hard on you," he says after we leave the village. "Seeing Alex that way and all . . ." his voice trails off. "I've seen men broken over less." He doesn't speak for a moment, just clears his throat and looks away. What is he remembering? My grandfather never talks about the past, nor has he told me stories of his youth. He always lives in the present, no matter what the occasion, as if the past is too painful to recall.

He never gossips and never speaks of anyone unless he knows it to be the truth, which means he doesn't talk much at all. His words are measured and weighed so when they come I consider them carefully because I know they cost him dearly. But there are times, when he drinks the liquor that is brewed deep in a long-exhausted cave, when he speaks of things I don't understand and curls up in his bed and weeps with regret.

He puts his hand on my shoulder, something else he rarely does. He's never been demonstrative in his affection yet I've never doubted his love for me.

"I just want you to know I'm proud of you. Of the woman you've become." Once more he clears his throat of the emotion that gathers there. "I know I don't say it enough." He laughs, once, a sharp bark that's rarely used. "I reckon I've never said it at all."

The words and his random attempt at affection should warm me. Instead they fill me with a horrible sense of guilt. The first time in my life he tells me he's proud of me and I'm lying to him.

"Don't you let them down there scare you with their talk," he continues. "Nothing that's happened is your fault. It could have been any one of them with Alex when he died." We continue on, him assuring me that everything is fine and me knowing that everything that's happened is my fault since the moment Lucy told Alex she didn't want him. I don't know what to say. I can't find the words that will take us back to the way things were before. So I walk with him and listen and fight back the tears of my shame until we come to the stable.

My pail is right where I left it, on the barrel next to the orange cat who seemingly hasn't twitched a whisker since I left. My grandfather packs my lunch into it carefully and turns to go. "I'm working guard duty tonight. Tunnel twenty-three."

I nod. Twenty-three is the cross tunnel where I came down the day Pace chased me. It's the one escape hatch the bluecoats know about. Even though it has been nailed shut it is still a risk because they know where it is and where it leads.

"I'll be seeing you in the morning then," he says and turns away and walks up the tunnel from the stable.

"Wait!" I call out just as he reaches the bend. He turns to look at me. His hair is wild around his face and his goggles hang haphazardly around his neck. His face is lined and streaked with the coal dust that never seems to go away. I run to him and throw my arms around him. His hands come up as I cling to him and then slowly and tentatively he puts them on my back and awkwardly pats me.

"There, there, gel," he says. "Everything will work out in the end. You'll see."

"I love you," I cry out. I hold him as tight as I can, as if tight will squeeze out all the lies between us. So there will be no room for them.

He pats me again and clears his throat. "That's good to know." He coughs and I feel his lungs laboring within his chest as they fight the coal dust. "I love you too." His voice is gruff and low, as if he's afraid someone will hear him. "Now let me go before we get called a couple of slackers."

I give him one last squeeze and he returns it with one last pat and I let go. I watch him until he fades into the blackness of the tunnel, and then with a sigh I turn and go back to the stables.

◆

Telling my grandfather I love him does not erase the lies between us. It doesn't do much to make me feel better either. I'd like to think that I said it for his benefit, but I know in my heart that I told him I loved him to alleviate my guilt. I am miserable as I work my shift, agonizing over my choices. The problem is, being honest with my grandfather will result in Pace's death.

You don't know that for certain . . . My argument with myself continues. *He could surprise you.* I go back and forth with the debate. I cannot find a way to tell my grandfather about Pace without the end result being Pace turned over to the filchers.

If I could just make my grandfather realize that even if we turn over Pace, they'll still come after me. That after they kill me, they will go after him because of me. That it will continue with the blue-coats killing anyone and everyone who might know their secrets.

The only way to beat them is to make sure everyone knows their secret. And Pace is the only one who truly knows. If only he would tell me where he thinks Alex got out. I've got to figure out a way to get outside and bring back proof that there are no flames. I've got to convince Pace that it's the only way he will survive. I've got to convince my grandfather that it is a risk worth taking because I know that without his help it will be an impossible task.

Another question haunts me as I try to figure out where and how. Why? Why aren't we allowed to leave? Is it because they are afraid that once the tide turns to the outside, there will be no one left to care for the royals? Are their lives so much more important than ours? Who has the right to make that decision for those of us who, like Alex, want to go? Who has the right to kill someone, just because they want something different from what has been prede-termined for them? It's something else I will ask Pace, a list of ques-tions that constantly lead to more. I am afraid he doesn't have the answers either.

My mind continues to chase through the never-ending tunnels of the different scenarios where each conscious decision will lead. I am so distracted that it takes me a long moment to realize that something is terribly wrong when the earth trembles and I am thrown to my knees.

The ponies rear up in their traces and whinny in fear. Luckily the cart had just been dumped so I'm in no danger from falling chunks of coal. I scramble to my feet and grab the halter of the lead pony, which is Ghost. He butts his head against my chest and snuffs at my jacket. My presence calms him. Blue, who shares the traces with Ghost, tosses his head up and down and I quickly place my hand on his nose, which settles him.

Shouts echo off the tunnel walls. The shiners pour forth from the tunnels where they were working. Questions ring out.

"What was it?"

"An explosion of some sort."

"Methane?"

"An attack?"

"Where?"

As I calm the ponies I suddenly know where and I can also say who. I take off at a run. Ghost and Blue follow me at a fast trot and the coal cart bounces and careens against the tunnel walls as they try to keep up with me. I can't worry about them now. I have to get to my grandfather.

The tunnels fill with people as I get closer to twenty-three. I see workers from the day shift along with the night. Someone grabs the pony cart and leads them away, back to the stables I can only hope, as I continue on my way. Voices that are raised in questions suddenly go silent as I turn in to the tunnel. Jasper is there, and James, Adam, and Peggy, all half dressed as they were awakened from their sleep and looking as dazed as I feel.

The throng separates as I continue onward. Hands reach for me, much like they did with Alex's mother. I ignore them. My heart knows what has happened but my mind refuses to acknowledge it until I see it for myself.

Mary is with my grandfather. I walk through the circle that surrounds him. A few hold lamps aloft and I see that there's been an effort to dig him out. It's no use. Even I can see that it is too much for men who only have picks and shovels.

"She's here, Elias," Mary says. She holds his hand in hers and I can see the strain of his grip. The other arm is beneath him as he is pinned facedown, caught in the cave-in after he rigged the charge.

I can't help but wonder how many filchers are dead beneath the rubble. How many came down this time in an attempt to find me? How many more will follow? I drop to my knees beside him and Mary places my hand where hers has been.

"Back up, everyone," she says. "Give them some room. Give them some peace." I hear the shuffling of their feet as they back away. Someone puts a lamp by my grandfather's head. I stretch out on my stomach beside him so I can see his face. He turns his head to me.

"Just wasn't fast enough this time," he says. "I used to be the fastest one. No matter what." He coughs, agonizing and harsh, and blood comes up. He makes an effort to spit it out. I wipe it away with his kerchief. No one has to tell me what happened. No one has to tell me that he set the charge because he'd lived the longest and he'd thought his time to die was long past. That he did it so a younger man would have more years with his family. That he made the choice to keep me safe. Those words go unsaid because his time is short.

He uses the last of his strength to pull me closer until we are cheek to cheek and his mouth is by my ear.

"I want you to fight, Wren," he says so low that only I can hear him. "I know you've got that boy hidden. It's a good thing you've done."

I shake my head and his grip tightens. "I believe in you. I believe you'll find a way. I believe you'll fly free, just like the little bird I named you for." His breath rattles and stops.

I move, twisting my head so I can see his face. His eyes are still open, deep and brown, and staring upward, through the roof of the caves, through the dome, and at the sky beyond it. The shine is gone. Mary comes to me and puts her hands on my shoulders. She pulls me up.

"There, there, child," she says. "Come with me."

I wrench away from her hands. They trap me. "No."

My grandfather is dead. He knew about Pace. He knew I lied.

He told me to fight. How can I fight when I don't know who the enemy is? How can I fight when I don't know what I'm fighting for?

"No," I say again. I look at the shiners gathered around. I see the guilt on the faces of the ones who were with him. The ones he saved. I see Peggy, with tears pouring down her face, start toward me and I hold my hand up to stop her. I don't want to cry. Grandfather told me to fight and fight I must, even against the tears that scream to be let out.

James stands beside Adam. In his hands are my grandfather's goggles. Why does he have them? Does he think that he will step into his place? That I will go to him because I have no one else? He holds out his arms as if he's going to hug me. Trap me. I take the goggles from his hand.

"Wren, wait!" Peggy calls after me as I start down the tunnel.

"Let her go," I hear Jasper say. "Leave her to her grief."

My grief.

My fight.

I am alone.

· 16 ·

My route to Pace takes me by the stables, so I stop to pick up the stash Lucy brought below and stuff my grandfather's goggles and my lunch pail inside it. Most of my ponies are back and sharing their stalls with the day shift. As usual, the news of my grandfather's death has already traveled through the mine and others have stepped in to do my job. There will be no more work this night. Instead, they will dig out my grandfather's body and prepare it for burning.

They will leave me alone with my grief, for which I am grateful. I run through the tunnels as if I'm the only one who exists in our world, and those I pass don't say a word. They will save them for the funeral tomorrow. I don't care if anyone sees what I carry, but I do have enough presence of mind to go the back way after I leave the stables, darting into caves and taking the escape routes until I arrive at the river cavern.

Pace is crouched in the cave entrance with the lamp by his side. I don't bother to whistle. I throw the bundle to him and vault up to the ledge. He pulls me in and I go directly into the cave without a word. I can see the questions on his face, along with worry and exhaustion.

My first instinct after my grandfather died was to go to him. Now that I'm here I don't know what to do or say. I turn around and around, searching for something that isn't there. The only thing to see is Pip, sitting on the perch in his cage, staring at me. There is nothing to see, no answers to be found, and no sensible reason given as to why my grandfather died. He just did. I back up to the wall and slide down until I'm sitting with my head on my knees.

Pace carries the bundle in and sets it aside. I admire his restraint as he must be starving, yet I am beyond telling him to go ahead and eat. Just the thought of talking seems impossible. He sits down beside me with the lamp by his side and takes my hand. He cradles my hand in both of his and his thumb strokes my palm as he talks.

"I heard it, whatever it was, in here. The walls shook and I thought they would come down on top of me." As every shiner thinks whenever there is a cave-in. "I'm guessing that whatever happened was bad and occurred because they were looking for me?"

I let out a deep and slow sigh, and with it comes the last breath my grandfather took. Had I been holding my breath all this time? Impossible, yet I feel as if in this exact moment everything about my life has changed. His death was the catalyst and the breath I let out was the acceptance. I can never go back to what was. From now on, everything about my life is up to me.

"My grandfather is dead." My voice sounds disjointed, as if it belongs to a stranger. "He blew a tunnel to stop the filchers and he was crushed."

"I'm so sorry," Pace says. He puts his arm around me and without thought I lean into him. He pulls me closer until my face is pressed against his chest and his hand strokes through my hair.

"You've got to take me above so this doesn't happen again," he says. "Before someone else dies."

"No."

"Wren, enough people have died."

"My grandfather knew I hid you. He told me to . . ." my voice breaks. I swallow it back as Pace strokes my hair. "He told me to fight. It was the last thing he said to me. To fight and fly free, like the birds."

"How are we supposed to fight them?"

We . . . I didn't have to ask. He already knows he has to be part of the battle. That without him, there is no battle. "I don't know. I just know I have to fight."

"You don't have to fight this minute, do you?"

I shake my head. "No . . ."

He bends over and kisses my hair and just with that gentle touch the tears come forth and I shake with the sudden violence of their appearance. "I got you," Pace whispers as he pulls me closer and wraps both his arms tightly around me. "I got you."

I've never cried like this before. I've never felt this much gut-searing pain. I can't think of anything but the pain that washes over me, wrenching at my heart and leaving nothing inside but a great empty pit, with me screaming my way into the abyss. Yet through it all Pace holds me and talks softly although I cannot comprehend the words.

Finally the tears stop and I am too exhausted to move. All I can do is lie there, in Pace's arms, and feel the sensation of his fingers combing through my hair. At some time during my weeping he removed my goggles and the band from my hair. I was never conscious of him doing it, yet he must have, because I can see them lying on the cave floor beside the lamp. Finally, the sound of his stomach rumbling penetrates the fog that covers me and I push myself up. I take my kerchief from my neck and wipe my face dry.

My eyes are swollen and my hair is wild from his hands. I swipe at the lingering tears and smile tremulously. Before I can blink Pace has his hands on my face and he kisses me again, hungrily this time, as if I am the food he so desperately craves. I return it and more. We both rise to our knees and press against each other, twisting and turning our faces and mouths because we want to get closer and kiss deeper, if that is even possible.

My grief has turned into something else. Something wild and uncontrollable that sings in my veins. My craving for the light has been replaced by a yearning for something different, something tangible and so very real. Something that is right in front of me. I can't stop kissing him, yet I must to draw in air. When I do his mouth moves along my cheek and down my neck. He kisses the place where my neck and shoulder meet and I gasp as I feel the kiss all the way through my body, and it warms me in places inside of me I never really knew existed.

I want more. More of Pace. I tilt my head to the side to give him better access to my neck and he kisses it again.

"Wren," he sighs and my name has never sounded sweeter.

I want you to fight, Wren . . . My grandfather's last words ring in my ears. This thing that I'm doing with Pace, it will not honor his memory, it will taint it.

I don't want to make the same mistakes my mother made. I don't want to end up like her.

I turn away from Pace and his wonderful kisses. His arms are still around me and I have to fight the urge . . . the want . . . the need to turn back to him. I have to stay strong. I have to fight. This thing with Pace is not fighting, it's giving in, it's doing what is easy.

Yet it feels so right.

He senses my withdrawal, for which I am very grateful. I'm not certain how strong I am when it comes to his kisses. He leans his forehead against the side of my head and swallows hard. Then he jumps up and goes to the outer cave.

I need time to gather myself. I've gone from one extreme emotion to another. My head is spinning and I must make sense of things. I must come up with a plan to win this fight.

My face feels hot and flushed. I can only imagine what I look like with my wild hair and swollen eyes . . . and now swollen lips.

I must not look as bad as I think. I look good enough for Pace to kiss. This thing between us, if there is something between us, it's happened so fast. It has only been a few days. I have to make sure that this, whatever it is, is real, that there is something between us and not just a result of the dire situation we've found ourselves in.

Pip flutters in his cage and drops down to the bottom and pecks at a large rock. I look closer and see that it is bowl-shaped and full of water. Pace must have left the safety of the cave and taken the light with him. If I had known I would have been angry at him for taking such a risk. Now it all seems kind of frivolous in light of what else has happened.

I open the bundle and spread one of the blankets to sit on. I laid out the food Lucy brought and add the things from my lunch pail. As I pull them out I stop suddenly with the vision of my grandfather placing the things inside. It was the last thing my grandfather ever did for me. The funny thing is there is much more food than usual. He *did* know about Pace and made this provision for him.

If only I'd confided in him. Maybe he wouldn't be dead, maybe we could have figured something out. So much of what I've done of late has been reacting to the circumstances I find myself in. *Like*

Pace's kisses . . . I've got to figure things out and decide what the next step will be.

Right now that step is a meal for Pace. As if he knows what I'm thinking, he returns. Without a word he sits down on the blanket and eats, and occasionally drops some crumbs into Pip's cage.

"You can thank Lucy for most of this," I say.

His blue eyes widen in surprise. "She came below? Does she have news?"

"Just what we already know. The filchers will try again because of the reward. It's much bigger now."

"What is it?"

"A house on Park Front with full privileges."

Pace shakes his head in disbelief. "I'd turn myself in for that. To make sure my mother was cared for."

"I asked Lucy to find out what she can about her."

"Thank you," he says with sincerity. He starts to say more, then doesn't. He doesn't have to; I know what he's thinking. He's terribly worried about his mother but he won't say anything out of consideration for me and my grandfather's death. His mother must be a good woman, to have raised such a son. Still there are things I need to know about his life above.

"Have you ever heard of the seekers?" I ask.

"Yes. The seekers are an illegal gathering of radicals whose main purpose is to undermine the authority of the government. My orders were to report any suspicious activity to my training commander. Suspicious activity consisting of any gathering of three or more people who were not related and who were from differing bodies of the population."

"From what I've heard the seekers are those who think there's an entire world outside the dome that is free of flame."

"Was Alex a seeker?"

"I thought he was. It turns out he was just foolishly in love with Lucy."

"What about you, Wren?" He looks at me with his beautiful blue eyes. "Are you a seeker?"

Am I? For the past few years all I've done is wonder what is outside the dome. But wondering about something and acting upon it are two totally different things. Am I ready to believe in something so much that I'm willing to die for it? Am I ready to die to protect Pace as my grandfather just died to protect me?

"I guess I was," I admit. "But now I don't know if I'm strong enough," I say truthfully. My answer leaves my insides more twisted, as if my heart is held in a vise. If only things could go back to the way they were. Would I do anything different?

"Watch this," Pace says. He opens the cage door and sticks his finger inside. He whistles quietly. Pip tilts his head and pecks at Pace's finger. Pace wiggles it and whistles again. Pip jumps on it and Pace brings him carefully from the cage and sits him on his crossed leg. He drops a few crumbs onto his pants and Pip pecks at them while keeping a close watch on me.

"It passed the time," Pace says with a shrug. I smile my approval.

"We should save some of this," he says.

"Good thing there's plenty," I agree as I pack up the rest of the food in my pail. There should be enough for another day, maybe two if he's careful.

Pace puts Pip back in his cage. Then he picks up the other blanket and spreads it against the cave wall. He lies down and stretches out, wiggling and shifting until he's found a comfortable place. He lies on his back with his arms folded beneath his head. "What do we do now?"

"I don't know," I say truthfully.

"We don't have to decide anything right now," he says.

"I know." I'm suddenly very sleepy. Too sleepy to think about fighting battles that will more than likely result in more people dying. I can't help but yawn widely.

Pace swiftly moves to my side in that way he has of just doing things. He's impetuous. He takes my arm and leads me to the blanket. "Lie down," he says softly.

I start to protest but he stops me by putting his finger to my mouth. "I just want to hold you," he says. "Nothing more, I promise." He pulls the other blanket over me and wraps it tightly around my body, which makes me feel somewhat safe. He turns the lamp down as low as it will go and stretches out beside me. Then he gathers me into his arms. Just that act gives me such a sense of relief. A sense of comfort.

"Tell me about your grandfather."

I don't know what to say. How do I explain my grandfather to someone who didn't know him? He was a man of few words. He let his actions speak for him in his everyday life, even down to his last sacrifice. He didn't like fish but he ate it anyway. His pinky finger was crooked because he once broke it and it didn't heal correctly. Is that all I have to say about him?

"He loved me. He raised me by himself, with no help from anyone." Then something I didn't even realize until this moment. "He taught me to believe in myself."

"I believe in you."

"Why? What made you believe in me when you came to me that morning? What made you think you could trust me to help you?"

"Because you didn't leave Alex when he was dying. Because you went to him."

Once more I have no response. I just did what I knew to be right. Doesn't everyone? Maybe I'm wrong. Maybe everything I've done is wrong. The things Lucy said and now Pace have made me more confused than ever. I'm not special, I'm not a leader, and I'm definitely not a fighter, nor do I want to start a war with the bluecoats. Yet it seems as if everything is leading me to that place.

"I can't do this."

"You don't have to do anything right now." Pace strokes my hair. "Just sleep. You need time to grieve."

I look up at the ceiling as he strokes my hair. The people before the dome used to bury their people in the ground. What if we're digging for coal and we find the bodies? What if they come crashing down from above and their boxes splinter and the bodies, what's left of them, fall out? I can't imagine putting my grandfather in a hole. And worse, having to cover up his body with dirt. But would it be any different from watching his body burn until it's nothing but ash and then spreading the ashes on the river to be carried away?

Where does it go? The ash and the river? Does it go to the seas that I've read about? Or does it just fall deeper into the earth? What would happen to me if I just jumped into the river and let it carry me away? I can hear the heavy rush of its current now as it pounds through the earth, going where it wants because it is stronger than the rock.

Fly free like the bird I named you for. The birds in my village are trapped, just as the ones who live above in the dome are. Just as Pip is. We're all in a cage, beating against the bars and looking for the way out. There has to be a way out. There just has to be.

My eyes drift shut and I enjoy the sensation of Pace's hand stroking my hair. He is so kind, so gentle. I concentrate on his touch until all the troubled thoughts fade away and I fall asleep.

· 17 ·

I dream of hands reaching for me, dead hands that come through the earth and capture me, only to throw me into the flames. I fall into them screaming. Pace is there, Lucy, David, and of course Alex, who holds on to me with his flaming hands and tells me over and over again about the blue sky.

I wake with a start. I'm exactly as I was when I fell asleep, wrapped safely in Pace's arms. His eyes open as I stir and he smiles at me. "This is getting to be a habit."

"How long did we sleep?"

Pace laughs. "I have no idea. I don't even know if it's night or day, much less how long I've been down here. I just know it has been a good while because I woke up for a bit and just now lay back down." He looks at me intently. "How do you feel?"

I take a moment to decide. "Rested. Hungry." I look up into his blue eyes. "Scared."

"What are you scared of?"

Falling . . .

"Everything," I confess. I sit up and throw the blanket aside. My body aches from sleeping on the hard ground, and I take a moment to stretch out my stiff muscles. "I've got to get back."

"I wish I could go with you."

"No, you're safer here for now."

"Not because of that." He holds out a hand to help me to my feet. "So you won't have to be alone during the . . ." His voice trails off.

How easy it would be to say yes, come with me and stay with me so I don't have to go through this alone. So I'd have somebody to lean on. "Oh . . ." I'm surprised to feel tears welling in my eyes. I would have thought there wouldn't be any more after all the crying I did before. All the crying . . . My cheeks flush in embarrassment. At my crying, at the kissing, at what could have happened between us. Being with Pace is so strangely different. It's confusing and comforting, scary and exciting. Like flying over the pit. You feel the wind yet you're scared of falling.

I find that I'm glad nothing more happened between us, although the thought of it still gives me a strange sensation inside. I'm not ready to take that step. I'm definitely not thinking clearly enough to make such a life-changing decision.

"Thank you," I say. "But it's something I've got to do alone. I'll be back as soon as I can."

"I know you will." Pace comes to me and with a grin wipes away the residual tears with his thumb. "I'll be waiting. Maybe Pip will have something new to show you."

I can't help but smile, and regretfully I leave once more to make my secret way back to the village that no longer feels like home.

◆

"Where were you?" Peggy hurries toward me as I pass by the stable. Both shifts of ponies are still inside. No one is working. It's late afternoon, the time I usually wake up. I'm not worried about missing my grandfather's funeral. I know they won't start without me. I'm glad for the rest. I needed it as I need a clear head to make the decisions that lay before me.

"I needed to be alone," I say. "Have they . . ."

"Everything is ready," Peggy says. "We were just waiting for you."

We walk together, with this strange awkward silence between us. Peggy seems nervous but I attribute that to not knowing what to say. It's been a long while since we lost anyone to something other than the black lung, and since it is such a long and lingering death, it is usually met with gratitude.

Have things changed so much between us that she doesn't know what to say? Or maybe it isn't us, maybe it's just me. I'm not the same person I was before Alex died. I'm certainly not the same person who James accused of treachery. I'm the sum of my experiences and there's nothing I can do to change things back. I can only move forward and hope . . . no . . . fight for the best.

No matter what has happened in the past or will happen in the future, Peggy has been a good friend to me and I will not forget it, so I accept her silent company for what it is: an attempt to offer me comfort.

The village is prepared. My grandfather's body lies on a pyre in the middle of the river. It is covered with a tattered blanket, except for his face, which was not touched in the cave-in. Someone had to prepare him. More than likely it was Mary, who was always a good friend to him. It should have been me. It's just another regret that I can do nothing about. Adam, James, and the other young men are busy placing coal and tinder around the pyre.

"We'll wait on you to get cleaned up," Peggy says. "Lucy brought something for you to wear." Peggy goes on down to the river and Lucy comes out of her parents' home as I climb the steps to mine.

Someone has cleaned inside. The floor has been swept, our beds are made up with clean linens, and our dishes washed and lined up neatly on the shelf. On my grandfather's bed are his possessions. His bandanna, his pail, a few coins, and his pocket watch. I pick up his watch. The crystal is cracked but the minute hand still moves. I hold it to my ear to hear the steady tick-tock as I used to do as a child when he would sit me on his lap and hold me until I fell asleep. It's my watch now. My legacy from two hundred years of MacAvoy shiners. I wrap the chain around it and slip it into my pocket.

On my bed a cat lies curled up on a pale blue dress. I shoo the cat away and he stalks off with an indignant swish of his tail. I've never had a dress before. My life has never called for it. I have to admit this one is pretty. I hold it up against my clothes. It has a high waist and short puffed sleeves and it is made of the softest cloth I've ever felt.

"It belonged to a girl who disappeared," Lucy says as she comes inside. "Her mother told me to take it because it was too painful for her to look at."

"Do they know what happened to her?"

"She's just gone. It's been happening more and more. Girls and boys disappearing off the streets with no explanation."

"That's the third time I've heard that. I heard it from the dome washers and from Alex, the day before he died."

"It was the reason he insisted on walking me to work. It's the reason he saw me with David," she confesses.

"Do you think it could have anything to do with everything else that's happened?" I ask.

"I don't know," Lucy says. She checks out the window to make sure no one is approaching. "We don't have much time," she begins. "I'm not sure when or if I'll be able to get back down here. Did you know that the shiners are going on strike?"

"No . . . I've been with Pace since my grandfather died."

"You're growing close to him, aren't you?"

I go to the washstand. There is fresh water in the pitcher and a full bucket sits beside it on the floor, courtesy of whoever cleaned our . . . my home. I scoop some up in my hands and press them against my face. It feels so good against my skin, especially since I could feel it burning as soon as Lucy asked me about Pace. I take a good long look in the mirror. "Is there time to wash my hair?"

"If you want to," Lucy says. "They can't start without you." She comes up behind me. "I'll wash it for you, if you want."

"Please," I say. "I'm not ready to go out there yet." And I'm not ready to talk about Pace.

Lucy moves our one chair out on the stoop in front of our house. Everyone will see what we're doing, but it doesn't matter. They'll understand that I want to look my best to honor my grandfather and give me the time. There's no rush. Especially if they're going on strike. I see them gathering below, standing in small groups, all of them talking about my grandfather and me. Across the way the guard stands in front of the council chamber. Already they are discussing who will replace my grandfather.

"When does the strike start?" I sit and Lucy rolls up a towel to place under my neck as I lean my head back.

"It already has." She pours the water over my hair and it dribbles into the bowl. "I was allowed down because of the funeral but after that I won't be able to use the lift or any of the escape hatches because I don't want to give them away. Can you tell me how you got through the tunnel David showed you?"

"Yes, but you'll need to dig it out. It was tight. Too tight for Pace. I dislocated his shoulder when I pulled him through."

"David will take care of it," Lucy says with some pride. "They need escape routes above too." She lathers up my hair and I give in to the sensation of her fingers on my scalp, much as I did when Pace stroked my hair.

"Is it bad up there?"

"It will be when the coal runs out and the fans stop blowing. They'll have to make concessions."

Concessions that include Pace and me? The shiners won't care about him. They might accept something for me. There has to be something more for us. Something that will guarantee his survival.

"Have you heard anything about Pace's mother?"

"They had her in for questioning. Apparently she works as a governess for one of the royals. The family she works for wasn't happy about it and let it be known. They let her go, but they are watching her closely in case he tries to see her." Lucy rinses the soap from my hair and wraps it up tightly in the towel.

"That's better than what I expected. I'm sure Pace will be relieved."

"And that will make you happy?"

I look up at her, upside down, as she crimps the towel through my hair to dry it. "How do you know, Lucy? How do you know if you love someone?"

"You just do." Lucy smiles. "Just like you know when you don't. The thought of them not being in your life hurts. The notion that they might not be rips your heart out." We go back inside. Lucy brings the chair and once more I sit down as she combs out my hair. "Has he kissed you?"

"Yes," I admit.

"And?"

"It's strange to think about because of the circumstances. He doesn't know if he's going to live or die. Neither do I, for that matter. I just don't know."

Lucy puts the brush aside and grips my shoulders with her

hands. "You need to grab your happiness where you can find it, Wren. Don't push it aside because of what might happen. Hold on to it while it's in front of you."

She walks away suddenly, leaving me to think on her words. Does she have any regrets about Alex? I cannot say and it is long past the time to ask her.

"I'll leave you to get dressed," she says and goes out the door without another word.

Yes, I believe she does have some regrets about Alex. She loves David, I am certain, but that doesn't mean that she didn't love Alex too. She made a choice, and like me, she has to live with it.

I follow the trail of ashes down the bank of the river until they disappear under the cave wall. Is it really that simple? If I was able to completely follow what was left of my grandfather would he show up in the pool with the glow fish and from there into the rapids by Pace's hiding place? Has anyone mapped the course of the river as it runs underground? Is the place where the royals have access before our gentle flow, or after? Will my grandfather's ashes end up in the washbasin of a royal after they travel through a pipe into a grand home? Or will they go deeper into the earth?

To the sea, my heart sings . . . but only because I so want it to be true.

"You look very nice," James says. He comes up behind me while I watch the water flow beneath the wall. I know he is there but I keep hoping he will go away. I don't want to talk to him. I need time to think. I have got to come up with some way to save Pace. To save both of us.

"There's to be a feast," he continues. "To honor him."

I finally turn to look at James. "Shouldn't we be conserving our food since we're on strike?"

"Everyone has contributed a little." He smiles his charming smile. "Because of your grandfather."

I gather up my dress so it won't drag on the ground and walk up to the village with James by my side. "He'd be the first one to say not to. To save the food because we don't know what's going to happen."

"Don't worry, Wren. We have our ways around the bluecoats." He sounds so cocky, so self-assured. He has no idea of what we're up against.

"The escape hatches? Don't you think they'll be watching for someone to pop up through them?"

"They can't watch them if they don't know where they are."

"They have eyes everywhere. All they have to do is offer a reward to anyone seeing a shiner above. The scarabs, the filchers, even the tradespeople will gladly give us up."

"We've got it all figured out," he assures me.

But he doesn't know what it's like up there. He's never been chased as I have. He doesn't have a price on his head. "You sound so confident, James. Do you know something I don't?"

"I've been elected to council," he says proudly.

"Congratulations," I say. I know it is the one thing he's always wanted. I knew he had to have been disappointed when Adam was elected before him. I am genuinely happy for him. And for Peggy. Her husband-to-be and her brother are both on council. She will have the life *she* always dreamed of.

He touches my arm and I can't help but recall how he held on to both of them in the tunnel when he kissed me. The look on my face must have reminded him too, because he quickly pulls his hand away. "I hate that it came because of your grandfather's death."

"It isn't your fault, James. My grandfather lived a long time. Longer than anyone. I know he would rather have gone the way he did than coughing his lungs up." I hurry my steps, anxious to be away from him.

"There's something else you should know." James stops me once again by taking my arm. What makes him think he can just touch me whenever he wants? I stare at his hand on my arm but he doesn't release it, instead he slides it down and takes my hand. "The council wants you to give up your house to make room for a new family."

His announcement is not surprising, except for the timing. I would have thought the council would have given me more time. "I will gladly give it up for Peggy and Adam," I say. I mean it. The thought of Peggy living in the house I grew up in makes me happy. When I look into my future I can't see myself there. I don't see myself anywhere. My future at the moment is a blank slate. There are too many questions and too many possibilities, and most of them end with my death.

"There's a way you won't have to," James continues.

"How?" I ask, mostly because I'm curious at to what the council has to say about me.

James turns my hand in his. I can't help but recall Pace's gentle touch of my palm as I told him about my grandfather's death. I don't pull away from James. I know that people are watching us. I don't want to give them cause to talk about me, or to presume some control over me because they think I am irrational with grief.

"They said they would allow us to marry first, since you're alone now."

I study James for a long moment. His light brown hair, his green eyes, his wiry body that hides his strength. His charming smile. He is so much like Peggy, but then again he is not like her at all. I imagine Alex's last moments as Pace described them and then I try to see James in the same situation. Someplace where he can't talk his way out of the situation. Where no one falls under his spell.

I can see him in the council meeting; pleading his case and making it seem as if it's all for me and everyone eagerly agreeing to it, because, in spite of what they think of me, they loved and respected my grandfather.

"Why do you want to marry me, James? Why me, of any of the girls in the village, or above for that matter." I was being honest. James could have his pick, if he could convince one to come live below. And I'm certain he could.

James squeezes my hand. "Because I love you, Wren."

"No, you don't. I believe you think you do, but deep down you don't."

"Of course I do," he says with his smile.

"I'm not really certain right now I know what love is. But I am sure of what it isn't. It isn't pressuring someone to do what you want, or forcing them to, or lying about them because they don't fall under your spell. It isn't betraying them to their friends and it isn't trying to change them to meet your expectations." I pull my hand away. "I don't know why you chose me, James, I really don't. I'm sorry I can't fall in with your plan for us."

Tears threaten again and it makes me angry. Why am I so weak? "I really wish I could. I wish I could be content to stay below and not wish for things beyond the dome. But I can't. I can't stop any more than I can stop breathing. My marrying you won't change it and it certainly won't make you happy. Choose someone else. Someone who will really appreciate who and what you are and not what they think you should be."

His smile fades and is replaced by the same look of disgust and frustration he turned on me in the tunnel when I rejected him. "You need to grow up, Wren, and quit fighting the inevitable." The notion that James was the one who killed the filchers and dumped them into the pit won't let go. I know in my heart that he is capable of it in the same way I know that Pace would never murder someone.

In spite of my fear of him I remain firm in my resolve. I had tried to be nice. I had tried my best not to embarrass him in front of the village. "No," I say clearly so he does not misunderstand. "You need to grow up and accept the fact that not everything is going to go your way."

"You don't mean this, Wren. If you don't marry me what are you going to do? Where are you going to go? No one will take you in."

"No one will take me in because you'll tell them more lies about me? Just like you did at the seekers' meeting?"

"You don't know what you're saying," he continues. "You need time to think."

I can see that his pride won't allow him to accept my answer. Only time will make him see the truth. I also have to admit I'm frightened by his insistence. After my experience with him when he kissed me I know he's not above forcing me into compliance.

"You are right, James," I say. "I do need to think. About a lot of things. So much has happened lately. There's just too much to comprehend."

James smiles his charming smile once more. He touches my hair and smooths a lock of it back from my face. "Take all the time you need," he says. He leans in and kisses me, quickly and chastely, before I have a chance to protest, and then he turns and walks away.

I watch him go, knowing he's happy with what everyone saw. He was able to save face in front of the village. I don't want to think about what he would've done if I'd embarrassed him. I know in my heart James is capable of many things. I'm just not so certain that all of them are good.

◆

I am exhausted after the feast to honor my grandfather. Many spoke about him, some telling things that happened before I was born. There were none there who could speak about him as a young man because there were none alive who knew him then.

So much about his life I will never know. But the stories I heard, and the gratitude expressed by those who were with him when the decision was made to blow the tunnel, give me comfort.

"I could stay with you tonight, if you want," Peggy says as I am finally able to break away from the feast.

"Funny, I can't remember the last actual *night* I slept in my bed." I don't say that I don't think I'll ever sleep in it again. That it no longer holds the sense of comfort it once had.

"Adam thinks the strike won't last long," Peggy says. "And then things will go back to the way they were."

Have I become so jaded because I've seen death and how ugly it is? How can Adam and the rest of the council believe that it will be that easy? Do they seriously think they can get what they want because they control the coal? I believe with all my heart that things will get a lot worse before they get better. That more people will die. And that I will be one of them. But I can't say these things to Peggy. Peggy who is full of hope and love for her world. Not my world anymore. Was it ever truly mine?

"I don't think it will ever be the way it was before," I say.

To my surprise, Peggy begins to cry. She puts her hand to her mouth to hold back the sudden onset of tears. "I know," she sobs. "I'm so sorry. I hope . . ."

I know what she hopes for. What she's always hoped for. "I'm not going to marry James," I say. "I can't, not after what he said at the seekers' meeting. But that means you and Adam can marry now." We stand at the bottom of the steps to my home . . . her home now. "It makes me happy that you and Adam will live here."

"But where will you go?"

I take her hands in mine, because she's always been my friend, and I don't want to lie to her. "I don't know. I just know that for now, I have to go."

"I don't want you to leave."

"I know," I say, simply, because suddenly everything has become clear to me. "I don't belong here anymore. I don't think I ever have."

Peggy shakes her head in an attempt to make it all go away. "It's all Lucy's fault," she says as she watches Lucy make her way up the ramp. "If she hadn't rejected Alex—"

"Peggy . . ." I recall Lucy's words to me. How she said I inspired her to go up and go after what she wanted. If Peggy blames Lucy, then she is indirectly blaming me. Something I'd already done plenty of. "None of that matters now." Lucy's later words came to me. The ones she had spoken before the service. "What does matter is you love Adam and he loves you. So hold on to that and enjoy the moments that are right in front of you."

"They won't be the same without you here," Peggy cries.

"Yes they will." I know in my heart that she won't even miss me when I am gone. None of that matters. I hug her tight, remembering all the happy times we had as children. "I'm leaving tonight, after everyone goes to sleep. Don't try to find me. If the filchers come for me I don't want you anywhere close."

She hugs me. "I will see you again," she promises. She leaves. I watch her go before I climb the steps one last time to the place that was once my home.

· 19 ·

I never thought I would actually leave this place. A week ago I was certain I would live out my life here, marry, have children, and eventually die of the black lung. I certainly had my dreams, dreams of things that I thought were impossible to obtain. Now I know that if I want anything more, including a life, I will have to fight for it.

I take all that I can carry. My clothes, my grandfather's clothes, our toiletries, the mirror, the slate, my grandfather's lunch pail and coins. I empty our larder of every bit of food. Everything that I have in this world except for my grandmother's Bible goes inside the two quilts, which I tied into a bundle. It is awkward and heavy but I have no choice. I will . . . Pace and I will need it all to survive. The Bible I leave on a table for Peggy and Adam. My benediction on their marriage. I wish them well, I wish them happiness. I wish them peace, something I know I will not have for a long while.

The village is serene. It has been so long since I've seen it at night, since I am usually at work. The overhead lights are dim and the birds quietly sleep on the wires. The goats sleep in their pen across the river. The only sound is the lap-lap of the waterwheel and a soft lullaby coming from one of the houses. A few lights wink through some of the windows. All is peaceful. All is calm. The only way for it to remain that way is if I leave. I won't bring my troubles down on these people. They've done nothing to deserve it.

I turn to say good-bye to my home. It's not as if I won't ever come back, I just know that it will be different from now on when I do. To my surprise a cat follows me up the ramp. It's the big gray striped one that likes to sleep with me.

"Stay here." I swing my leg out to discourage him. "This is your home." He gives me a plaintive meow and continues to follow me. And so I go, carrying my bundles with a cat trailing behind me through the tunnel.

Guards are still posted. I pay them no mind as from here I must pass the stables and I know they will assume that is where I'm heading. They don't say much, except to acknowledge my passing and say something about my grandfather.

The cat stays with me and is still with me when I wearily come to the river cavern. I whistle as soon as I pass over the cave. Tonight of all nights I'm not concerned about being followed or anyone finding us.

Pace meets me at the bottom of the long ledge with the lamp in his hand. He takes the bundle from me and without a word we make our way back to the cave. I'm still wearing my dress, which is foolish considering the trek I made and the rocky pools I have to navigate. I feel ridiculous with my skirts rucked up and my work boots, which are the only shoes I own, showing my bare legs as I jump from rock to rock. More so with the cat following me and mewing its distress at all the water.

"I told you to stay home," I say as we come to the cavern. "I didn't think you'd like it."

Pace shoves the bundle inside and turns to me. He stops with the lantern held high and stares at me.

"What?" I'm standing on a huge rock and thinking about how I will manage to make the climb into the cave while wearing the dress. I should have changed before I left. I should have tied my hair up instead of having it fall in my face every time I bend over.

He smiles and shakes his head. "You are so beautiful."

No one has ever said those words to me before. I don't know what I'm supposed to say, or do. I feel the heat rise on my cheeks as Pace just stands there with the lantern held aloft and looks at me while the cat twines around my ankles and meows its unhappiness.

"Who's your friend?"

"Cat," I say. "There are too many of them to name so they are all just Cat."

Pace crouches down and does his little whistle that he does with Pip. Cat butts his hand questioningly. "We have one rule here, Cat. No eating the birds." He stands. "Hold this," he says and shoves the lamp at me. In the next instant he picks me up, so suddenly that I can't help but let out a little yelp.

"What are you doing?"

"Your castle awaits, milady." He swings me around and kind of sits and kind of shoves me up on the ledge to the cave.

"What is a castle?" I ask.

He picks up Cat and sets him on the shelf then jumps up beside me. "You don't know what a castle is?"

"No."

"Can you read?"

"Yes. I went to school until I was twelve."

"What did you study?"

"Reading and writing and numbers. How much coal makes a ton, how long a ton will burn, things like that."

"How about history?"

I shake my head. "Before the dome? Just what is in the Bible, and I think I know it by heart." It was the only thing available to read.

"You never go to the library?"

"We're only allowed once a year," I say. "And I always looked at the drawings."

He takes my hand and I stand, arranging my skirts as I do so. I suddenly realize the finality of what I've done. It's just Pace and me in a very small cave. At my home we had curtains for privacy, and while I did bring them, I have no way to hang them. Did I think this through? Should I have stayed at the stable and made a home in the loft?

It's too late now. Pace carries the bundle and drops it on the blankets. "This is your castle," he says. "It's where the royals used to live in the before time. They had more rooms than you can count and servants and stables full of horses and fields of grass where they would ride their steeds and the men would do daring deeds."

I smile at his foolishness. "Daring deeds? Like what?"

"Slaying fire-breathing dragons." He waves a pretend sword around and then thrusts it forward.

"If only it were that easy," I say.

Pace suddenly realizes what he said. He runs his hand through his hair and sighs heavily. "I guess there is no escaping it," he says. "We're going to have to figure this out."

"Yes, we are," I say. "But not tonight. I just said good-bye to my grandfather and my home and I'm exhausted." I sit down on the blankets to unwrap the bundle. Cat has already made himself comfortable and I shove him aside to make room. He moves to the corner of the blanket and licks a paw.

"You didn't leave your home because of me, did you?" Pace sits down beside me as I start to sort through my possessions. I can't help but notice he's been busy while I was gone. He's set up a shelf with two block-size rocks and a long board and has the food arranged on it. Pip sits on one rock and he sets the lamp on the other next to the lunch pail I'd left behind.

"Where did that come from?" I ask, pointing at the board.

"I found it stuck in the rocks." He shrugs. "It must have washed down from somewhere." He puts the food I brought on the shelf. "You didn't answer my question."

"No, I didn't leave because of you. I left because I had no choice."

"They kicked you out?"

"No . . . I could have stayed. All I had to do was get married."

He sputters. "What?"

"I said no of course."

Pace shakes his head in disbelief. "Why?"

"Because I didn't love him," I say simply. I get the feeling he wants to say more but he doesn't. Instead he takes the lamp and pail I brought from home and places them with the others.

"I should change out of this dress," I say.

Pace picks up the pail and lamp. "I'll go get some water."

I start to call after him, start to tell him to stay inside, where it is safe, to not take the risk but I don't. I don't think anyone will be roaming around tonight, except for the guards stationed at the cross tunnels close to the hatches. Later, when people get tired of the strike, they will wander, but for now I think we are safe.

I turn on the other lamp before I take off the lovely blue dress and put my work clothes back on. I don't know what to do with the dress, I don't want to mess it up but there's no place to hang it. Finally I fold it as neatly as I can and place it on top of the pile of clothes and set them against the wall. I set all the toiletries on the rock and lean the mirror against the wall behind it. Then I spread the two quilts out. Cat protests again at this interruption and waits until I have things arranged how I want before lying back down, right in the middle of them.

Pace is sitting on the ledge with his back against one side of the cave wall and his feet propped on the other. I crouch down next to him, inside the cave, and look out into the darkness. The lamp is as low as it will go and still put out a bit of light. It gives me some reassurance to know that he's using his head.

"Ever since I found that board I've been thinking about the river," he says. "Is there anything else lying out there, that came from someplace else? Where does the river start? Where does it end? Where does it go?"

"Does it go outside?" I finish for him.

He puts his arm around me and I lean into him. "Or does it fall deeper into the earth?" His questions echo my own. "I'm glad you didn't get married, Wren. But that doesn't mean you shouldn't have."

"I couldn't."

He puts his chin on top of my head. Being here with him feels so right, so natural, like breathing and walking and talking. "They will find me eventually," he says.

"Which is why we have to find the way out first."

I feel his heavy sigh on my cheek. "Do you really think it's worth the risk?"

I sit up so I can look at him. "Don't you?"

"I don't want you to get hurt. I'd rather think about you living and having children, and growing old, and," he smiles, "thinking about me occasionally."

"It's too late for that now. Too much has changed. I've changed. I could never be content living down here, knowing there is an entire world out there."

"We don't know that for sure."

"Don't you?" I turn so I am facing him. "I feel it here." I touch my heart. "I just know it's out there. A big blue sky and trees and real grass and an ocean that goes on forever."

"I believe it is there too, it's just that I'm not sure if it is worth your life to prove it."

"If not this then what? What could be more important than this? There's got to be something more to this life than what's been decreed to us for the past two hundred years. If not, then why bother?"

"Wren, you're not listening to me . . ."

I start to protest but he stops me by taking my wrists into his hands. Funny how I don't mind when he touches me in such a possessive way, but let James try it and I cringe. I look into his beautiful blue eyes.

"I agree with what you're saying, Wren. My point is I don't want you to die because of it. I know my life is a given, that as soon as they find me I'm dead. I can only hope and pray that it's fast and not like what they did to Alex or Tom. And it will all be worth it, if I know that you're safe. I'll go upside right now and tell everyone that there is a way out and we're all being held prisoner, as long as I know that you'll be all right."

"Pace . . ." My heart swells at his words, the sweetest words I've ever heard, yet also so tragic and without hope.

He pulls me to him and kisses me, hungrily, possessively, as if he is going to die in the next minute and I'm the only thing that can save him. The kisses we shared before were good, but this kiss, this desperation, is overwhelming. My insides catch fire and I cling to him, once more not able to get close enough to satisfy the burning that courses through my veins.

More . . . I want more . . . Pace pulls me into his lap without stopping the kiss. I love the way he holds me, the way he moves me, tenderly and gently, but without effort, as if I'm a bird in the palm of his hand that he wants to keep safe, yet he doesn't want to hurt if it decides to fly free.

His touch shows he wants me, but it doesn't trap me; it gives me the freedom to make the choice. And I choose him. I chose him the second I held out my hand to him when he asked me to help. And live or die, he will always be my choice.

Please, God, let it be live.

He is stronger than me, much stronger because he stops the kissing and leans his forehead against mine in a position that has suddenly become so dear to me. "I'm not like the ones you left behind," he says after a moment.

"What do you mean?"

"They put conditions on you. You could stay if you married someone. I won't do that. I won't make you think you have to do something you're not ready to do because you're here with me."

I start to protest, to say I am ready, but deep down I know I'm not. There are too many uncertainties, too many things that have happened in too short of a time. I slide off his lap and once more sit by his side with my head on his shoulder and his arm around me.

"I wonder where it goes," Pace says after a long moment.

Another question without an answer. For the moment, I am content with not knowing.

· 20 ·

I learn more about the history of the world from Pace. He has this amazing way of telling it, as if it's a story, which keeps me captivated for hours. He tells me of a kingdom long ago called Camelot. He tells me that we live on an island called Great Britain in a part of it called Wales. He tells me of an exciting country across the sea called America. He tells me about different countries that speak different languages and about people who have skin a different color from ours. He tells me about exotic animals that I've only seen pictures of. Elephants and giraffes and bears and cats that are larger than any man. He uses the slate to draw pictures of castles and great sailing ships and the animals. His pictures amaze me even though they are the barest of sketches. I wonder what he could do with paint and a canvas. I have heard that the royals own wonderful paintings with bright colors that depict people and scenes from the world that was. Once more I am stunned by how unfair it is that they have everything and we are nothing more than servants to their way of life.

I cannot help but wonder if any of these people or places or animals that Pace speaks of and draws survived the comet. I dream that night of castles and large animals being consumed by flames as I watch from a glass cage that hangs above the fire, much as Pip's cage hangs from a hook. In my dream I beat against the glass and scream because I'm roasting inside, but no one hears me. They are all too busy trying to run from the flames. I wake with a start.

I lay next to Pace on our makeshift bed. I'm against the cave wall, and he is on the outside, something he insisted on, to protect me, in case someone discovers us. Cat lays half on, half off my legs and Pip, who also entertained me with his new tricks, is in his cage. The lamp is turned down low and casts a soft glow across our little nest.

Pace lies on his side, facing me. His hand is tangled in my hair and his mouth partially open as he breathes softly. A slight stubble darkens his cheek but it is still supple beneath my hand as I stroke his cheek. He doesn't move, just sighs, and a quick smile dances across his lips.

He asked if I would take him back to the glow fish, for a bath, and to learn how to swim. I am torn because I know the people of the village will get restless the longer the strike lasts. But I also want to make him happy and there is little enough down here for him to do.

My body clock insists that I should be up now and working. My grandfather's watch confirms it. It is almost midnight and I would normally be halfway through my shift and eating my lunch. I've caught up on my sleep and need to move and do something. I pull my hair as carefully as possible from Pace's hand and creep from the bed. Cat, disturbed by my movement, mews sleepily and curls up against Pace's bent knees.

We will eventually need food. I need to make an appearance, to remind everyone that I am still alive and make a contribution by work in order to eat. I decide to go to the stables to check on the ponies.

The tunnels are so quiet. Even though I am not on the usual path, there is usually the knowledge that people are about, doing their jobs, traveling back and forth from whatever tunnel is being mined to the village and onward to the lifts, whatever their work entails. Tonight the stillness is ominous, as if even the mine is waiting for something to happen. The noise of a pebble skipping ahead of my boots is enough to make me jump, and it seems as if the support joists creak with the strain of the weight they bear as I pass through them.

The ponies are happy to see me. They whicker as soon as they catch my scent and put their heads out of their stalls in anticipation of my arrival. I touch their heads as I walk through, greeting each one in turn. The chickens stare at me sleepily with their beady eyes and ruffle their feathers before settling back into their sleep.

I let the ponies out. I lead Ghost, confident that the rest will follow, down into the mine to give them exercise. It is their current route so they won't be hesitant, even without the familiarity of their harnesses. I find Hans at the current dig site. He is the night-shift supervisor, so it makes sense that he would be as restless as me.

"Where have you settled, Wren?" he asks. He stands in the middle of the dig site with a chunk of coal and tosses it back and forth between his hands.

"A cave," I say simply. I am not about to offer details in case someone decides to come looking for me.

Hans grins. "You are as cryptic as your grandfather. Everything with him was on a need-to-know basis. I reckon you don't think I need to know."

I can't help but smile. "Nope," I say. "You don't." I'm pleased at the comparison. I'd never realized it before, but he is right. I tend to keep my thoughts to myself. Except with Pace . . .

"You take all the time you need, gel. When you're ready to come back, we'll find a place for you."

"Thank you," I say, genuinely grateful for the offer even though I know that it will never come to fruition. My gratitude is also tinged in guilt as I am certain he wouldn't be so kind if he knew I had Pace below. I turn the ponies to make the return trip to the stables.

Would he feel the same as my grandfather? Could I go before council and tell them everything, including the fact that I have Pace hidden? Their reaction from my first time tells me no. The questions I asked when they interrogated me about Alex's death went unanswered.

Maybe it's because they *are* council. They have the difficult job of making the choices that are best for the whole, not just one or two. What I consider to be best for Pace and me would not benefit the village, it would only harm it.

This is something I have to do on my own.

Once we are back at the stables, I feed and water the ponies, clean out their stalls, and leave them with a reassuring pat that I will be back tomorrow and take the circuitous route back to Pace. Now would be a good time to take him to the glow fish to learn how to swim. Hans was the only person I saw while I was out. Everyone else is enjoying the luxury of a night without work and spending the time with their families and staying close to home. And looking forward to the wedding of Peggy and Adam. This day will be filled with preparations for both their families. I am torn about going to the ceremony. On the one hand, I don't want to be anywhere near James, but on the other, Peggy is my friend.

I have plenty of time to decide.

I return to find Pace still asleep. He lies flat on his back with his arms thrown over his head and with Cat curled up on his chest. I can't help but laugh at the sight of him, which rouses him from his sleep.

"Where did you go?" he asks as he stretches, which sends Cat looking for another pillow.

"I took care of my ponies," I said.

"Ponies?"

"My job is to carry the coal in the pony carts from down in the mine to the lift. The ponies still need to be fed and watered even though we're on strike. So I took care of them. No one is about, so if you want to learn to swim, now would be a good time."

His grin is all the answer I need. I grab some soap and towels and we take off for the cave with the glow fish.

Pace is much more patient this trip through the tunnels. We have to go up and then back down and I wouldn't let him take the lamp, just in case we came across someone. He holds on to my hand and follows my lead until we crawl through the low tunnel that leads up to the cave.

As soon as we get inside and see the light from the glow fish he grins broadly. Pace picks me up and swings me around and laughs. He amazes me with his capacity to find joy in the direst of circumstances. He carries me to the water and pretends like he's going to drop me in, which makes me laugh, and I bury my face in his shoulder to quiet it.

If only we had met under different circumstances. If only we had a lifetime to get to know each other, instead of these few stolen moments. I could waste the precious time we have agonizing over what will more than likely happen, or I can embrace the here and the now.

Pace puts me down and goes about the business of shucking out of his clothes, down to his undershorts, much like he did the first time we came here. He takes the soap and wades out into the water. I take my time as I strip down to my underclothes. I sit on a rock and tie up my hair as he lathers with the soap and then lowers himself to rinse it off with the glow fish darting around the angles and planes of his hard body.

He grins as he comes up and pats the water. "Come here."

"No," I say playfully and kick water at him.

"How am I supposed to learn how to swim?"

"Just let the water hold you."

Pace looks dubiously at the surface of the water. "You're going to have to show me."

"Only if you promise to be nice."

"What? I'm always nice." His grin is mischievous.

"I will let you drown," I say as I wade out.

He puts his hand over his heart. "I'm wounded." He pulls his hand away. "Seriously, can't you see the blood?"

I shake my head. It's too real of a statement to make fun of. Maybe he's just trying to forget for a while. As I should. Pace crouches down in the water as I come closer and waves his arms lazily back and forth beneath the surface.

"That's a good start," I say.

"This is swimming?"

"Close." I sink down beside him. "First you need to learn how to float." I talk him through it and he turns over on his back and carefully stretches out. "Keep your arms moving," I say. He picks it up quickly, but given his athleticism I'm not surprised. Soon I have him paddling around the water with the glow fish racing ahead of him.

"We should be getting back," I say finally. My body tells me morning is approaching with that same familiar yearning for the light. We dry off and dress quickly by the light of the glow fish.

"Thank you," Pace says when we are dressed once more. He puts his hands on my waist and kisses me. His touch is gentle and his hold loose, giving me the choice as to how close and how much I want. I put my hands on his shoulders and surrender once more to the touch of his lips on mine.

Which is why I don't hear the laughter until it is too late.

"Someone is coming," I whisper as I break away. I recognize the laugh. It's Peggy, which means Adam is probably with her.

"Where do we go?" Pace asks.

The escape tunnel is on the opposite bank and in the far corner behind a large boulder. We won't make it. I can hear them in the short tunnel now. Pace takes my hand and we race to the opposite side of the entrance. There's a bit of an alcove where the wall fades back. We can only hope that whoever is coming through will turn straight to the water and we can sneak out while they are going away from us. Pace pushes me behind him, even though I protest. I can see better than he can in the dim light, and if it is Peggy I'm hoping I can convince her not to tell. Adam I'm not so sure of since he's on council. Pace is determined to protect me and won't budge as he has me trapped in the corner. I have to stand on my tiptoes to see over his shoulder.

I hear Adam's deep voice and Peggy's answering laugh. I have my hands on Pace's back at his waist and we both hold our breath as a head emerges from the tunnel.

It is Peggy. Pace has no way of knowing that she is my friend. He pushes back against me, flattening me against the cave wall. Peggy turns automatically to the water just as Adam's dark head emerges from the tunnel. He scrambles and catches up with her, throwing his arm around her. Then another head comes out.

"Hey," James calls out. "You dropped this." He stands with the soap in his hand. Adam turns and James tosses it to him. It hits the ground because Adam and Peggy are both looking at us. They can see Pace clearly and know by the absence of the shine in his eyes that he does not belong here.

"Wren?" Peggy says cautiously.

"She's a friend," I say to Pace and he moves enough to let me step in front of him.

"Are you sure?" he says quietly. I hold my hand up to assure him that everything is fine.

"Tell me I'm wrong now." James's disgust is obvious. "I should have known you'd bring him down here."

Just as quickly as I stepped before Pace, he once more steps before me. James's hostility is evident and oppressive. He stands before us with his hands curled into fists at his sides.

"I did what I had to do, James," I say. "He was there when Alex was murdered."

"What do you mean murdered?" Adam asks.

"It's all part of her lies," James says.

"I wouldn't," Pace warns. I feel his body tense beneath my hand.

Before I can say anything to Peggy and Adam to defend my actions, James attacks. He lowers his head and charges at Pace with his arms outstretched. He crashes into Pace with his head angled into his chest and pushes him against the cave wall. I am caught in the corner and thrown forward. My head hits a rock and I am dazed. I try to crawl away. I put my hand to my temple and it comes away sticky and wet with blood.

Behind me I hear grunts and the sounds of flesh pounding against flesh. I can't concentrate. I want to stand up. I want to stop James and Pace from fighting, but I can't. All I can do is crawl away, on my hands and knees, and hope that my head doesn't cave in upon itself as it feels very fragile on my neck.

Peggy screams. I sense Adam moving past me. Pace can't fight two of them. Not with a recently separated shoulder. Adam and James have the advantage of their eyes also.

But their eyes make a target for Pace . . . I've got to stop it. Before someone else dies.

It takes every bit of my willpower to come up to my knees. Someone slams against me and knocks me forward again. I feel Peggy's hands on me and she urges me up. My head spins and my stomach protests the movement. Lights spin before my eyes like the glow fish in the water. Peggy gets me to my feet and we stagger away as once more bodies roll at the back of my legs.

"Stop them," I gasp. "Please."

"I can't," Peggy cries out. "I don't know how."

I am finally able to focus my eyes. It's hard to tell who is where in the mad scramble of bodies, especially since Adam and Pace both have dark hair. Their clothes are all the same browns and grays. But then I realize that James is on Pace's back when Pace flips him over. Pace is taller and broader than both Adam and James, but they have a wiry strength from years of work that is easy to overlook because of their smaller stature.

As soon as Pace flips James off, Adam kicks out and sweeps his feet from beneath him and Pace falls backward onto the ground, nearly missing a large rock that would have crushed his skull had he landed on it. James staggers to his feet and shakes his head before rushing back into the fray. I have to stop it. I have to.

"*STOP!*" I scream. I throw my body at Pace, who is momentarily stunned by his fall. I turn around to face Adam and James as I crouch over Pace, who backpedals away from me. James keeps coming and I rise to my feet and meet him. I shove with all my strength and he staggers back.

Anger distorts his face and he clenches his hand into a fist and raises it.

"Stop!" Adam shouts. He stops the forward motion of James's punch. Pace climbs to his feet behind me and once more shoves me behind his body, using it as a shield for me.

All four of us are breathing hard. Peggy stands behind Adam and James with her hand over her mouth and her eyes wide with fear or horror, I cannot tell which. The cut above Pace's eye has come open again and he moves his left arm gingerly. James and Adam don't look much better.

"We've got you now," James says. He spits out a gob of blood. "All we have to do is turn you in and we can have whatever we want."

"They'll kill him," I say.

"Why should I care?" James spouts. "Because you love him?" He sneers, like it's something nasty and disgusting.

"Because they'll kill her too," Pace says.

"And you, if they know you've been with us. And you and you," I say, looking at Adam and Peggy.

"Why?" Adam asks. Peggy comes to his side and he puts his arm around her.

"Because Alex got out and he survived until they caught him and brought him back in. Because he saw the sky and knew it was safe. Because they murdered him, by burning him alive, and Pace saw it."

"They're afraid I'll tell," Pace says. "They murdered my friend Tom, who was with me when they murdered Alex, and then they framed me for it because I got away. They beat him to death with their fists and pipes because of something they thought we might know. It's the same reason they want Wren. Because they saw her talking to Alex before he died and they think he told her where he got out."

"Alex got out?" Adam asks. "Out of the dome?"

"You can't seriously believe them," James says.

"Shut up, James," Peggy says. "Let them talk."

"Are you crazy?"

"No," Peggy spouts. "But you are. Crazy with jealousy. So let them talk. I want to know how Alex got out." She looks at Pace. "Do you know where he got out?"

"I have an idea," Pace says.

"Why don't they want anyone to know?" Adam asks.

"Would any of us stay here if we had a choice?" I say. "Without us, who would serve the royals?"

"There've been rumors," Pace says. "Of some of the higher-ups in the enforcers, what you call the bluecoats, of them going out and meeting with someone on the outside."

"Lucy heard it too," I add. "And there have been a lot of girls disappearing and some boys too."

"What does people above disappearing have to do with us?" James asks.

"It's why Alex was above. He wanted to make sure it didn't happen to Lucy," I say.

"It could be any of us," Peggy says. "It could have been you, Wren. You went above every day."

"To see him," James says.

"We didn't meet until the day Alex died," Pace says. "I saw her with him. I knew they'd murdered him as a lesson to anyone who tried to escape. I needed to know why. Why it was such a bad thing, so I chased her."

"Then he followed me the next morning, when I followed Lucy," I add. "That's when we met. I wanted to know what he knew about Alex's death so I agreed to meet him the following day after my shift."

"They killed Tom the morning we met," Pace continues. "If I hadn't stopped to talk to her, I would have been dead too. I walked in when they were beating him to death and he told me to run, so I did. The next thing I knew, I was wanted for his murder and would be dead if not for Wren."

"You brought all this trouble to us by bringing him down here," James spouts off again. "I killed someone because of you. Your grandfather is dead because of you."

"James," Peggy says. "Stop." She looks at me. "It's not true. Don't believe him."

I am suddenly so very weary and my head hurts. I urgently feel the need to sit down, so I do, on a rock beside the water.

"You're bleeding," Pace exclaims. He immediately touches my face, pushes my hair back and examines my wound. Peggy picks up a towel, either mine or hers, I could not tell in all the excitement, and dips it in the water before she comes to me and wipes the blood from the side of my face.

"Can you see it? How bad is it?" Pace asks her.

Peggy holds the towel to my temple to stop the bleeding. "Wait until it stops," she says to Pace. "I can't see it clearly now."

"I'm sorry that you had to kill those men," I say to James as Peggy ministers to my cut. "If I had known . . ." I look at Pace. I see the guilt and anger and concern in his eyes. "It doesn't matter. I wouldn't have done it differently. I still would have brought him down."

"Even though it meant your grandfather's death?" James asks incredulously.

"James," Peggy says in a low voice. She puts the towel in my hand and steps in front of her brother. "Stop it now." Her jaw is set and she grinds out the words. In all my life I cannot recall seeing her angry. Nor did I ever expect her to stand between me and James. My heart swells with love for her. My friend.

"My grandfather knew I brought Pace below," I say. "His last words to me were to fight them."

"How do we fight them?" Adam asks. He looks at Pace.

"There's a series of doors where the furnaces for the exhaust fans are located. They are heavily guarded by men who aren't part of the enforcers. There are also tunnels that run beneath the fans. You can see them if you get close enough. They have to lead somewhere."

"What makes you think this is where Alex got out?" Adam asks.

"Because I saw the men drag him through those doors. Tom and I were reporting to our squadron commander for our next assignment. They turned Alex over to him and they took him into this large warehouse and roasted him alive."

"Tell them what he said," I say.

" 'The sky is blue.' Over and over again. He didn't stop screaming it, even when he was burning up," Pace says in a harsh whisper.

"It's the same thing he said to me before he died," I add.

"We have to find the way out," Adam says.

"Yes," I say, and this time I believe it with all my heart. "We do."

"Why should we help you?" James asks.

"Don't you get it, James?" Peggy says. "If we turn them in, they're going to think that we might know something too. The only way to beat them is to let everyone know that Alex got out. If not they'll kill Wren and her friend and anyone else they think they might have come into contact with. They won't stop until we're all dead."

"But they need us," James protests. "To dig the coal."

"The coal is running out," Adam says. "Hans said that they haven't found a new deposit in any of the exploratory tunnels this year. And the one we're working now is about exhausted."

"My grandfather said the same," I add.

"And they'd just send below people from above to mine," Pace says. "They don't care who digs it up, as long as they continue to bring it up."

"We need to tell the council this," Adam says.

"We can't," Peggy says. "They won't agree. Some of them might, but not all." She looks directly at her brother. "And if they vote to turn Wren and Pace over, it will be as if they signed their death warrants."

"We've got to make sure Alex's death counts for something," Adam concludes.

"Exactly." I find it hard to believe that Adam has sided with us. That he's agreed not to mention it to council. James I'm not so sure of, especially since he looks at Pace with such venomous hatred. He was, however, good friends with Alex. Will that be enough to overcome his hatred for Pace and me?

"So what do we do?" James asks.

I let out a sigh of relief. "We find the way out," I say.

· 21 ·

Heads need to cool and Peggy and Adam have a wedding to get ready for. I'm still uncertain about the tentative truce I have with James. "I'll take care of him," Peggy assures me as she hugs me good-bye. "Will you come?"

"I'll try," I say. I look over at Adam and James. Adam has James by the water and is talking intensely to him. James shakes his head no. It frightens me to think of what James might or could do. All he has to do is tell someone that Pace is below and the entire village will be out searching for us.

"Don't worry, we'll make sure he doesn't follow you," Peggy assures me. "Your secret is safe."

"Lucy knows," I say. "If she comes down you can talk to her. She can help. She wants to help."

"You could have told me," Peggy says. She looks over her shoulder at James and Adam. "But I understand why you didn't. We'll meet you tomorrow morning at the stable. We'll figure something out."

"Not tomorrow morning," I say. "Tonight is your wedding night. Day after tomorrow."

Peggy once more looks over her shoulder at Adam. "I think sooner is better than later where James is concerned."

I have to agree. "Tomorrow morning then."

Pace waits for me at the tunnel. He lets me go first. I crawl through, almost expecting him to be dragged back by James, but thankfully he is right on my heels. When we are both through I put a finger to Pace's lips so he'll remain quiet and pause long enough to make sure we're not being followed. I can hear them talking on the other side but can't make out the words.

"Let's go," I say to Pace and lead him quickly away. I stop at each twist and turn, checking the tunnels and carefully listening. My head is pounding from my wound and I'm dizzy and nauseous. I have to stay on my feet or else Pace will be trapped in the darkness. It's the middle of the morning and I know there will be people about. I can't relax until we are both safely back in our cave. Finally, after what seems like hours, we arrive and I sink down onto the quilts with a grateful sigh.

"I'm guessing James is the one you were supposed to marry?" Pace joins me on the quilt.

"How could you tell?"

He touches the cut over his eye. "It felt kind of personal when he was pounding on me." He twists around and grabs the lamp. "I need to get a look at your cut," he says. He pushes my hair back and holds the lamp up while he looks. He touches it with his finger and I wince. It hurts.

"How bad is it?"

"Deep and swollen. You should have it stitched closed but . . ." He picks up the mirror and holds it before me. "See?"

I make a face as I look. The side of my face has already turned a vile yellowish green and the inch-long cut is raised and jagged. "I will probably have a horrid scar."

Pace puts the mirror aside and very gently and tenderly kisses my temple by the cut. Just that slight touch makes it throb, but I appreciate the thought behind it and I lean in to him.

"Take this off," he says and tugs on my jacket. I let him guide my arms out and then he moves down to my feet and pulls off my boots. He picks up the curtains from the neat pile I've made in the corner and places them on the quilt for a pillow. I watch him, as if from a distance. My head is throbbing. "Lie down," he instructs and I do so. "Do you feel like eating?"

I shake my head no and just that simple movement is enough to make me want to cry.

"Hey, we're missing someone," he says. "Cat isn't here."

"He's probably out looking for something to eat," I say. My voice sounds like it belongs to someone else.

"Hope he knows how to fish," Paces says, or so I think. Maybe I just dreamed it. All I know is that I closed my eyes and everything went dark.

◆

"Wake up, Wren."

"What?"

"Who am I?"

I reach out my hand. It's hard to open my eyes. I don't want to open them. He grasps my waving hand and squeezes it. "You're Pace."

"Good. You can go back to sleep now." I want to ask him why he woke me but my mouth doesn't want to open. I hear a rumbling sound and realize that Cat must be back and once more I fall asleep.

◆

My head still throbs when I wake up again, but not as bad. The pain is more centralized around my temple. I touch it tentatively and feel a lump the size of an egg.

"You're alive," Pace says. He's sitting cross-legged with Pip on his shoulder. Cat lies by his side with his tail twitching.

"Barely," I groan. "How does it look?"

"On you? Beautiful." He grins. "And like you lost a fight."

"I can't go to the wedding," I say. "If James and Adam are banged up and I show up with this, everyone will know we were fighting each other."

"Or you could make up a story about filchers coming below and the three of you beat them up."

"No, nobody would believe it. But only because it means the filchers got by the guards. We don't need any more guards in the tunnels."

"You mean they'd believe the part about you beating someone up?"

I throw my jacket, which was lying on top of the quilts, at him and wince in pain at the sudden motion.

Pip flies straight up in the air and Cat hisses and jumps into the outer cavern. Pace laughs as Pip lands on his lap and ruffles his feathers out. He picks him up and puts him back in his cage.

"I think you need to stay still until you feel a lot better," he says. "Are you hungry?"

"I could eat. Do we have anything left?"

"We can make it through another day, I think," he assures me.

"I can go to the village later to get food," I say. "There will be a feast for the wedding."

"A feast." Pace sighs. "That sounds wonderful." He puts out some of our larder on the quilt. "My mother is the best cook," he continues. "She makes this stew with sausage and apples . . ." His voice trails off. "I hope she's still safe."

"Lucy will let me know if anything happens."

"There's not a whole lot I can do about it if it does."

I can see the worry in his eyes. "Tell me about her," I say. "Tell me about your life before all this happened."

Pace sits down beside me and we divide up the food. I make sure his portion is larger. I'm not sure how much my stomach can handle at the moment. Even chewing hurts my head.

"My mother works as a governess for one of the lesser royal families," he begins. "It's not a live-in position so we have a small flat on the outskirts of Park Front. She teaches the children their lessons, along with painting, music, things like that. She moves from family to family as the children reach the age where they don't need her anymore. It was always nice for us because she was always bringing home clothes, toys, and treats—castoffs from the royals." He shrugs. "It was always just the two of us. When I was younger I was allowed to go with her and study with the royal children. That's how I learned so much about history and geography."

"What are they like?"

"The royals?" Pace breaks off a chunk of bread and chews on it. "Just like us, only with nicer clothes, nicer homes, more to eat," he says after he swallows. "Their lives are nothing but strolls on the promenade and parties and fussing over their dogs and tracing their bloodlines." He breaks off a piece of cheese. "You know they don't get to choose their mates?"

"Mates. As in husbands and wives? Why?"

"After all these years and a limited number of families they have to preserve the lineage. So all the marriages are arranged to keep the different bloodlines from crossing each other too much. There's someone in charge of it. They pick the couples and then negotiate the deal."

"That's horrible." Almost as bad as James's ultimatum, I don't add. "I can't imagine being forced to live with someone. What if you couldn't stand them?"

"As long as the line is preserved. That's all they care about. That's all any of us are supposed to care about."

I can't eat much. My stomach is still too weak and my head throbs. So I slide what I can't eat over to Pace's side of the quilt. He doesn't notice, just keeps picking up food and eating as he talks.

"What did your father do?" I ask.

"He was an enforcer. So it made sense that I wanted to follow in his footsteps."

"How did he die?"

"He fell off the catwalk. He was chasing a thief."

I know the catwalk. It bisects the dome and runs parallel to the promenade. It is suspended from the girders that support the dome like a bridge suspended in the air. I've always wished I could go up there. It is so high and practically invisible when the air is bad.

"That's where I touched the dome," Pace says. "One of my father's friends from the force took me up there when I was twelve."

"What was it like?"

"Like touching a very thick window or a mirror. It wasn't hot, and it wasn't cold. It just was."

"Did you see anything? Sometimes, when I'm up on the rooftops I see shadows."

"It was bright. The middle of the day. I thought it was because of the flames but now I know better."

There is nothing left of the food he put out. We've eaten it all. Pace sweeps up the crumbs from the quilt into his hands and lets Pip out of his cage. Pip jumps on his shoulder and nibbles the crumbs from Pace's open palm.

"So you decided to follow in your father's footsteps. What do you have to do to become an enforcer?"

"Well, there's school. And there's a physical test."

"Which you passed with no trouble at all," I tease.

He grins and shrugs sheepishly. "This morning was the first time I was ever in doubt about winning a fight."

"There *was* two of them."

"I was the fastest of the applicants also. That's why I was able to catch up to you so easily that first day."

"Your lungs are clearer than mine. That has a lot to do with it."

"So that's your excuse?"

"Okay, I admit it; you can beat me in a footrace."

"And?" he says mischievously.

"And at wrestling. But I win at swimming."

"I defer to your prowess in that area."

"You defer to my prowess?" I laugh and then wince at the movement. "Is that a fancy way of saying I win?"

"Yes, you win." He grins.

"What about your friend?"

"Tom?" He's suddenly serious again.

"Yes, Tom."

"We grew up together. We were the same age. His flat was below ours. His father worked for the administration. His older brother apprenticed with his father. Tom wanted to do something different so he decided to try for the enforcers with me." Pace runs his hand through his hair. "If not for me he'd still be alive." His voice breaks. He takes Pip down from his shoulder and into his hand and strokes his feathered head with a finger.

I touch his arm. "I know how you feel. I feel the same way about Alex. It is my fault he went out."

"How is it your fault?"

"Lucy said that it was because of me, and my independent streak, that she went above. If she hadn't gone above she wouldn't have met David. If Alex hadn't been worried over her he wouldn't have seen her with David."

Pace shakes his head. "That's a roundabout way of taking blame."

"No more than yours. At what age do we start taking responsibility for our own actions? Sure, Tom was inspired to be an enforcer because of you. But what if he never met you? What if someone else lived above him who wanted to be one? What if it was Tom that saw me with Alex and he was the one who chased me?"

"All right, I understand," Pace says. "You're making *my* head hurt now."

"We're responsible for our own decisions. It's that simple," I say. "We make our own choices and, win or lose, we suffer the results. Saying someone made me do it doesn't change the fact that we make a conscious decision to do it. That was the last lesson I learned from my grandfather."

Pace puts Pip back on his shoulder and picks up my hand. He cradles it in his just as carefully as he held Pip. "Did that blow to your head make you wiser?"

"No," I say. "But it might have shaken something loose."

Pace lifts my hand to his mouth and kisses the back of it, so lightly, so gently that I barely feel it. It's more of a sensation than a touch. Then he lowers my hand and looks at me with his extraordinary blue eyes. "I love you, Wren. I just wanted you to know that before all the madness starts."

All my questions, all my wondering, all my agonizing over love, and it is really all so simple when it comes down to it. "I love you too."

· 22 ·

Are you sure you want to do this?" I look at the faces gathered around me. Peggy, James, Adam, and Alcide. Even though I'd meant what I said to Pace the night before about being responsible for our own decisions, I still can't help but feel guilty about those standing here with me, ready to take on the bluecoats.

"For Alex," Alcide says.

"For Alex," James and Adam echo.

"Lucy said they'd be ready for us," Peggy reminds me. "That there are others who want to help."

"Meet us at tunnel three in two hours," I say. "It leads to Lucy's."

"We will be there," Adam assures me. I wasn't ready to give up my hiding place yet, so that is why I asked them to meet us. In case we didn't make it above, I wanted a secure place for us to come back to.

Adam, Peggy, and Alcide turn to go back to the village. James lingers for a moment. I wish he'd go on with the rest of them. I'm not ready to talk to him. I don't know if I'll ever be ready.

"Did I do that?" He points with some hesitancy at the bruise on my face.

"It was an accident," I say. "I fell when . . ."

"When I attacked your friend."

"He has a name, James," I say. "It's Pace."

"Yeah, Pace." James looks around the stables. I don't know what he's looking for. Maybe it's just that he doesn't want to look at me. "Wren, if all of this hadn't happened, would we have had a chance?" He looks at me, finally, and I see the guilt over my wound plainly written on his face, and the things he's said and done to me. I also see something else in his green eyes that I've never seen before, something that I can't identify. I shouldn't trust him and I'm not sure if I do. But I'm willing to listen to his apology if that's what he's offering.

"I don't know, James," I say after a moment. "Until you kissed me I would have said yes. But when you—"

"Tried to make you see things my way?" James the charmer is back.

I fold my arms defensively. "I wouldn't have put it that way."

He sighs. "I admit it, Wren. I was an ass. I probably still am. But I'm smart enough to know when I've been beaten. I saw how you looked at him . . . at Pace . . . last night. And how he looked at you. I know that look when I see it. I guess I just need to have that look directed at me."

"It will be someday," I say. "You've got a lot to offer a girl, James. Don't settle for anything less."

"I'm truly sorry, Wren. About everything."

Is he? I search his face and all I see is his charming smile. "Me too," I say finally. I have to agree with him. To not respond in kind would be an insult, so I offer my own apology. His smile widens.

"I want you to promise me something, James."

His look conveys the same hesitancy that I felt just a moment ago.

"When we get above, if things go bad, you've got to save Pace. He's the only one who knows how to get out. The rest of us don't matter. Only him. Without him we don't have a chance."

"Are you planning something, Wren?" James asks. "Something you should let us in on?"

"No," I answer truthfully. "Just examining our options. Losing Pace isn't one of them."

"I'm not so sure about that."

"You owe me, James." I am suddenly angry. I am definitely not in the mood for games with him. "The only thing that can save us is finding the way out." I step closer to him, until I am right in front of him. Close enough for him to see the bruise on the side of my face, close enough for him to see the brown behind the shine in my eyes. Close enough for him to feel my anger. "I need you to swear you'll do it. That you'll protect Pace no matter what happens."

He stares at me a moment, the shine in his green eyes dim in the light from the stables. I do not back down from his gaze. I keep my eyes on him, strong in my resolve. "All right," he says finally. "I swear I will protect Pace at all costs."

"Thank you." I turn to go. "I will see you in a few hours."

"Yeah," James says. "I'll be there." He takes off.

I go back into the stable. I'd already taken care of the ponies, arriving long before Peggy and the rest. I'd left Pace sleeping since our body clocks were still running opposite of each other's. I knew he'd want to come with me because of my injury but I wasn't ready for that yet. I wasn't ready to let everyone know he was down here. Especially since I didn't know what to expect out of James.

We are all going upside. Going to the dome to search for the way out. Lucy, as I expected, had come to the ceremony. Peggy took her aside and told her about discovering Pace below. Peggy told her the conclusion we'd all come to. Meanwhile, Lucy shared the news that David and his friends dug out and shored up the tunnel Pace and I escaped through. It was a secret way up and back that only a handful of people knew about. It was the way she'd come down and was going back.

Things were worse above. The coal was already nearly gone and over half the fans shut down. People were complaining. They didn't care about Pace or what the bluecoats accused him of. They just wanted the fans back on so the air would flow.

Would they feel the same if they knew there was all the air they could ever breathe right outside the dome? Would they feel the same if they knew there was a blue sky and an entire world out there? Would they feel the same if they had seen one of their friends needlessly and horribly murdered?

One last time I walk down the aisle of the stables and say good-bye to my charges. The orange cat twines around my ankles as I stop at each stall. I give him an ear rub and go on my way, after checking to make sure I am not being followed.

Pace is awake when I return and sorting through the remaining food. "Is there a plan?" he asks.

"We're going above." I have to sit down. Being gone drained me more than I thought possible. I gingerly touch the lump on my temple and wonder if my skull could be cracked. It sure feels that way.

"Won't they be watching for us?"

"We're using the same route we came down in." His eyes widen. I know why. Crawling through that tunnel had to be one of the worst experiences of his life. So far . . . "David and his friends dug it out and shored it up, according to Lucy. She used it to come and go last night. And this time we can take a lamp."

"What about your eyes? They'll be looking for shiners to be above."

"Only half the fans are running because the coal is so low. The air will be thick."

"So everyone will have goggles. They can't make everyone they see take them off."

"Exactly. What would work even better would be the filchers' masks."

Pace shivers. "Not for me . . . I've heard rumors of what they're made of, and none of it is anything I'd want on my face. Besides, filchers would raise as many questions as shiners where we're going."

"David's friends want to help us. They want to be a part."

He hands me a sandwich made of the remaining bread, cheese, and dried pork I'd brought from the larder. "You make it sound like we're starting a revolution." He sits down next to me.

Until he said the word I really hadn't put a name to what it was we were about to do. I look into his earnest blue eyes and the full implication of what we've planned seizes me in a cold, hard grip.

That's when I realize that everything that's happened has led to this moment. My trips to the rooftops, Alex's death and my grandfather's. It is as if the hand of fate has been pushing me along and just like the story of Camelot Pace told me, my life is a result of the circumstances. "We are starting a revolution."

"You sound so sure of yourself."

I shake my head. "I'm scared out of my mind. Scared that we're all going to die." I lean into him and he puts his arms around me. "But I think I'm scared worst of not doing anything. Of not trying. Of not knowing what's out there."

He kisses my hair as he smooths it with his hand. "How much time do we have before we have to go?"

"Not much. I want to beat them to the ladder. So there is no danger of them figuring out where we are hiding."

"What about the rest of the family?"

"What?"

Pace tilts his head at Cat and Pip. "Shhh. I don't want them to know they're not really ours."

I can't help it. I laugh, which makes my head hurt. "Ow. Ow. Ow." I put my hand up to the bruise, which brings another burst of pain.

Pace grins at me and shrugs sheepishly. "I'm just kind of concerned, if we don't make it back . . ."

"Cat will be fine. He can find his way back to the village or even the stables. But Pip . . ."

"Pip can come with me. I'll put him in my pocket. That way he can at least go free."

"Instead of being trapped in his cage in the dark." I could never let that happen. Not to Pip or to Pace. Never again for either of them.

"Can you think of any way we can get word to my mother?"

"I don't know enough about the way things work above. But maybe Lucy or David can think of something."

"Any one of us steps onto Park Front and we'll be caught for sure," Pace says. "They are probably still watching her."

"She'll be all right," I say. "Soon this will all be over and you can see her again."

"I can't wait until you two meet." He smiles tenderly and smooths back a lock of my hair. "She will adore you. As I do." He kisses my forehead. He is so affectionate. He touches me constantly, yet he's not oppressive. For someone like me, who wasn't shown much affection, it's strange, yet I can't get enough of it. I love it when he touches me. More than anything I want him to touch me without the fear gripping my heart that this will be the last time we are together.

I want time with Pace. Time to be with him. At the moment, time is something that's in very short supply.

· 23 ·

Our trip through the sewers is blessedly without incident. I almost expected to see the two bodies lying where we left them after out altercation with the bluecoats on our trip down. I was never really certain if they were alive or dead when we ran, and at the time I didn't care one way or another. Still, it is a good thing to pass through that area and see nothing there. I know Pace feels the same way because he gives me a slight smile and a nod when we go by the broken-down section of pipe.

There have been no repairs made either. Of course the government has had other things on their mind since our escape. Knowing that doesn't help the smell. We all cover our mouths and noses with our kerchiefs as we navigate the long tunnels. I'm not certain if I will recognize the place where we're supposed to turn to get to Lucy's until I see the fresh supports in place. I am relieved when I see that not only have David and his friends shored up the tunnel, but they've also built a ladder that leads up to the hatch we originally escaped through. Adam goes up first, then Peggy, James, me, Pace, and Alcide.

"Welcome to the seekers," David says as Alcide comes into the kitchen from the closet. The rest of us laugh as David closes the hatch and slides the trunk back into place.

"That's what we're called," James says. He holds out his hand to shake with David and his usual charm oozes from him.

"So Lucy told me," David says as he grasps James's hand. The kitchen is full with the six of us, me David, and Lucy and three others. "This is Jon," David begins.

Jon's clothing is a hodgepodge of rags stitched together. His hair is long and unruly with curls, and he has pale blue eyes. His hands are wrapped tightly with cloth and I can tell by the fading bruises on his face that he's a brawler, even though he's slight. "I'm from the scarabs," he says roughly. "Like your lot, I'd like to get out of here."

"It's much the same with me," Harry, who has long, light brown hair and brown eyes, says. "My father is a butcher and they expect me to be the same. I hate it. The blood, the guts, the smell . . ."

"Harry, don't be disgusting," a beautiful girl with red hair and the nicest clothes I've ever seen says. "It's rude, especially when you first meet." She holds out her hand to Adam and I'm actually surprised that he doesn't bend over and kiss it. She has an air about her, an air that bespeaks privilege. "I'm Jillian Pembrooke," she says.

We greet the three of them, cautiously and shyly, especially Jillian. All our lives we've been told we can't and shouldn't mix with those from above, especially the royals, and yet here we stand with the exact ones we are supposed to fear and worship. All three of them study us intently and I know they are staring at our eyes, which really do set us apart from the rest of the dome's inhabitants.

Pace doesn't stop to greet the strangers. Instead he takes Pip from his pocket. "Do you have someplace to keep this little guy safe?" he asks Lucy while we're being introduced.

"What the hell is this?" James asks.

"Couldn't abandon him," Pace says. "And it's my problem, not yours."

James rolls his eyes and Peggy elbows him hard in the stomach.

"I'm sure I can come up with something," Lucy says. She goes to the cupboard and comes back with a loosely woven basket. She pours some water onto a plate and sets it on the counter. Pace puts Pip on the plate and Lucy turns the basket upside down over him.

"Good idea," Pace says.

As David gives us the introductions, I can't help but notice Jillian's hands. They are soft, unblemished, and clean with nails that are perfectly formed. I feel filthy and lacking next to her, even though I just bathed.

"Do you remember me, Pace?" She goes to where Pace stands with Lucy by the counter. Her goggles are the best, shiny and new, along with her boots, which are made of the softest leather I've ever seen and practically scuff free. She wears a skirt of a fabric that seems to change colors in the light, going from a dark rusty color to a bright orange like a flame. The collar of her blouse shows around her neck and it's of a fine and delicate lace. She wears a short coat that's finely brushed dark brown suede.

I've never owned anything new in my life. Everything I have is secondhand and well used, even my boots have been resoled more times than I can count. The only thing I've ever had that is nice is the blue dress, given to me by Lucy, and even that belonged to someone else first.

Pace looks at her with some confusion showing in his blue eyes. "You seem familiar."

"Your mother was my governess once upon a time. We used to study together."

Recognition lights his face. "Jilly?" Pace shakes his head. "It *is* you. What are you doing here?"

I move closer to Pace, jealous and curious all at once. Who is this girl to Pace and why is she here? "You're a royal?" I can't help but ask. I hate myself for saying it. There are more important concerns right now than my relationship with Pace, but I can't get over the fact that they have *history*. As I do with James . . . I spare a look at him. Was his capitulation this morning too easy? His apology and regret were so sudden. Can I trust him? He watches the three of us with a curious look and I can't shake the feeling that he's planning something that I don't know about.

"I hear that is what you *shiners* call us," she replies with spirit, drawing my attention back. Her eyes are extraordinary, clear and green with gold tints. They are so different from what I am used to, just like Pace's. I can't stop looking at them. "Yet here we are in the same place with the same purpose," she continues.

"Jilly is like us," David explains. "She wants out."

"But why?" I can't help but ask.

"I think it a better alternative than marriage," she says. "Pace." She turns to him as if the matter is closed. "They took your mother in this morning."

His face turns a ghostly white and he slumps into a chair by the table. "Where is she? Where did they take her?"

"I don't know. It was enforcers, but not the type I've ever seen before. Their uniforms were different. And the carriage was nice, not the usual wagon they pile the criminals in. Her employer went round to the station to ask about her and they had no record of her being brought in.

"The maids talk to each other," Jilly says as an aside. "'Tis a great source of information, if one knows how to listen."

"I've got to find her," Pace says. "I've got to help her."

I kneel down next to his chair and take his hand in mine. His blue eyes are full of despair and frustration. It is as if his soul lives behind them and they are the windows to view it. Beautiful windows framing a beautiful soul. "We will help her," I assure him. "The best way we can help her is by finding the way out. Then we'll have some power over them. They won't need to keep her once we prove there is a way out and that we can survive outside."

"It all sounds so simple," Jon says. "Yet we're not the first ones to look for it. I've heard stories. Stories of it being found and those who found it being killed."

"Maybe for the same reason Alex was killed," Alcide says. Alcide is still devastated by his cousin's death. I know he feels as if he could have stopped it, if only he'd known. I notice that he gives Lucy a wide berth, as if she's also to blame. Maybe we all are, or maybe we should just accept the fact that Alex made a decision that led to his death.

"David told us about what happened. To you and your friends," Harry says. "Do you really think it's there? By the fans?"

Pace still looks ghastly and his mind is on his mother, not the questions at hand. "It's where he was when they carried Alex back in," I finally say as I stand. "There are tunnels that run beneath."

"Alex always thought that would be the logical place," Alcide adds. "The fans have to have some sort of exhaust system."

"We've got to figure out a way to get close to them," James says.

"We can't just walk up to them," Peggy adds. "Is there a way to get to them underground?"

"Isn't that where you come in?" David asks.

I listen to them talk, glad to see how quickly we've come together as one group with one purpose.

"We need maps," Adam says. "Maps of the dome and maps of the systems beneath. We could compare them to the tunnels in the mines and see if there's a way to come up from beneath."

"That's simple," Jilly says. "They have those in the library. 'Tis just a matter of going there to look."

"Except we're not permitted in the library," Lucy says.

"Really?" Jilly asks. "I never realized."

"You always thought we were just too busy with work?" David asks.

"Jilly is all right," Harry says. "There's no need for any of this."

I can't help but wonder what their connection is, how these three people found one another and how they in turn found David and Lucy.

"We have enough to fight out there with the filchers and the bluecoats," I add. "Whatever we're going to do, we need to get on with it."

"I could take two of you in with me," Jilly says. "Preferably someone who knows the tunnels."

"Adam and Peggy," I say. Adam works on the blasting crew so he knows our tunnels well and would know what was possible once he saw the maps. Plus, I think it would be easier for Peggy or Lucy to pass unnoticed in Jilly's company than two rough-looking young men.

"What about the rest of us?" Alcide asks.

"We go scout out the fans," James says. "Let Pace show us what he knows. That way if something happens to him, at least there's someone else who can carry on."

I knew there was a good reason not to trust him. James will

have his way, apology or not. Unfortunately for Pace, his plan makes sense. Still, I glare at him, letting him know I'm on to his plan. He has the audacity to smile back at me.

"Does anyone have a clue how to find out about my mother?" Pace asks.

"I'll see what I can come up with," Lucy volunteers. "I'll just ask if there's another place where the enforcers take special prisoners. Someone will know something, or know someone who knows something. It's the way things work up here."

"Now would be the time to go," David says. "The streets are busy and it will be easier to go unnoticed. We should all try to be back here by five o'clock. Agreed?"

"Agreed."

"One more thing," I say. I look directly at James as I speak. "If one of us gets caught, the others have to run, especially if it is before we figure out where Alex got through. As long as some of us are free, then we all have a chance. But if we're all caught . . ." There's no need to finish. We all know what the penalty will be. We also know it will be like Alex's death, a swift retribution with fire so that we too may be an example. The faces around me show their resolve, even Jilly's, which surprises me.

But that doesn't surprise me as much as I've surprised myself. When did I become the leader of this tiny revolution? Why do they listen to me when I speak? When did my opinion become so valuable, when it has never been considered as such before?

It is Lucy who gives me the answer. She steps up beside me and squeezes my hand. "I believe in you, Wren," she says, and just like that, I realize that it's because I now have something to believe in that I have changed.

I watch Jilly as everyone readies to leave. I can only hope that she doesn't consider this some sort of great adventure. Yet her reasons are so similar to my own. Risking her life to get out is a better alternative than marriage. I can only imagine what her designated mate must be like.

We disperse. Lucy on her own, Jilly, Peggy, and Adam to the library. Pace and I with David and Alcide. James, Harry, and Jon in another group and taking a different route to the exhaust fans as the seven of us traveling together would surely draw attention. James, Alcide, and I are unfamiliar with the streets so we divide accordingly so we won't get lost.

The streets are dark and gloomy and covered with a dense gray cloud that is hard to breathe. It's a situation that makes it easier for us because we're just among the several that wear goggles and have their lower faces covered with kerchiefs. Pace pulls the hood in place over his dark hair and I wrap a knitted scarf Lucy gave me around mine. In just a matter of seconds we are totally separated from James, Alcide, and the rest as we go our separate ways.

Pace is exceptionally quiet. It's his concern over his mother that makes him this way. Still, it worries me as even in the direst of circumstances he would usually say something in his dry way that showed me he saw the humor in the situation, if there was any to be found.

I'm used to taking the lead. I'm used to forging the path. Most of our time together has been underground, where I am comfortable and where everything is familiar. Today he takes the lead, pounding ahead with a purpose so I have to hurry to keep up with his long-legged stride.

"Slow down," David says. "We need to blend in, not shove everyone aside."

"Pace." I grab his arm. David is right. We're practically running. "Stop."

His head swings around to me. There's moisture on his face.

That's why he walked ahead. He didn't want us to know he was crying.

"It won't help her if we get caught," I say.

"I know." He stops, pushes up his goggles and wipes at his eyes. "I'm just scared of what they'll do to her. You know what they did to Alex. What might they do to her if they think she knows where I am?"

I squeeze his arm. "You can't dwell on it," I say. "You want to help her? Show them they can't control you anymore. That they can't control any of us. Show us the way out."

"She's right," David says.

Pace nods in agreement. A swarm of people move around us and a few give us curious looks. Pace's blue eyes will surely give us away. He slides the goggles back into place. The goggles that were my grandfather's.

"Let's move," David says, and we do, pacing ourselves to the others on the street and doing our best to blend in.

I've never been in this part of the dome. My innate sense of direction tells me we're going away from the coal lift to the opposite side of the dome. There is a noticeable lack of scarabs in this area, which makes sense if this is where the exit exists. The bluecoats would want to be able to control the area and having people living on the streets would make that close to impossible.

The buildings here are larger. There aren't any homes in this area, just places of work, large depressing buildings with narrow windows and cracking and peeling paint and large stains from soot-filled water that drips down from the dome. The roofs here don't hold gardens as there is too much smoke from the industry contained on this side of the dome. The buildings are close together with narrow alleys barely wide enough for two people to walk side by side.

The workers on the street all walk with their shoulders hunched and their heads down, as if they carry the weight of the dome on their shoulders. There is no joy here, no happiness, just the everyday drudgery of lives with no choice. Like those of Harry and Jon and even Jilly, who'd rather rebel and face the flames than face a future with a husband not of her choosing.

We're close to the public works now. The offices of air quality, water, disposal, and waste management—the latter needing to have a serious look at the pipes beneath the street, but only when we're not using them to travel back and forth. Pace walks with a purpose, he knows where he's going.

We see the rest of our group on an opposite corner. The roar from the fans is deafening now, as we are so close to the engines. Most of the people we see on the street are men, in old and stained work clothes. They are all headed in the same direction. A steam cart with a half load of coal nearly runs us down as we cut across a street; the blast of its whistle is followed by a long line of curses that can be heard in spite of the fans.

Pace holds up a hand as we come to the corner. The rest are opposite us on the street and they look over our way as we stop.

"Tom and I went into that building," he's practically shouting due to the huge fan that hangs behind the building he points out. There's no sign on it to identify it as anything in particular. "We went down a flight of stairs and that's where I saw the tunnels that go beneath the fans. We crossed over a catwalk and then went up. There's a huge space, like a warehouse beneath the ground. That's where they killed Alex."

"Did they bring Alex in the same way you came in?" David asks.

"No. They carried him in through a door on the other side."

"We should go around it," I say. "See what's behind it."

Pace points up. "We can't," he says.

I follow where he's pointing and see a guard stationed on top. He's carrying something I've never seen before. It's a weapon of some type, but I can't imagine what it would be.

"Let's swing out a few blocks and see if we can work our way around," David suggests. He gives some hand signals to the rest of our group and Harry nods in agreement. We disperse again, us going left and the rest right.

We round a large square building with black smoke pouring from the chimneys. It must house the furnaces that power the fans. The men we passed on the street pour into the door. They work the furnaces.

"Look at the smoke," I say. There are two huge fans behind it, one on top of the other. The smoke is moving directly to the lower fan and disappearing into it.

"It's shooting it outside," David says. "So?"

"Which means there has to be an opening for it to escape through."

"But is it big enough for a person to fit through? And how can you with the blades going?" Pace says.

"Look at the top fan."

David and Pace both shrug.

"If the one below is taking air out, then what's the top one doing?"

Pace and David both stand and look at the smoke drifting into the lower fan. It looks as if someone placed a board on top of it to flatten it.

"It's bringing air in," they both say at the same time.

"Fresh air," I add. "If it was flames wouldn't it be hot? Wouldn't the flame shoot right through it?"

"I wonder how long it's been like this," David says. "And nobody realized."

"Or maybe they did and they were killed. Just like Alex," I say.

"We need to move," Pace says. I look around and see that we've been noticed by a pair of bluecoats. It's not surprising as we're the only ones on the street. We've been so involved with watching the smoke that we lost track of our surroundings. We also did not notice another guard on the roof who waves at the two bluecoats following us.

"With the strike they will eventually run out of coal," David says as we move at a quick walk. "Then all the fans will shut down."

"They'll still have guards," Pace says.

"And we might not have enough food to outlast them," I add. "It's amazing how your resolve weakens when you see your children going hungry."

"Could be a moot point," Pace says. "We better run for it."

I glance over my shoulder and see that the bluecoats are getting closer. Pace grabs my hand and the three of us take off, running for our lives.

· 24 ·

The sound of the steam whistle fills the air. At first I think it's the alarm, but when men pour into the streets I realize it's the shift change and the whistle stops as suddenly as it started. The men who fill the street are sweaty and covered in coal dust. If not for their eyes you would not be able to tell the difference between them and a group of shiners. I even hear the familiar cough that is a sure sign of black lung. The three of us head straight for them in hopes we can blend into the crowd and make our escape.

To my horror I see a pair of filchers coming toward us from the other side. David sees them and we turn in the direction the workers are going. We weave our way through, passing men, crashing into them, and moving on as they grunt and curse us. There is no time to apologize. There is no time to explain. We must keep moving. Pace keeps a tight hold on my hand, only this time he leads me as he and David are much faster than I and their lungs are cleaner.

At a distance in front of us I see three men dash across the street. James and Alcide I easily recognize. They moved so fast I didn't have time to identify the other. It is either Jon or Harry. Since there are only three it means someone got caught or else they split up. I hope and pray it's the latter.

We finally break free of the group of workers, which puts us out in the open and makes us easy to spot. Something whistles by my ear and David, who was ahead of us, tumbles onto the pavement. Pace and I both stop and pull him up.

"Something hit me," he gasps as we stumble forward with him between us. "Go on."

I know what I said and made everyone promise. But I can't go off and leave him. I barely know him, but I know Lucy and I couldn't do that to her again. Blood pours from a wound in his stomach and back.

"What happened to him?" Pace asks.

"It looks like something went through him." I look over my shoulder. The bluecoats are gaining on us, racing the filchers to see who will get to us first. The filchers are driven by the reward and will use any means possible to get it. I know we will never make it. Not as we are now. We dash for the cross street where James and Alcide ran.

"James!" I scream. I see him ahead of me. Alcide turns and sees us. He comes back to us with the third person, who I recognize as Harry. I see James's mouth move as he shouts at Alcide, then he shakes his head and comes back toward us.

"David," I say in a low voice. "Pace has got to survive. Do you hear me? Once he's gone it's all over for the rest of us."

"What are you talking about?" he gasps.

"Keep him safe."

Alcide reaches us. "Get Pace to safety," I say to him and I slip out from under David's arm and Alcide slips in. "As long as he's alive we've all got a chance." I turn to James. "Remember your promise," I say before I turn and run as hard as I can back out to the street.

The bluecoats are the closest to the intersection. I put my shoulder down and I plow right through them. I yank off my scarf and pull my goggles down around my neck. I run down the middle of the street and I scream at the top of my lungs.

"The sky is blue! There's a world outside and they don't want us to know! The sky is blue!" I scream it over and over again as I run right for the main body of workers.

I hear yelling behind me. I know it's Pace because I hear my name. I can only pray that James has him. That he'll get him back to safety. If he doesn't then my sacrifice is meaningless, as was Alex's and Tom's and my grandfather's.

"It's the girl!" someone says. I know it is the bluecoat behind me. I can feel them on my heels as I run. I'll never outrun them but I can make sure they get me, instead of the filchers who are coming straight at me from the other side. Hopefully I can buy Pace and the others some time to get David safely away. I can make enough of a commotion that they'll put all their attention on me. They won't kill me. Not as long as Pace is free, because they want him the most. They'll keep me alive until they find him.

I turn away from the filchers, knowing it will put me closer to the bluecoats. Suddenly I pitch forward, flying headfirst toward the cobblestones beneath my feet. I put my hands out to catch myself as I fall. I hit hard, my hands skid and my head crashes forward and blessed darkness fills my vision.

I am caught.

◆

The throbbing in my head wakes me. I'm lying facedown on a wooden floor that is rough, splintered, and covered with dirt. My face is sticky with blood. Someone is beside me. As I open my eyes I see a bent leg. My hands are tied behind my back.

"Pace?" I say, hoping and praying that he doesn't answer.

"It's Jon."

I manage to turn myself around and prop myself up. My head swims and I swallow back what little I've had to eat today. Jon is sitting with his back against the wall, facing me. The room is empty except for us and a pile of rags kicked into a corner. "What happened?"

"We turned a corner and walked into a group of filchers. There were about ten of them. They grabbed me and said that we were trespassing and they were hired to make sure no one did. Everyone else got away."

"The filchers have us?" A sense of dread fills me. At least with the bluecoats I had a chance of staying alive for a while. The filchers are ruthless. There is the reward, but it was offered for Pace, not me.

"What do they want with us?" I convince myself not to panic. I know it won't help.

"Nothing good, I'm sure," Jon says. I don't know him at all but I admire him for staying calm, even though I can tell he's as frightened as I am. "Are you all right? Your head looks bad."

I roll my eyes up as if I can see my forehead. "I guess now I have a matching set," I say. "Does it really look bad?" Not that I'm concerned about my appearance at the moment. Two hard blows to the head in less than a day can't be good.

"It's hard to say with all the blood. But it looks like it's stopped bleeding, so that's a good sign."

"If you say so." I groan in pain as I try to move. "Are we the only ones?"

"As far as I know."

"Where are we?" I look around and can tell that we are in a small room. There's a high narrow window that lets in a minimum of light. I can see the shadow of another building close by.

"I don't know. They put a bag over my head and marched me here. I didn't even know they had you until they dropped you down beside me. It wasn't far from where they caught me. And we haven't been here that long." He looks at the thick door. "It's locked," he says. "With a chain."

"I would be surprised if it wasn't. I guess the fact that not much time has passed is a good thing."

"We're still alive," Jon says matter-of-factly. "What happened to you?"

"Bluecoats," I say. "They did something to David. One minute we were running, in the next he was on the ground. We got him up and he was bleeding from his stomach and back. We caught up with Harry, James, and Alcide. They took him and I provided a distraction."

"So you think they got away?"

"If they didn't, then I'm certain we will all be dead soon." I know it is not what he wanted to hear, but I will not lie to Jon or myself. Being caught by the filchers is almost as bad as Pace being captured. Almost. As long as I know Pace is safe I can handle anything.

Maybe if I say it enough times I will actually believe it.

We hear a door slam. Voices. Footsteps that grow closer. The heavy thump of a chain moving. The creak of the door opening. Four men walk into the room, all of them wearing the masks of the filchers. Hands grab me and jerk me to my feet and my head reels with dizziness. Jon is treated to the same and we're marched down a hallway and up a flight of steps into a room with dingy windows that let in streaks of light.

Five men stand in the room. They all wear masks except for one, who is short and stout as a keg with arms that look as thick as support beams. His face has a scar that goes from his temple to his neck and one of his ears looks as if it was mangled years ago. His hair is shaved close and he's missing two bottom teeth in the front.

Jon and I are jerked before him and hands push on the back of our necks until we are both kneeling before the man without the mask. For some reason this angers me more than anything else that has happened so far, and I fight against the hands and the pressure until I have the choice of kneeling or having my neck broken.

A sound of rage slips through my lips. Rage and frustration at the injustice. I am determined to fight them until my last breath. Jon narrows his eyes at me, asking for something that I cannot give. I fear we will both soon be dead. I am certain we will be begging for it to happen.

The stout man grabs my hair and wrenches my head back. "A shiner," he says. "Are you Wren MacAvoy?"

"I am," I spit out. There is no need to deny it. If I'm going to die I don't want to die nameless. There is also the chance that it will give me . . . us . . . more time.

He smiles a humorless smile and moves to Jon. He does the same with him, grabbing his hair and pulling his head back so he can look at him. "This ain't Bratton," he says.

"Brown hair and blue eyes," one of the masked filchers replies. It is hard to tell who because their mouths are covered and the words are muffled.

"Bratton is taller and his hair is straight." He jerks Jon's head back and forth. "Are you worth anything, boy?"

"More than you'll ever know," I say.

"Really?"

I stare him down, daring him to strike me. If I had a weapon I know without a doubt that I would attempt to kill him. I'm not foolish enough to think I'd succeed, but the rage and anger are so great within me that I can taste them. I'd rather have the anger than the cold, dark fear.

He stares at me for a moment. Laughs. And then he swings his leg back and kicks Jon in the side of the face. Jon falls over onto his side with a grunt. Blood pours from his nose and mouth.

"Bastard!" I yell.

Man grabs the front of my jacket and pulls me to my feet. He's not much taller than me; still, my toes barely touch the ground as he holds me up with his fist. "There's a bounty on your head." His face is inches from mine. His breath is disgusting and I fight the urge to retch. "It didn't say what condition you needed to be in, so I'll leave your tongue. They want you to be able to talk, is all."

"Get your hands off of me," I grind out between my teeth.

"Oh, there will be more than my hands on you. That you can count on." He drops me and I fall to the floor. Since my hands are tied behind my back I have no way of catching myself or supporting myself. I try to roll and protect my head, which feels like it is about to split in half. He sticks his hand in my hair and half carries, half drags me from the room.

Jon still lies where he dropped. He's as still as death and I'm afraid he's gone from the kick to his face.

"What do we do with him?" one of the masked filchers asks.

"See if they'll trade for him too. If not, kill him and drop him in the fires."

"Go tell Randall we've got the girl," he says to another one. "And no rush. The reward ain't going nowhere." He continues to drag me across the hall. He kicks open the door and pitches me forward onto a pile of blankets. I land face-first on them. The stench is horrible and I gag as I try to flip myself over. I hear the door slam shut behind me and the turn of a key.

I flip over on my back. Stout walks toward me, unbuttoning his pants as he comes. "Oh yeah, we're going to have a good time before I collect that reward. And maybe, if you're nice, I'll let you come stay with me in my new house on Park Front."

"I'd rather die." As soon as he gets to the end of the blankets I kick up with all my might. My feet land squarely in his crotch and he flies backward and crashes against the door.

I can see that he's dazed. His hands go to his crotch and he rolls onto his side. I scramble up and kick him in the face. He swings an arm out toward me but I sidestep it. I feel the squish of his jaw through the soles of my boots as I kick him again. And again. I feel his bones crunch as I keep on kicking. Each time I kick I scream as if I can't believe what I'm doing.

Finally, I cannot lift my leg to do it again. I look down at what I've done. His face is no longer recognizable. I stumble into the corner and throw up.

When I am done I wipe my mouth on my shoulder. My hair is stuck to my face and I am covered with sweat. My hands are numb from the ropes. I lean against the wall and slump to the floor.

I can't believe the other filchers didn't hear what I did. Or maybe they thought what they heard was their leader having his way with me. Whatever they think, it won't be long before I am discovered. I've got to get out of here. And I can't leave Jon behind.

· 25 ·

Before I can do anything I've got to have the use of my hands. I try to pull them apart. The ropes cut into my wrists and my palms are raw from when I tried to catch myself when I fell on the street. I squirm around until I'm able to loosen the ropes enough to slide my arms under my bottom. From there it is just a matter of bending and stretching enough to get my legs through. Every time I move I feel as if the filchers are listening right outside the door. I wonder how long I have before someone comes to investigate. I pick at the ropes with my teeth until they come loose enough for me to wiggle my hands out.

The door is blocked by the filcher I killed. I stare down at him with the knowledge that I killed a man. I stomped the life from him because I was angry and frustrated and scared. I stand there, looking down at him, and try to justify what I did in my mind. I tell myself he deserved it. I tell myself he was a horrible man and deserved to die.

I know what he wanted to do to me. I am not sorry he is dead. I refuse to be. Yet tears course down my cheeks. I mourn for the innocence I've lost. For what he changed me into.

I hear shouts coming from outside. Then strange noises that are sharp and stinging to my ears. I've got to get out of here. I've got to help Jon, if he can still be helped.

I wipe my eyes and pull the dead man away from the door by his ankles. Before I can open it, it crashes against me and I fly forward. Someone grabs my arm and pulls me around. It's another filcher and he has a knife at my throat.

He drags me into the hall with one arm around my neck and the other holding the knife against it. "Stop or I'll kill her!" he yells. Has it come to this? Did I kill a man just so I will be killed myself, nothing more than a pawn in a game of who is mightier, who is more desperate, who wants to win, and who will most definitely lose?

Two bodies lie on the floor, both bleeding from wounds I cannot see. Another lies in the room with Jon, who has crawled into a corner. He holds his hands against his head. I don't know if he can see me. I take some small comfort in knowing that he is alive for now. Through the open door that leads to the street I see bluecoats, six or more, it's hard to tell. They hold strange weapons, long and black and made of iron.

"Give her to us," a bluecoat says.

"I want the reward." I feel the knife press against my throat and a sting that tells me the skin is broken. Yet more blood trickles from my body. "You promised a reward."

The bluecoat raises his weapon and a projectile comes out of it, so fast that all I see is a blur. I jerk away and feel the blood splatter my cheek and hair as the filcher falls to the ground. "As if we'd let the likes of you live on Park Front," I hear the bluecoat say.

As soon as the filcher falls away I run to Jon. "You're alive."

"If you say so." The side of his face is swollen and covered with blood, but his grip is strong as I pull him to his feet. Before we can move, bluecoats surround us. They herd us outside, throw us into a wagon, and slam the door shut.

I untie Jon's hands and help him to the low bench that runs along the walls of the wagon. "You've got to pretend like you don't know me," I say. "You don't know anything about me. It's all just a coincidence, nothing more."

"Why?" Jon pulls up his shirt and wipes the blood from his face. He puts his fingers to his jaw and pushes against it. "I think he knocked some of my teeth loose."

"I'm pretty sure I stomped his down his throat."

"You killed him?"

It is something I will never escape and can't deny. It is something that will haunt me for as long as I live. "I didn't like what he had planned for me." I can't understand why tears gather in my eyes and I quickly wipe them away. I cannot be weak. If whoever they are taking me to senses a weakness they will use it against me. I will be strong. I have to be.

"I never really thought they would go this far . . ." he begins. "I guess I should have known after what they did to your friend."

"Which is why you've got to stay out of it. We don't want them to know what we're doing. Pace and I are the only ones they care about right now. I'd like to keep it that way."

Jon nods. I know he's frightened. He has to be because I'm scared out of my wits. I can only keep reassuring myself that as long as Pace is out there they'll keep me alive. Jon moves down the bench and looks out the tiny barred window in the door.

"Can you tell where we are?" I ask. Like Jon, I pull out the tail of my shirt and wipe at the blood on my face, in my hair, on my neck. I look at my shirt when I'm done and wonder how much of it is mine and how much belonged to the filcher they killed. What was that weapon they used? What does it do to kill people instantly? Is that what happened to David? Is he still alive?

"We just turned onto the promenade," he says. "They must be taking us to the enforcer headquarters. Wait . . . I think I see Harry," he whispers. "And Jilly. And your friends."

I join him at the window. It is hard to stay upright in the jolting carriage. I'm incredibly dizzy and my head throbs with waves of pain. I finally focus and manage to look out. I quickly recognize Adam and Peggy worming their way through the crowds on the streets as they try to keep up with us.

Try as I might, I don't see any sign of Pace, James, Alcide, or David. I'd like to think they're safe, but they could very well be in another wagon.

Or dead.

If only there was some way to signal them. I'm afraid if I do, that it will put them in danger. The wagon turns a corner. I'm thrown back on the bench and I stay there, but I still keep watch out the window. Buildings loom up on either side and I realize we are in an alley. I see Adam and Peggy, and then Harry and Jilly pass my line of sight as they stay on the promenade. I see bluecoats following the wagon and then the light gets dim and a door closes behind us. We're inside. There is no way for our friends to help us.

I hear the clatter of chains and the door opens behind us. Six bluecoats stand before us in the dark. Do they realize I can see them clearly or do they think the darkness will intimidate me?

"Get out," one says. Jon gets up. It's impossible to stand straight so he bends over awkwardly. Two bluecoats grab his arms and pull him out. They do the same with me.

We are marched through a door that leads into a long hallway lined with more doors, all of them closed. The two bluecoats with Jon shove him forward and to a flight of stairs. They go down.

I stand with four bluecoats by the lift in wait for it to appear before us.

"Where are they taking him?" I ask.

"None of your concern," one answers.

I don't say anything more. The only way I can protect Jon is to pretend like I don't know him. The lift arrives before us with a hiss of steam. One bluecoat opens the door and another pushes me inside. I stumble forward and luckily stop myself before I crash against the back wall. I'm not certain how many more blows to the head I can stand before my skull fractures into a million pieces.

Only two ride up with me. I suppose my risk of flight is reduced now that I'm confined. I know I don't have a chance of escaping as long as I'm inside. I can only take comfort that my friends know where I am. It might be the last time I see them.

I spread my legs to keep my balance. The two bluecoats face forward, neither one looking at me, and neither one speaking. The lift keeps going up and up until we finally lurch to a stop on the top floor.

One throws back the metal cage door and the other puts his hand in the small of my back to propel me forward. I stand in a long hall. Elegant lamps alternate between beautiful paintings that lead all the way down to a set of double doors. I can't help but stare at the paintings as I walk down the hall with one bluecoat in front of me and the other behind. The colors are extraordinary, like nothing I've ever seen before, not even in the books in the library. I never realized such riches existed, not even in my wildest dreams could I have conceived of such things. I wonder if Pace has seen paintings such as these. The artist that I know exists in him would thrill at their existence.

I don't even realize the bluecoat in front of me has stopped until I bump into his back. The one behind me puts his hand on my shoulder and jerks me back and I stumble. I am weak and dizzy and I don't know how much longer I can go on. I desperately need to rest. I need water. I want to wash away the blood and the grime that covers me. But most of all I need to know that Pace is safe.

The bluecoat before me raps on the door.

"Come in," a voice says. The bluecoat opens both doors and I'm shoved forward into a large room.

The ceiling is twenty feet above me and covered in dark wood paneling with detailed molding. High arched windows line the walls on the three sides with lamps in between each one, and live trees sit in pots in the light. They are unlike any tree I've ever seen, with thick wedges of bark on the trunks and long spiky leaves around the top like an umbrella.

I quickly realize that the room covers the end of the building. The wall behind me is windowless; however, there are doors on either side of the one I came through and books fill the shelves that go from the floor to the ceiling.

The carpet beneath my feet is as plush and as soft as my mattress. In the middle of the room is a huge, ornately carved desk. A leather chair with a high back sits behind it and two deep-red wing-backed chairs are set before it. I'm guided to one of these chairs and forced into it.

I hear a tinkling sound but I can't see anything as the bluecoat keeps his hand on my shoulder as if he wants to smash me into the chair. "You may go," a voice says. "But wait outside the door."

A tall man wearing the dark blue uniform of the enforcers comes around the desk. He sets down a clear vessel that holds liquid. It must be a glass, made from the same substance as the windows. Yet it is so much thinner and lighter than the dome. I've heard of them but never seen one. We drink from crocks and tin cups in my world.

His uniform is embellished with the double row of gold buttons and has gold epaulets on the shoulders and a series of gold bands on his right sleeve. He is tall and solid with broad shoulders and thick, lustrous hair that is as black as coal. He sits down in the chair and folds his hands before him as he leans back and stares at me. I see that his eyes are as dark as his hair. They are deep and mysterious, but suddenly they widen and he drops his hands onto the desk as he leans forward.

"Maggie?" he says questioningly.

And that's when I know I am looking at my father.

· 26 ·

I find it hard to believe that he recognizes me with my bumps and bruises and my face covered with blood. But the fact that he knows my mother's name is all the proof that I need. "My name is Wren," I say. "Maggie was my mother, as you well know." At last I have the proof that I do look like my mother as I was always told.

His face changes completely as he laughs. He looks boyish . . . almost. His eyes crinkle and dance with some sort of secret joy. Is this what attracted my mother? I can see how it would. He has the same charisma as James. I can feel it already, drawing me in. "Spirited like me," he says. "I'm glad to see it."

I won't be drawn in. Just because he sired me doesn't mean he has any authority over me. "I'm not."

He sits back in his chair. "I always wondered if it was a boy or a girl."

"It?" My anger rises. "*It* is *me* and as I said, I have a name. Given to me by my grandfather who raised me. Wren MacAvoy."

"Your mother didn't name you?"

"My mother died giving birth to me." I watch his face carefully, hoping for something that will make me believe . . . I don't know what. An explanation? Something more than acknowledgment that he knew my mother and sired me? More emotions than I can count rush through me and all are compounded by the constant throbbing in my head.

"Perhaps if she had stayed above, something could have been done . . ." He shrugs his shoulders. "But you—"

"Are not what you expected?" I finish for him. It dawns on me that I am having a conversation with my father and I don't even know his name.

He places his fingertips together and looks over them at me. "Let's just say that I did not expect the source of all this trouble to be my daughter."

"Will it make a difference?"

"That depends. Where is the boy?"

"What boy?"

He picks up a piece of paper that lays facedown upon the desk. "This boy. Pace Bratton. The one you were seen with."

Did it occur to him when my name was put on the paper that I could be Maggie MacAvoy's daughter? Did the connection ever cross his mind, or maybe he just assumed that we all shared the same names. All the dirty, filthy shiners that lived beneath the dome were the same.

"I have no idea," I say in answer to his question. "What makes you think I would know?"

He laughs. "As I said. Spirited." He leans back in his chair and studies me for a bit. "Did my men do that?" He raises a finger and points it at my forehead. I touch it and it comes away sticky with blood.

"It was the filchers," I say. "And I'm lucky to escape with only this. They promised they'd save me the use of my tongue since you wanted me to be able to talk."

"Filthy lot," he agrees. "But they serve their purpose."

"And were stupid enough to believe you would actually reward them with privileges and a house on Park Front."

"You would be surprised at the lengths some people will go to when they believe what they want to believe."

"More so when what they believe is the truth."

His eyes widen slightly. I've surprised him again. "How about the cut on the side?"

"No, that was me. I tripped."

He laughs again. "I have to admit, my dear daughter, this is the most interesting conversation I've had in ages."

"Just look at all you missed," I say.

He gets up, still laughing, and goes to a table behind me. He returns with a glass of something amber in color and a wet cloth. "Here." He hands me the cloth. "Clean yourself up." He places the glass down in front of me and returns to his chair. He watches me as I wipe my face with the cloth. It feels so good against my skin. Cool and clean. I dab at the place on my forehead until no more blood shows on the cloth. I'd like to look in a mirror and see how bad I look, but I don't want to show any weakness in front of him. My hands are raw from where I fell forward, and one of my knees feels like the skin has been torn off. The first time I meet my father and I look like a wreck.

"Drink that," he says.

I pick up the glass and sniff the amber liquid. It burns my nose.

"All at once," he says.

I have no reason to believe he'd poison me and I'm desperate for some relief from the thirst, although I'm not so certain this will do it. I tilt back the glass and drain it. I choke and sputter but manage to swallow it down. It burns all the way down my throat and lands in my stomach like a charge that's been lit in the mines.

"What is this?" I finally gasp.

"Whiskey. I know it burns, but it will help you get through what's ahead."

That does not sound reassuring. Should I be grateful that he is considerate of me? That in some strange and bizarre way he actually cares? "What is your name?" I ask. "Or is that privileged information?"

"Your mother never told anyone?"

"As far as I know, she didn't."

"My name is Sir William Meredith. And as you can see, I am the master general enforcer."

"Does this mean I have royal blood?"

"It does."

"Why?"

He knew what I was asking. Even though we did not know each other, we had an instant understanding. I found it annoying but also fascinating. Was it because we share the same blood?

"Your mother was a beautiful young woman. As are you. I found that I could not resist."

"So you took what you wanted."

"I always get what I want, Wren. As you will soon find out." He shakes his head. "Wren. What a strange name. Like the bird?"

"Yes. We have several of them down below."

"Really?" He looks at me curiously. "Birds down below? I never would have thought it."

"Oh, my world is quite extraordinary," I say.

"So why are you so anxious to leave it?"

"Why are you so determined to make sure I don't?"

He laughs again. "Concise and to the point. It is too bad your mother took you down below. You would have been quite the success on Park Front."

"As your bastard daughter?" I sneer. "I think not."

"You're not really surprised that I didn't marry your mother, are you? She really expected me to, for some strange reason. It wasn't until she finally realized that I wouldn't that she left."

"Because having a shiner for a wife would have held you back? Because you could either have us or this?"

"I see you have it all figured out."

"Except for why we can't leave the dome."

"Why would you want to leave? Don't you know that there's nothing but flames out there? Nothing but fire and destruction."

"I know that what you say is a lie to keep everyone inside." I look into his eyes. "I know that you murdered my friend, Alex, because he made it outside and you didn't want anyone to know." As soon as the words leave my mouth I realize my mistake. I've given away what I know and therefore, given up the fact that I've talked to Pace. The smile that graces my father's lips lets me know that he's caught onto my mistake also.

"Where is the boy?" he asks.

"I don't know." It's not a lie. I know where I hope he is, but at the moment I honestly can't say.

"I don't need you to find him, you know," he says. "I have his mother and I hear they are very close. I am certain he will trade himself for her if he knows it will save her life."

"The opposition has principles," I say. "How convenient for you."

"How many other people know?"

"Everyone. Didn't your friends tell you what I was doing when they caught me?"

"They did." He shakes his head in agreement. "It might have worked had your audience been larger."

"Word has a way of getting around," I say. "Soon enough everyone will know."

"Why is it so important to you that everyone knows?"

"Because I want out."

"But you are safe here. We all are." He says it as if he's talking to a child.

"No, we are all slaves here," I say so there is no mistaking my intent. "Slaves to the royals and their way of life."

"Ahhh. So now we get to the heart of the matter. You don't want to be a coal miner."

"Why is that a surprise? Why shouldn't I want more for my life than what was dictated two hundred years ago?"

"Because you were born to a purpose, just as the rest of us were."

"What if my purpose is to do something more? What if my purpose is to free everyone from the dome?"

He laughs. He laughs long and he laughs hard. I know he's mocking me, but I also think that perhaps I might have scared him a little. Not enough to let me go, but enough to make him think. To make him doubt his purpose. I know I succeeded in that when he rises and walks to the windows. He folds his hands behind his back and looks out at the view.

"Will you join me?" he says after a moment.

I do. By now I know I have nothing to lose and everything to gain. And my curiosity about him is boundless. As I come to the window I realize that we are in the tallest building in the dome. From here I can see all the way to Park Front even though there is a slight haze. Of course the fans on the royal side of the dome are still running. The royals will have the best until the very last. Light is fading with the day. I am closer to the top of the dome than I've ever been, even when I was on my rooftop. Lights blink along Park Front and the elaborate homes of the royals.

The office he occupies is arranged to have the best view. The wall behind us hides the industrial side. The ugly side. From these three sides everything is beautiful. Everything is perfect. We stand there, side by side, and gaze at the world within the dome. At the efficiency of it. A well-oiled machine still running after two hundred years. But the parts are wearing thin and some will soon be broken beyond repair. It's only a matter of time. It is something that I have to make him realize.

"Beyond those walls is a horrible place." He says it quietly, as if he's talking to himself. Or maybe he's just sharing a secret with his daughter.

"Have you been there?" I don't have to look at him. We can see each other's reflection in the glass. He, tall, straight, and clean; me, looking as if I've rolled in dirt and blood after being severely beaten. It is very seldom that I've worried over my looks, but this is one time I do. I wish I was clean and my hair neatly brushed and I had on the blue dress. I wish my hands weren't dotted with scars and my nails rimmed with coal. I wish I looked my best so he would look at me with pride. Or love. Or regret.

"Yes, I have been outside many times."

"What is it like?" I can't help but ask. I want to know. I want to know everything about it.

"It's very beautiful. As if the fire purged the earth of all the ugly things and it began anew. But if you look closely, you can still see the remnants of what was."

"And?" I look up at him. He's taller than I imagined, although

I can't really describe what it was I expected. As tall as, if not taller than, Pace.

"We are not the only ones who survived. The ones who did, who live out there, are ruthless. They want what we have. They want in. And we have no way of fighting them. The weapons they have can kill a man at one hundred yards or more. We have nothing to compare with it. When this place was built, all the weapons were left outside. Our makers thought we would have no need of them."

"You have weapons. I saw them."

"Yes. We used it on one of your friends. The one who wasn't Pace Bratton. Did he survive?"

"I don't know. He was alive the last time I saw him."

"It was a brave thing you did. Sacrificing yourself so the others would get away."

"Are you saying you're proud of me?"

"I suppose I am." He turns from the window and walks back to the desk. I follow as I have no place else to go. The height has made me dizzy and my head still pounds.

"May I have some water?" I ask.

He retrieves my glass from the desk and fills it from a pitcher on the table with the other liquids. He hands me the glass. This time I examine it. I am amazed at how light and delicate it feels in my hand. Almost like holding Pip in my palm. Almost the way I feel when Pace holds me. I raise the glass to my lips and drain it. He pours me another and I take my time now. Sipping it. Enjoying the feel of the cool liquid on my parched throat.

"How did you get the weapons?" I ask.

"We traded for it."

"What did you trade?"

He smooths my hair back from my face in a motion so much like Pace that it makes my heart hurt. "We traded girls like you," he says. "And a few boys," he adds so easily that I want to hit him.

He returns to his desk and moves a few papers around. Straightens a pen and a letter opener. Sits down and adjusts the sleeves of his jacket.

"I have been charged with a duty. A duty I take very seriously. As seriously as you take your tiny little rebellion."

I want to speak, to tell him that my rebellion is not tiny, that it is important to me, and not only to me but to several others like me. That people have died because of it. That I'm willing to die for it as well. That I've already consciously made that decision and proved it by sacrificing myself to save Pace. But I don't because I know that he won't really listen. In his mind, his agenda is much more precious than mine.

"The bloodline must be preserved at all costs. It's a line that goes back thousands of years. They are the nature of our race, the very foundation. And until we can protect them from what is outside, no one is going out."

"You've made this decision for everyone? Including the royals?"

"I have."

I think of Jilly. "Have you ever thought to ask them what they want? What any of us want?"

"That isn't up to them. It's up to me."

"You're wrong," I say. "It is up to all of us. The people you are protecting, that you are sacrificing the rest of us for, aren't the foundation. We are. The shiners and the rest of the workers that keep your royals' perfect little world running. And I've got more news for you. The coal is running out. It has been over a year since we've found a new deposit. So what are you going to do when it is all gone? Let everyone boil beneath the dome?"

"By then we'll have enough weapons that we can fight them. By then we will have an army that will know how to use them. How to beat them."

"And until then the rest of us are sacrificed to the royal gods."

"I see you understand."

"I understand this is what you believe. I don't. I believe in a higher power. And I believe that he has a different purpose for us. That he gave us this life to thrive and to strive for better things. That he gave us this world to live in. That if life has returned out there then he wants us to live it. That he gave us this place so that we may survive and return to the earth and grow once more. Not lie stagnant beneath the glass."

"Those are powerful words, Wren. Words that I cannot allow to be spoken outside this room."

"You can't change what I believe. And I'm not the only one who believes it."

"No, but I can change what people perceive. Just as I did with your friend. What was his name . . . Allan?"

"Alex," I correct him. "How did he get out?"

"Through the tunnels. Beneath the fans. It's amazing how quickly he slipped through. He was outside before my men even realized it. If he'd kept on running he'd be free now, possibly dead at the hands of those outside, but most definitely free of this place. But he didn't. He wanted to come back. He wanted to show some girl . . ."

"Lucy."

"Yes, Lucy, that there was a world out there. He couldn't understand why my men didn't agree with him. He kept screaming something about the sky."

" 'The sky is blue.' "

"Yes. It is. A most extraordinary shade of blue."

"Why are you telling me all this?"

"Because I'm going to give you exactly what you want. I'm going to show you the world outside the dome."

· 27 ·

My father. It is a hard word for me to comprehend. My life in the past few hours feels as if it is happening to someone else. As if I'm not living it, but just watching it unfold. The pounding in my head and the ache in my heart assure me that everything has actually happened. The fact that I have finally met my father is not any stranger than anything else that has happened to me in the past week. Has it only been a week? Has it been longer? I find that I can't even identify the day, much less how many have passed since it all began.

My father summons the guards from the hall. "Take her and the other one to trade. Get as much as you can for them."

Just like that I'm gone from his presence. No one but the two of us knows that he is my father. As far as he is concerned, no one will know. To him I am nothing more than a means to an end. Something to be traded for weapons.

My trip from my father's office is much like my trip to it. Except this time the lift goes down a level. I am relieved to see Jon sitting in a cell. He looks much the same as he did when I last saw him. Jon is taken from his cell by another pair of bluecoats and we are marched down a hall to a door, then up a flight of stairs and to a wagon. I cannot tell if it's the same one we arrived in or not.

"What did they do to you?" Jon asks.

"Asked me questions." There is no need to tell Jon who I talked to or about what. The result is still the same. "You?"

"Nothing. They just put me in that cell. Do you know what they plan for us?"

"We're to be traded. For weapons."

"Traded to whom?"

"Whoever they are afraid of that lives outside the dome."

Jon looks at me incredulously. "What?"

The engine starts and the wagon vibrates and jerks as the doors swing open and we pull out. The dome is dark except for the streetlamps that light the promenade. I look out the small barred window, hoping to see a sign of someone we know, but the streets are deserted.

As we ride I tell Jon what my father told me. The reasons we are lied to and the reasons we are still kept prisoner inside the dome.

"Those must be the weapons they used when they got us from the filchers," Jon says.

"And on David. I've never seen anything like it. One minute he was fine and the next he was bleeding. It happened so fast. There's no time to react or defend yourself." I recall the moment the filcher that held me was killed. "Whatever it is, it's accurate," I say. I'd hate to think that the bluecoat with the weapon was counting on luck to get me through.

"Do you think there are people out there? Like us?"

"What else could they be? They survived the comet. They've been living out there all this time while we've been locked inside."

"So what are the bluecoats so afraid of?" Jon asks.

"Losing control."

"Aren't we all," he says as the wagon turns a corner.

We are back where it started to all go wrong. The roar of the fans beats against the wagon and the large square building that houses the furnaces looms into view. We drive behind it and once more doors close behind us.

"I guess we're luckier than your friend was," Jon says as we come to a stop. "We'll just be more on the list that have simply disappeared."

I'm still trying to decide if that is true. My mind is racing, trying to catch up with everything that has happened in the past few hours. Trying to come to the realization that I'm about to go outside and not really believing it. I am expecting something horrible to come, just like it did for Alex.

The bluecoats haul us from the back of the wagon. Everything that has happened catches up with me. My legs are weak and my body trembles. I don't know if I can walk but I'm determined not to be weak. Our hands are tied, but this time they do it in front instead of behind. The bluecoats lead us into the furnace building.

We are on a catwalk that takes off in several different directions. Below us are the furnaces. They are huge, with fire blasting from open ports. Men are around them, stripped down to their undershorts. Their arms and backs are great with muscle and their skin glistens with sweat. They shovel coal from a large pile that sits in the middle of the floor. A cart, much like the one that almost ran over us earlier, dumps a load from our level onto the pile. The chunks are getting smaller. The strike had a quicker effect than any of us imagined.

Jon and I are herded around the exterior of the catwalk to a set of stairs that run behind the furnaces. The heat hits me like a wall, pushing me back while the bluecoat behind me shoves me forward. I raise my hands to my face to protect it as it feels as if my skin will melt away. We go down several flights of stairs that are slick from the heat. Jon and I both hang on to the rails to keep our feet from sliding out from under us. We come to the bottom and another set of doors. One of our guards beats on the door and we hear the rattle of chains. It opens to reveal a set of guards, both of them with the weapons. Jon can't help but stare at the weapons as we are pushed on down another hall.

The heat is above us now. I look up to see the ceiling is a metal grid and large square metal pipes that cross over us and go through a wall. They carry the heat that powers the fans.

We travel on through the tunnel. My legs feel like they are made of rock. I'm not sure how much longer I can go on. I just want to lie down and forget everything that has happened. I want the world to go on without me for a while. I want to go back to the cave by the river with Pace and pretend like everything is good and fine and no one wants to kill us. I want to lower myself into the water and let the river carry me away.

This has to be the way Alex came. How did he get in? Was security that lax a few days ago that he just walked in and followed the route until it came to a way outside? Is it truly that simple? I will know the answer soon enough.

We come to a large room. It is several stories high with windows around the very top. A table and chair sits along the opposite wall next to a set of large double doors with another regular-size door beside it. Empty crates are piled up behind it. At one time it clearly served as a warehouse for the dome. The supplies it undoubtedly stored are long gone, leaving behind nothing but an empty space, all the more barren because it serves no purpose.

The middle of the floor is blackened and scarred. We walk around it as if the bluecoats don't want to tarnish their boots.

This is where Alex was burned. The room is just as Pace described it. I can feel the horror of the moment as we pass by. I'm glad the bluecoats shove me on. I'm afraid if I stay, if I linger, that I will break down. That I will lie down and they will kill me because I can't go any farther. That they will burn me alive, just as they did Alex.

We go through the smaller door and into another tunnel. One of the bluecoats turns on a lamp. As soon as I pass into the tunnel I know that something is different. The air feels lighter, if that is possible. The walls are strange, thick and polished like the dome. I want to reach my hands out to touch it but I am shoved onward. It is dark but I can see well enough with my shiner eyes to know that the world I have so desperately sought is right on the other side of the walls. We continue moving, uphill now. Jon is in front of me and he looks over his shoulder at me, questioning with his eyes.

I have no answer. All I can do at the moment is put one foot in front of the other.

We come to another door. "Stay put," one of the bluecoats says. Jon and I are shoved to the side while our four escorts go ahead. I can't see what they are doing because their bodies block my view. I hear several sounds. The click of bolts. The slide of chains. The slow creak as something heavy is moved aside.

Wind howls inward. Fresh and clean and tinged with salt. My hair blows back with the force and I turn my face into it, sucking it into my lungs. It is so clean that it hurts to breathe. My lungs, full of coal, rebel and I double over with a hacking cough that grips my sides like a vise.

"It's real," Jon says. "It really exists."

The bluecoats motion us forward. I can't move and I can't stop coughing. Jon helps me by putting his arms before me, which gives me some support to move forward.

Before I can take a step the ground falls away from me and we both fall. The noise is deafening. The wind howls over us with a great whooshing sound and we both slide back the way we came.

"What is it?" one of the bluecoats yells.

"An explosion!" another one says. They run past us and over us as Jon and I fight to regain our feet. To my surprise we are left alone. We go to work on the ropes and are able to untie each other's hands.

"What should we do?" Jon asks.

I look upward, toward the door the bluecoats opened. They shut it and bolted it but the chain still lies on the ground. Everything I have dreamed my entire life about lies right outside that door. All I have to do is open it. I've waited for this moment for what seems like forever. I've imagined it. I knew it existed; all I had to do was find the way to it.

Yet everything and everyone I love is still inside. And something is desperately wrong in there. "I can't leave him."

"I understand," Jon says. He looks toward the door. "I'm going for it. I have no one inside. No one to hold me back."

"Good luck." He hugs me, fiercely, and runs to the door. In just a few tries he has it unbolted. I feel the air on my face once more as he slips through it. The door slams shut behind him with the force of the wind.

I turn and go back the way I came.

Dreams are nothing unless you have someone to share them with.

· 28 ·

*C*haos. *Complete chaos.* The world is on fire. A great wall of flames dances up the wall of the huge room where Alex died. It's the way we came in. I can't go back that way. The doors we came through are on fire.

I hear the screech of strained metal and a crash that shakes the floor beneath my feet. I fall forward and scramble to my feet. The wall behind me, with the door that leads outside, is now on fire. I watch the flames shoot up and outward, a dazzling mix of bright yellows and oranges and reds, as bright as the paintings I saw earlier. They hypnotize me until I realize that I will die right here if I don't move. I feel the flame inside my lungs and throat and they threaten to consume me on the inside. I have to find another way into the dome. Outside is lost to me, the path now engulfed in flames. I couldn't go back even if I wanted to.

There has to be another way out. Which way did the bluecoats go? The room is dark, yet bright with heat. I run to the far dim corner, farthest away from the fire. To my relief there is another door there and it is unlocked. I dash through and I am outside of the building and into the street.

I cannot believe what I see. The furnace building is on fire, along with the building behind it that housed the fans and the warehouse I just escaped from. The fans are not running, I'm not even sure if they are there anymore. The smoke is so thick. My eyes water and my throat burns. I've got to get away from it. I've got to get back to Pace.

To my surprise I find my goggles still hanging around my neck. I cover my eyes and raise my kerchief to protect my nose and mouth. I run. I become part of the masses that are trying to escape the fire. People and dogs and cats and rats, even a donkey runs with us. From the other direction come the fire crews with their steam engines and their pumps and the long hoses that will be attached to hydrants that pump water up from the underground river.

Fire is the enemy in the dome. There's no place to escape it. We always believed it to be outside, and we lived in terror of it consuming everything and everyone in its path if it came inside. Fire is the death sentence for the more horrible crimes. Fire is the consummate ending.

It is like living my worst nightmare. Except I'm not on fire, my world is. I was so close, so close to escaping, so close to the outside, so close to proving what I knew all along and I walked away from it.

Because it is nothing without Pace.

What if I can't get back to him? What if he's not there? What if my father already put his mother out as bait to capture him? What if he's dead?

I've got to know, one way or another. I know that the outside world exists. The way out is gone, but the outside isn't going anywhere. It will always be there. I will just find another way. A way for all of us.

I don't know how I'm still on my feet. I don't know how I'm

running or even breathing. I just know I've got to keep going, got to keep moving until I get back to Pace. I come to the promenade. It's full of people, all running from the burning side of the dome to the other. Bluecoats try to make sense of the utter panic that fills the streets. They form a line to keep the people from crossing over into the royal side. They try to calm the people and when that doesn't work they beat at them with their thick clubs. There are not enough bluecoats to handle the streams of people coming at them. Some slip through and disappear into the darkness of the alleyways that run like spiderwebs away from the promenade.

I stand in the middle of the screaming and the yelling while people run to and fro around me. I look up at the enforcer building and the wall of windows that I know is my father's office. Is he up there staring down at this mess? Does he wonder if I'm outside, or maybe he thinks I am once more responsible? I hope it's the latter.

I'm not trying to reach Park Front, as the rest of the people are. I just want to get to Lucy and David's. I try to turn down an alley that is as full of people as the promenade; something blocks the other end and their cries of panic rise to the rooftops. I cut over and over again until I'm on the correct street. The people who live here are outside, watching the fire flicker and talking in excited tones. They ignore me as I pass through until finally I pound on the door in the alley.

Harry opens the door. The look on his face is pure shock. I can't say that I blame him. "You're alive," he says. I have no more strength. Whatever got me here is gone. I fall through the door and he catches me in his arms.

"Pace? Where is Pace?" I gasp.

"Here. He's safe."

Harry half drags, half carries me into the kitchen. I don't see

Pace anywhere. Peggy runs to me and hugs me but I look beyond her. Adam, James, and Alcide are all there. All safe. Where is Pace?

"Pace?" My throat is so raw I can barely form the words. Alcide fills a cup with water and hands it to me. I gulp it down and he fills it again. "Pace?" I say, clearer this time. I can't stand on my own and Peggy and Harry put me in a chair. I hold on to the edge of the table. I'm afraid I will fall over if I don't.

James shakes his head and goes to the closet beneath the stairs. He moves the trunk and opens the hatch. "You can come up now," he says.

My body shakes with relief or shock, I don't know which. I look around the kitchen, trying to focus. I can't believe I made it back, alive and whole. David and Lucy's home is an island of peace and calm compared to the chaos outside.

Alcide and Adam come back from the front of the house. "They're calling for volunteers to fight the fire," Alcide says. "Someone on the street said they're starting a backfire to control it. They're trying to save the stockyards. As long as we can get below we should be okay."

"The streets are a madhouse," Adam says. "I can't believe you made it through."

"How did it get started?" I ask. Not that its advent wasn't timely for me. Still, it seems like it couldn't have been a coincidence, could it? I look around the kitchen, where things seem as normal as they can be. On the counter sits the makeshift cage for Pip and a bag that looks like the one Adam carries charges in when he's working on a tunnel. I recognize it because my grandfather had one just like it.

Peggy wets a cloth with water and wipes my face. It comes away black with soot. I'm surprised they recognized me. "What happened to you?" she asks, ignoring my question about the fire.

Where do I begin? There's so much . . . "David?" I ask.

"He's alive," Peggy says and I feel another burden drop from my shoulders. I'd felt so responsible for all of them. Knowing that everyone is safe, in spite of the fire, almost makes me crumple. I won't. I won't do anything until I see Pace. Until I see with my own eyes that he's here and unhurt.

"Whatever hit him went right through," Peggy continues. "But we think he will be all right. Lucy and Jilly are with him. What happened to you?"

"You won't believe it," I say.

"We lost Jon," Harry says. "Have you—"

"He's alive," I say. "He's outside the dome."

"What?" Harry sinks down into a chair and Peggy looks at me as if I've grown two heads.

"When Pace gets here," I begin. I am interrupted by Pace exploding out of the hatch and launching his body at James. They crash into the table and onto the floor. Chairs and dishes fly across the floor as they grapple with each other, twisting and turning and punching until Pace scrambles on top of James's midsection and punches him in the face. Harry and Peggy both grab for Pace. My chair tips over and I fall backward.

"You son of a bitch," Pace yells at James. "Now we'll never find her!"

"She's here!" James yells back. "She's right here!"

Adam and Alcide pull Pace from James. Pace fights them and all three of them slam him against the wall.

"She's here," Adam says. "She's safe."

Peggy helps me to my feet.

"Pace?" I don't know how much longer I can last. He sees me and his beautiful blue eyes widen and his glorious soul spills out and I know it's all for me. It was worth it. Not going out because of him. He stops fighting the ones who hold him. The last thing I see is him coming for me and then everything goes dark.

◆

When I come to I am in Pace's arms. He holds me close while Peggy wipes my face. I realize I wasn't out long as the only thing that's changed is the furniture has been returned to its proper place.

"Don't you ever do anything like that again," he says softly against my ear so only I can hear him. For the first time today I feel safe. The entire dome may be on fire but I don't care. Pace holds me close in his lap, against his chest, sheltering me with his arms and his head that is bent over me.

I know my friends are concerned. I know everyone wants to know what happened, especially since I said Jon was outside. I don't want to talk to anyone. I don't want to be here. I want to be back below, in our cave, with Pip and Cat. I want to feel safe again, if just for a while. I just want to be with Pace, to listen to him make silly jokes and play with Pip. I want this all to be over but I have a feeling it has just begun.

"Why were you below?" I ask, just as quietly as he spoke to me.

"Because your friends put me there. To protect me."

"He went a little crazy when you ran off," Peggy says. She holds a clean cloth and goes to work on my hands, which are black with soot.

"We had to drag him back," Alcide says. "Because James knocked him out."

"We put him down there to keep him safe, just like you asked," James says with a smirk.

"You can't do that, Wren," Pace says. "You can't make decisions for all of us like that."

"If they had gotten you you'd be dead now," I say in my defense. I am certain James enjoyed every minute of it, from knocking Pace out to dropping him into the tunnel and making sure he couldn't get out. Still I am grateful that he did it, no matter what his motives.

"I thought for certain you were gone," Pace says. "So it didn't matter to me if I was alive."

"Don't ever say that." I look into his beautiful blue eyes. "Ever."

"I hate to interrupt this lovely moment," James says. "But you need to tell us what happened."

"Can't it wait?" Peggy says. "The fire? Shouldn't we go below?"

Alcide comes in from the front. "Word is it's under control, but that part of the dome is completely gone."

"The fans?" James asks.

"I don't know," Alcide says. "I'm just picking up what they're saying on the street."

"It doesn't matter if the fans are gone," I say.

"What do you mean?" Adam asks.

I look at the group gathered in the kitchen. They've all risked so much this day. They all deserve to know what I know. "Can David be moved?" I ask. I only want to tell it once. I'm pretty certain I won't last much longer.

"I think so," Harry says. "He was sitting up." He goes up the stairs to get David, Lucy, and Jilly. Peggy fixes me a bite to eat while Lucy and Harry help David down the stairs. He settles gingerly into a chair and Lucy pulls another one up close to him so he can lean against her. He's pale but strong enough to sit. I am certain he will recover.

"Thank you for what you did," he says. "You probably saved my life. I just wish I knew what hit me."

"I can sort of answer that," I say from the comfort of Pace's arms. There aren't enough chairs for everyone and I don't want to move so I stay safely on his lap with his arms around my waist. I'm not so certain I could hold myself up without them there.

"Jon and I were captured by the filchers." I leave out the details of my time with the filchers. There are things I'm not ready to share. The things that would have happened to me and the reason why they didn't. "They tried to collect the reward but the blue-coats killed them. They took me to meet with Sir Meredith . . ."

"He's over the enforcers," Pace adds. "I don't think I've ever seen him, at least not close enough to talk to him."

"He's quite driven," Jilly adds. "A real stickler, according to my father. There are rumors afoot that he killed his competition for the position, although it was all deemed an accident upon investigation."

I am not surprised by Jilly's statement. I had come away with the same impression after spending half an hour with him. He abandoned my mother and me and thought nothing more of me than to trade me off for some weapons. I fully believe him capable of murder.

I tell them what my father told me. About the world outside, about the others who are out there, about the weapons and the reasons why he won't allow us out.

"What makes you think he's telling the truth about all of this?" Adam asks.

"Because he's my father."

The ones who know me and my history fall silent, as they digest this morsel of information.

"Well, that certainly puts things in a different light," Jilly says. "Meredith *does* have skeletons in his closet." She looks at me. "No offense."

I can't help but smile. "None taken," I say. "It was as big a shock to me as it is to everyone else."

"He recognized you," Lucy says. "Because you look like your mother."

"You would have thought he'd seen her ghost," I say. "But he recovered quickly enough."

"So what happened?" Peggy asks.

"He said he was going to give me what I wanted when I refused to tell him where you were," I say, turning to look at Pace. "He was going to put me outside. Jon and I were to be traded for more weapons. We were almost there when there was an explosion."

James and Alcide grin widely and exchange a look that puzzles me.

"The bluecoats took off to see what was going on. Jon went out. I came back," I say simply.

"Did you see anything?"

"What was it like?"

"I can't believe you didn't go."

The questions fly but I hear only one thing.

"You came back," Pace says quietly so that only I can hear him.

"Outside will still be there," I say. "We'll find another way to get there."

"We can't go that way?" Peggy says. "Why?"

"The fire," I say. "It burned everything. I wonder how . . ."

"We did it," James says. "Adam, Alcide, and I."

Now it is my turn to be surprised. "What? How?"

"Alcide went back and got the charges," Adam says. "They took you. We wanted to show them we could take something too."

"I'm pretty sure the fans are gone," I say. "And the furnaces."

"Which means they've got to let us out now," James says confidently. "Come on, Wren, you were the one who started this revolution. You didn't think we were going to sit around and just bide our time and not put up a fight?"

"You just decided to do it? Without thinking it through?" Even though I am exhausted my anger rises as the full impact of James's impetuous act sets in and my voice rises with it. I stand and lean across the table to face him. "They don't need us now. They don't have any use for our coal without the furnaces. You think they will just let us go?"

"He's *your* father, *you* tell me," James yells back.

"'Tis done now," Jilly says. "Right or wrong, there is no going back."

"Fighting amongst ourselves isn't going to help anything," Lucy adds.

They are both right and I am too exhausted to think.

"Tomorrow," I say. "We'll talk again tomorrow." The only problem is, I'm not certain if there will be a tomorrow for any of us.

· 29 ·

*W*e *part ways* with Peggy, Adam, James, and Alcide once we are back in the mine. At this point I'm not sure if it matters if they know where we are hiding. At this point I'm not sure of anything. Pace has the benefit of the lamp, but he still needs me to show him the way. I don't care if James follows us. I don't care if James falls into the pit. I just want to get back to our cave.

We finally arrive to the sound of the rushing river. The sound that means home. Pace keeps a tight hold on me as we walk down the narrow ledge. It's a good thing he does. I am so exhausted I am dizzy. I concentrate on putting one foot in front of the other so hard that I don't even know we've arrived until Pace puts his arm around my waist. When we get to the bottom he picks me up and carries me, gracefully navigating the rocks and pools until we are before our cave. If only we could crawl into our cave and never come out again. If only we could leave all of this behind us and wake up in a new and peaceful world.

I need to get the remnants of this day off of me. I'm covered with blood and dirt and soot and the smell of the sewers. My skin feels crawly and I don't think my clothes will ever come clean. "Put me down," I say. "I need to bathe."

"Shouldn't we go to the glow fish?"

"No, here is fine." I'm too weary to go on. I just want to wash the day away. I don't care that the water is cold. Maybe cold will make me feel normal again instead of like a monster.

"I'll be right back," Pace says. He climbs into the cave to put Pip back into his cage. While he is gone I strip everything off down to my underclothes and make my way out to a cluster of rocks that form a pool alongside the river. The water pours over and through but there is no danger of washing downstream because of the boulders that block the way. I sink into the water and let it pound against my back before I go completely under.

It would be so easy just to slip out into the river and let the water carry me away. To not have to think about anything. Just to let go and not have to fight anymore. To not have to tell Pace that my father is planning to trade his mother for him. To not have to admit to him or myself that I actually killed a man.

All I have to do is let go. It would be so very easy. Let go . . . I see myself floating beneath the water, pale against the darkness, with my hair spread out around me, at peace before I disappear beneath the cave wall. So very easy . . .

Pace won't let me. He splashes into the pool and pulls me against his chest. The heat of his bare skin against my chilled body jolts my insides. "Don't," he says.

"Don't what?" I gasp. I'm shivering now. The cold and the wet finally registering in my shocked and exhausted body.

"Don't leave me."

I open my mouth to respond, to tell him I'm not going anywhere, but one look into his eyes makes me realize he knew what I was thinking. How is it that he knows me so well in the small time we've spent together? Better than anyone who has known me my entire life.

"I killed a man," I finally say. "A filcher. He tried to . . ." I can't say the words. To speak them out loud would make it closer, scarier, more real, if that was possible. The thought of what could have happened is enough to send me over the edge.

I would very gladly go, if not for Pace. He pushes the wet and wrecked mess of my hair back from my face. The lamp sits on a rock beside us and he turns me so he can examine each cut and bruise on my face. He touches them gently and tenderly, almost as if he could heal them with his fingertips. He does the same with my hands, kissing each finger and finally the palms that are raw from my tumble in the street.

"You did what you had to do to survive." His voice is hoarse with emotion and his eyes narrow as his face turns deadly. "I would gladly kill anyone who tried to hurt you."

"Your mother . . ." I begin. I feel the need to confess all my sins. I feel so unworthy of his love, after what I did today.

"They expect to trade her for me," he says. "I know. It's the only reason to take her. It is not your fault that they have her. You can't be responsible for everything and everyone."

I nod in affirmation. Now that I've confessed I haven't got the energy to speak.

"We'll figure it out tomorrow," he adds. "For now let's just be."

He's carried out the soap and towels. He bids me to sit before him and I do, wrapping my arms around my knees and leaning against the warm skin of his legs as he washes my hair, my back and arms, quickly, as he can feel my chill. When he's done he wraps my hair up in a towel and puts the other one around me and once more carries me to the cave while I hold the lamp up so he can find solid footing on the rocks.

He puts me on the ledge into our cave and I slide back so he can leverage himself in. Then we both crawl back into the cavern. Cat lies on the quilts and meows sleepily, as if to say, where have you been?

"Do you want to eat?" Pace asks.

I shake my head. "I just want to sleep." I'm still shivering and need to get warm.

"Good, because we don't have much."

"I'll go get some in the morning," I say, with a yawn. I want to lie down but Pace won't let me. Not until he wraps me in a blanket and brushes out my hair as I lean against him, gathering his warmth while listening to the sound of Cat's rumbling purr as he lies next to me. I fall asleep as Pace cares for me and do not realize it until I wake from a dream with a start and find myself wrapped safely in his arms.

If only I could stay this way forever.

◆

"Wren!" I fight my way through the many layers of my dreams. Fire and blood and filchers chasing me and through it all I hear the sound of rushing water and know that escape is so close.

"Wren, wake up."

I open my eyes to find Pace sitting before me and Hans and his son standing over us. Pace clenches his fists and the muscles in his arms and across his back tighten. I touch his shoulder, gently, and rise up to my knees behind him, his body shielding mine from the wandering eyes of Hans's son.

We have been found.

"We need you at the council, gel," Hans says. He looks down at Pace. "Both of you."

"We'll be there," I say because I know we have no choice. They know where we are now, so they know how to stop us if we try to leave. Not that we have anywhere else to go. Hans nods and leaves while his son looks around curiously before following him.

Pace does not relax until they are gone. "What does it mean?" he asks.

I drop down to sit. My heart is racing and my mind is trying to find the path between my dreams and reality. "They want to talk to us. About what, I don't know."

"I wonder how bad it is," Pace says as he dresses. "If things above have gotten worse."

"Without the fire it was already bad enough," I admit when my brain finally focuses on the here and now. "It could be the bluecoats have sent word about your mother. Or it could be they found out about our involvement in what happened last night."

"Do you think they'll be angry when they find out what James, Alicide, and Adam did?"

"Yes." I don't even have to think about that response. I rise and put on the only clean clothes I have left besides the blue dress. "No one is allowed to put the rest of us in jeopardy. I got away with what I did because they didn't know you were below and they were trying to protect me, but now that they know you've been here the entire time they will be angry."

Pace looks up from pulling on his boots. "What will they do?"

"Banish me at the worst. But if they do, that means we have no place to go." My mind races as I try to conceive of a safe place for us to hide. The only one I can come up with is beneath David and

Lucy's, and that is no way to live. It would be like living in a grave, like the dead people from the time before the dome.

My boots sit right by the entrance. Sometime in the night Pace had retrieved my clothes and cleaned them the best he could. I pick up my boots and pull them on.

"We can't hide forever, Wren. And whatever happens, as long as we're together in it, we'll figure it out." As soon as I stand Pace puts his hands on my shoulders and tilts my chin so I have to look into his eyes. "I mean it, Wren. No more taking off on your own. From now on it's the two of us, facing this together. Both of us deciding, not just you." His blue eyes search my face. "Understand?"

His soul is right there shining in his beautiful blue eyes and bared for me to see. It is made up of sweetness and strength, resolve and fortitude. I don't understand why fate threw us together but I will not question it. Instead I will be grateful for it. For knowing he is there to help me and to protect me, even if it is from myself.

"I understand," I promise him. He smiles, puts his hands on either side of my face, and bends to kiss me. It starts tender and sweet but we are suddenly hit with the realization that this might be the last time we have a moment like this and it turns desperate once more, hot and demanding until I can do nothing but cling to him as he cannot seem to stop.

But he does, because we both know that we have to face the day and whatever it brings. He leans his forehead against mine as we both struggle to steady our breathing once more. "Should I bring Pip?" he asks.

"Yes," I say, because for some strange reason I know that we will not be coming back. At least not today.

Cat follows us, questioning as we walk with his raspy meows. We come to the stable and I take my time with the ponies, greeting each one and then introducing Pace to them. They sniff his clothes and shake their heads up and down as I scoop into their bins the little bit of feed that is left. They will starve soon if something isn't done. I have a feeling we all will and things have gone past the place where it is just a matter of Pace and me turning ourselves in. James took care of that when he blew up the fans.

"They need our coal and we need their food," I say. "This world was made so all parts worked together as a whole. Why did it all go so wrong?"

"Because it wasn't meant to last this long. Because we're people and we need to reach for greater things."

"Funny. That's the same thing I always said." I have to laugh. "Of course it was mostly to myself."

"You're not the first one to think it, Wren. You're just the first person to act on it."

"Why me?" I look at him, hoping for an answer or a sign that what I've done is right.

"Why not you?" he says. I forget when I look at him that he is young, like me, and doesn't have the answers. I forget because he has become my answers and my reasons. Should it be that way? I don't know. I just know what I feel inside.

I unlatch all the stall doors before we leave. Just in case. Because like Pace with Pip, I can't stand the thought of the ponies being trapped in their stalls to die. Because without the doors and the locks they have a chance to help themselves.

Pip sticks his head up from Pace's pocket and watches the chickens who peck furiously at Pace's boots in search of something to eat.

"Do you think they'll feed us first?" he asks with a lopsided smile.

"Is food the only thing you ever think about?" I tease.

"No. I think about you occasionally too," he teases back. He takes my hand and we walk onward to the village with Cat still trailing along behind.

· 30 ·

*A*mazing," *Pace says* as we walk down the ledge into the village. "I never dreamed there was something like this down here. It reminds me of the dome, only smaller."

"I always thought so." I felt as if I'd been gone from this place for weeks instead of only a few days. We passed several shiners on our way here, all of them patrolling the tunnels. Most all greeted me in our reserved way and looked curiously at Pace, who bore it all with good grace and his own curiosity.

"That was my house." I point at the little place up on the cavern wall as Cat runs down before us with his tail straight up behind him. He greets some other cats with a nose sniff before sauntering off into the village. "Peggy and Adam live there now."

"You gave up your home for them?"

"It is the way of our world," I say. I could say more. That my home is now with him, but I don't as I do not know what the next moments will bring. I look across the water to the council chamber. There is no guard before it so nothing has happened yet. They must be waiting for us to arrive.

I see Jasper coming our way and we both stop at the bottom of the ramp. Pace keeps a tight hold on my hand. "Thank you for coming," Jasper says to my surprise. He holds out his hand to Pace. "I'm Jasper."

"Jasper is the head of the council," I add so Pace knows the importance of who he is talking to and the greeting Jasper gives him.

Pace slowly takes his hand, as shocked as I am at the gesture. "Pace Bratton," he says.

"The wife has some food for the two of you," Jasper says. "Go eat and come when you're done."

"Thank you," we both say. Jasper goes on across the bridge to the council chamber and I see the others coming out to follow, Mary, Hans, Frank, and Rosalyn. I see no sign of James or Adam.

We go into the village proper. It is fairly quiet as the children are at the school in another cavern that is close by. They go there as it does not have the distractions in the village. Jasper's wife, Etta, feeds us. We sit at a table outside by the water and Pace puts Pip on his shoulder and feeds him crumbs.

"Well, I never," Etta exclaims as she watches the bird. Her youngest son, who is around two, sits on her lap and claps his hands with glee as Pace shows off Pip's tricks. Etta asks Pace questions about how he trained the bright little bird and he explains his methods to her. I listen with fascination as most of Pip's training happened while I was gone.

The waterwheel turns merrily along and the sound of the water flowing by is peaceful. People go about their chores as usual, but I can sense the worry that lies over the village. Those who are usually working at this time patrol the tunnels, while the night shift sleeps until it is their time to take over. The food that Jasper's family has so generously shared with us will run out soon, and no one knows when or if there will be more. Yet everyone carries on because there is no need to sit and be anxious about tomorrow. Being anxious will not change what will or will not happen.

I cannot help but think that we, as shiners, have made the best of our lot in life. We live our lives with honor and justice and take pride in our work. We have nothing to be ashamed of. My father left me with the impression that I missed out on much because I grew up below. I would have to say he is wrong. He missed out on much by rejecting my mother. How different a man would he be today if he had chosen her instead of success? I'd like to think he'd be a better person for it.

My musings are not enough to change the past. All I can do is learn from the mistakes that were made and hopefully make a better future for all of us.

Pace now has Pip sitting on the outstretched finger of Etta's son, whose eyes round with wonder as he tries to hold perfectly still so he does not frighten the bright little bird. I see Alex's mother by the water doing laundry and I excuse myself to go talk to her.

"I never got to say it," she says as soon as I walk up to her. "But I'm glad you were with him at the end. That he had someone he knew to talk to."

"You know what happened?"

"I've pieced it together," she says. "No one wants to say exactly." She wipes her hands on her apron and settles herself on a rock. "I would appreciate it if you would tell me. The truth can't be any worse than my imaginings."

I tell her everything I know, from the moment Alex decided to run until the moment he died. I tell her what Pace saw and I tell her what Alex said to me. "He made it outside," I tell her. "He found the way. It exists and he saw it."

"And they killed him for it?" she asks in a tearful voice.

"They did. But because of Alex we found it too."

"You saw it?"

"I did."

She grabs my hands. "Don't you let them forget it neither. Don't you let none of them forget that it was my boy that done it."

"I won't," I assure her. "We will never forget him."

She wipes her eyes with her hand. "Go on then. The bunch of you stirred up a mess of trouble and I'm glad for it. But you best go tell them the rest of it."

"I will." I look over my shoulder. Pace is waiting. Behind him on the bridge I see Peggy, Adam, James, and Alcide going up the steps to the council cave, and Abner is stationed at the entrance.

They are waiting for us.

◆

I told Pace what to expect as we walked to the village. Both of us are surprised to see Adam and James sitting before the council instead of with it. Two low benches have been carried in; James, Adam, and Peggy sit on one and we join Alcide on the other. Peggy and Adam are both pale and grip each other's hands tightly. Alcide slightly nods to us as we sit down. James just looks rebellious, which is not a good thing in my mind.

"Who is responsible for the fire last night?" Jasper asks without preamble.

He is met with shocked silence for a moment.

"I am," James says.

Then Adam speaks up. "We are," he says. "James, Alcide, and I." Alcide nods his head in confirmation.

"You fools," Hans says. His anger is tense and tangible and I cannot help but admire him for restraining it. "Do you know what you have done?"

"They did it to save me," I say. Pace grabs my hand and squeezes it. Without thinking I'd done what I promised I wouldn't do. I acted without talking to him first.

"No, we didn't." James's answer is belligerent. "They might have, but I didn't." I suddenly realize his reasons. He didn't do it to save me any more than he put Pace in the tunnels to save him. He did it because he was jealous of me. Jealous that the others looked to me for leadership. Jealous that I made the sacrifice to save David and Pace by drawing attention to myself. James wants the glory and the power.

I just want out.

"What was your reasoning, James, if not to save Wren?" Jasper asks.

"I did it to show them we are a force to be reckoned with." James's answer confirms what I suspected about his motives.

"We are a force?" Mary growls. "Do you mean you, yourself, or us as a group? Did you consult any of us when you were making this decision?" Mary stands. Her anger is no greater than Jaspers's or Hans's, but her restraint is not as strong. She jabs her finger toward James. "You fool," she says in disgust. "You have killed us all."

"What has happened?" I ask.

"The fans and the furnaces are destroyed," Jasper says. "Until they are repaired there is to be no trade, which means no food. Not only that, but the entire workforce above is put on half rations."

"Which means they hate us. Everyone above. No one will help us," Mary finishes.

I look at Pace. I don't have to speak; it has been the unasked question between us since this all began. He nods, knowing this is my world and he does not have a voice here. I look at the council. "What if we turn ourselves in?"

"It is too late for that," Jasper says. "They were looking for an excuse, any excuse, to destroy us. There are too many people for the dome to support. By making us the enemy they've assumed the right to come after us. To kill us all."

"We will fight them!" James jumps to his feet.

Adam leans over and puts his face in his hands. "I should have stopped you. I should have known better."

"It doesn't matter," I say. "The outside exists. We just have to find a way to get there."

"No more of your flights of fancy, Wren," Mary says. "That's what started this entire thing in the first place."

"It's true," Alcide interrupts. "Let her tell you."

The five council members look at me. I feel their impatience but I also know their ways. They will want to hear all of it. For the first time I tell them the entire story, from the moment Alex died until the events of last night. Pace tells his part also, and they listen with shock and wonder plainly showing on their faces as I tell them about my trip through the tunnel.

"What did you see?" Jasper asks.

"I saw nothing but darkness because it was night. But it seemed to go on forever. I felt the wind on my face and I tasted salt in the air. It was so pure that it hurt me to breathe."

"Why didn't you go?" Hans asks.

I pull Pace's hand into my lap for all to see and look into his beautiful blue eyes. "I came back because everything I love was still inside."

"We now know where it is and how Alex got out," Adam says. "I looked at the maps in their library. Our tunnels are not beneath it, but we can make one that goes there and come up from below. We can make our own path out."

I can tell by their faces they need time to think and time to plan. Nothing is to be decided now.

"You will do nothing until we talk this through," Jasper says. "James, because of your impetuous behavior, you are dismissed from council . . ."

James jumps to his feet to protest but Jasper cuts him off.

"Adam, because of the regret you have shown you may stay. We will elect another council member to replace James and discuss our options. The rest of you may go."

James is livid, but before he can say anything Abner comes in with another shiner. It is Peter, who was with us the night Alex flew. He's out of breath and bends over with his hands on his knees to catch it before he speaks.

"The lift has been taken," he finally says. "The bluecoats are coming and we can't stop them."

"See what you've done," Mary hisses at James.

"They have a flamethrower," Peter says.

I feel the chill all the way into my bones. A flamethrower in the mines is a death sentence for all of us. If there is a buildup of the methane gas anywhere there is a flame, the entire mine could be lost to an explosion. We will never survive it. The looks on the faces of the council and those facing them are much the same as mine.

"Sound the alarm," Jasper says. "We must stop these fools before they kill all of us." Peter runs out to do as he is told. "Those of you who are not on council leave us now. And James. Stay put until we tell you where to go. We don't need you making decisions for us."

We turn to go, urgency at the situation holding us in its grip.

"You!" Hans calls out. "Pace! We have need of words with you."

Abner herds James, Peggy, and Alcide out. James is livid, but

I am confident he won't do anything to lose face in front of the village. I know he wants to fight and is just waiting to be turned loose so he can grab his weapons and join in.

Pace and I turn to face the council.

"Where do you stand in this battle?" Hans asks Pace.

"I stand with Wren," Pace says without hesitation. "The only possible way for either of us to survive is to find the way out. But Sir Meredith holds my mother. If there is anything I can do to save her, even if that means trading myself to them, I will do it."

"We appreciate your honesty," Jasper says. "You may stay and we hope you will fight with us. If you decide to go above, we ask that you inform us first."

"Thank you," Pace says. "I will."

We are dismissed and go outside the cavern as the shrill whistle of our alarm sounds. James and Alcide are a few paces away and are in a heated discussion. Peggy has just set foot on the bridge while Cat jumps off and comes bounding to us with a curious meow. Pip pokes his head from Pace's pocket, looks around, and then dips back inside. I'm not sure if we should try to talk to James or just go on and wait for the council to speak to the village.

I am worried about the ponies. If there is an explosion, I can't stand the thought of them being at the mercy of fire shooting throughout the tunnels. I should be worried about my people, about the shiners who even now are fighting to protect us from the blue-coats. Cat twines between my ankles as I stand there, watching my fellow shiners gather by the bridge, and listening to the sounds of their questions as they wait to find the reason for the alarm.

Those who were awake don't know any more than those who were asleep. Mothers hold their babies close and the men, most of whom were awakened by the alarm, ask one another the news. Peter is already up the ramp and back to the fight. The council comes forth from the cavern and steps onto the bridge just as Peggy steps off. She continues on, past the crowd and to her house. She already knows the news. She already knows we have to fight to save ourselves.

Pace and I, along with Alcide and James, stay close to the chamber. To cross now would interrupt the announcement of the bluecoat invasion. The gathering grows quiet as the council members stand on the bridge.

"We have been invaded," Jasper says. "The lift has fallen to the bluecoats and—"

Before he can say another word the tunnels rumble and the earth beneath our feet violently shakes. The four of us on the cavern side of the bridge—me, Pace, Alcide, and James—are thrown to the ground. Cat yowls and dashes into the council cavern.

"What is it?" Pace asks as the shaking continues. The lamps above our heads swing to and fro and some fall, crashing to the earth with great popping sounds. The water sloshes from its banks and those on the opposite shore try to retreat as they are pitched to the ground.

"Methane," I gasp. "There's been an explosion."

The bridge swings back and forth violently. Those on the bridge dash for either side; Adam, Mary, and Hans come our way, the rest go to the other side. A huge groan echoes in our chamber and suddenly water spouts through the wall, spraying in every direction. There are screams and cries of terror as the cave wall above the bridge splits in half and a great wave of water tumbles through.

"We're trapped," Pace says.

"No." I pull him to his feet and into the council cavern. There is always an escape route. Always. But in this case, I am not so sure, as we never thought we would have to outrun the rising waters.

· 31 ·

The escape tunnel is still there. For one panicked moment I was afraid it might have caved in with the explosion, but it is still there, leading out, up, and away.

"Peggy!" Adam stands in the entrance to the council cavern and yells across the cave. The water is rising fast. Across the way we can see people, cats, and goats all running up the ramp. The birds circle around the ceiling, chirping their displeasure. The water keeps pounding and it is only a matter of time before the water-wheel gives way and the cavern is plunged into darkness. Against the far wall pieces of our lives are smashed in the frenzy of the rising tide of water. Tables and chairs, bed frames, blankets, and curtains twirl about in whirlpools before being sucked under, all traveling beneath the cave wall. Where will they end up? Will they tumble past our cave and will that cavern flood too? What about the shiners who are out fighting and patrolling and the ponies and the cats and chickens who all live in our world? Will everything and everyone be swept away?

I have no idea how many were washed away and smashed into the far wall with the first blast of water. Jasper and the rest? Those who stood on the bank when the great wall cracked and the water tumbled forth? Entire families? Mothers and fathers and tiny children?

Peggy is trapped. The water quickly rises and covers the steps that lead up to her home. It could be me up there. It could be me, standing in my doorway, screaming and crying for my husband who is being held back from diving into the water by his brother-in-law James and Alcide.

"Oh God, Peggy," I cry out. She is running out of time as are we, as we are only a bit higher on our side of the water than she is.

Pace grabs me from behind and pulls me back into the council cavern. Cat is already gone after scrambling into the escape tunnel. Mary leverages herself up to follow.

"We must be away," she says.

"Peggy!" I sob, echoing Adam as he screams her name over and over again. Hans grabs hold of him too as he is almost too much for Alcide and James.

"You can't help her," Pace says into my ear. "I know you love her. You can only save yourself." We are plunged into darkness and I know the waterwheel is gone, along with the rest of the village. Birds fly at us, quickly dodging our heads before shooting into the escape tunnel. They are gone before we even know they have passed.

"Get in the tunnel," Hans yells at us. The water is coming at us, splashing around our boots in its rush to get in. Pace picks me up by the waist and stuffs me into the tunnel and is on my heels before I crawl forward.

"Move it!" Hans yells. We scramble forward, moving on until

we can stand and then running along the slope that leads up. Alcide is behind Pace. He drags at Adam while James pushes him from behind. Adam is dazed and I know they must have struck him to get him inside and away from the water.

"It's coming behind us," Hans yells. I can hear it splashing. If it catches Hans, who is bringing up the rear, it will wash him into us and we will all fall and be drowned. I know Pace cannot see. He holds on to my jacket and pushes me forward.

"Come on!" Mary yells. The way is steep and the climb is arduous. I have to lean forward to climb. "Don't drag her down," Mary yells at Pace. "Just climb, there's only one way to go and that's up."

Pace lets go of my jacket and we scramble upward. It will level out soon, I know, but I don't waste the breath to tell him. Alcide is on his heels and Adam is climbing on his own, his natural sense of survival overcoming his grief at losing Peggy.

"Hurry, hurry, hurry!" Hans yells. The water splashes and sloshes behind us. We climb and we climb and we climb until I know my heart will explode if I don't stop soon. Maybe drowning will be easier. It has to be easier than this.

I fall forward and Pace falls on top of me. We've reached level ground. Mary drags us up as Alcide is almost on top of us. We scramble out of the way and bend over with our hands on our knees to catch our breath as the rest come up. A lamp hangs on a support in this tunnel and Pace, who has recovered quicker than any of us as his lungs are stronger, takes it down and holds it over the way we've just come.

"It looks like it's subsiding," he says. Mary and Hans stand beside him and peer down at the water.

"Poor bastards," Mary says. "All of us. God bless us all."

I wonder about their families. Hans's wife and two sons and

Mary's married daughter, who teaches the schoolchildren. Mary is a widow so she has no husband to worry over. No one to share in her suffering if her daughter and all those children are lost.

Please, I pray, but who and what to pray for escapes me. I've lost my best friend, Adam lost his wife, and James lost his sister. Entire families are gone. I look at Adam, who stands with his hands at his sides, curling them into fists. I don't know I have tears on my face until I see his and I run to him and throw my arms around him. He sinks to the ground in his grief and I go with him, both of us on our knees as we cry together.

"They will pay," James says. "All of them. For Peggy and for the rest." His voice breaks and he whirls around and pounds his fist into the wall. Hans grabs him as he draws back to strike again.

"We've got a long way to go, son," he says. "We need you whole, not with a broken hand."

James nods his head and comes to where Adam and I kneel in each other's arms. I back away and Adam falls against James. They are best friends and they were brothers through Peggy. I know they will always stay that way. But my connection to them is now gone with my dearest friend.

Pace wraps his arms around me and kisses the top of my head. I wipe my cheek against his shirt and Pip squeaks.

"I can't believe he's still in your pocket." My voice, heavy with emotion, is as squeaky as Pip's.

"He's not the only one who has stuck around," Pace replies. I look down and see Cat twining through his legs.

"We should follow the cat," Mary says. "He'll know the way out."

"We've got to move on," Hans says. "See if any of the others have survived."

We set out, going the only way we can. We're above the village and going away from the lift. Pace carries the lamp and we walk behind Mary and Hans with Alcide, Adam, and James behind us. Cat scampers ahead, meowing into the darkness. I don't know if he's calling out for his friends or mourning the ones he lost. He seems to know where he's going, and as there is no other way for us to go we follow until we come to a cross tunnel. There are only two directions for us to go in, as back is not an option.

We all stop. Cat sniffs the air and takes off to the right. Hans and Mary look at each other for a moment. "I trust his instincts more than mine," Mary says, so we continue on after Cat.

"Can't we use one of the escape hatches?" Pace asks.

"Most all of them are on the other side of the river," I say. "We'll have to find a way to cross over. We're on the outside boundary of the mines."

"This is where we were going to make new tunnels," James says. "Fat chance of that now as the charges are underwater."

"You don't know that for sure," I say. "We won't know anything until the water subsides."

"The explosion must have damaged the dome reservoir," Pace says.

"The lift was close to it," James says. "If they shot flames down one of those old tunnels that were flooded and there was a gas pocket it would have blown the walls for certain."

"I wonder where the birds went," Alcide says. "They flew by us, didn't they? Or did I imagine it?"

"They did," I say.

"Quiet!" Hans holds up his hand. "There's someone ahead."

We all hear the noise, but it echoes strangely, in a way I've never heard before. It is louder and harsher, not muffled by the many tunnels. We move on, cautiously as if we're afraid we will find something worse than what we've experienced before us. Cat keeps going but we turn off, drawn by the noise.

It takes me a while to realize that we're in what I called our cave. The cave with the rushing river where Pace and I had hid. This tunnel never led there before, but that is because the walls were still in place. Pace shines the lamp out; the cave is too big to show everything, but from what we can see, it looks as if the dome has fallen into it. Indeed it has. Dim light filters down from above through the tangle of debris that looms before us.

"Now we know where the birds went," Alcide says.

We all stand there, mouths agape as we stare at the destruction. "The explosion must have weakened it," Hans comments.

"Can we climb out?" James asks.

"There's no way to get to it," Hans says. Indeed there isn't. We can't reach it and even if we could, one misstep would send us tumbling into the river.

"Hallo!"

We look over to the top of the long and sloping ledge. How many trips did I make down that ledge, going to Pace? Now it's a death trap. Everything I had in this world is gone, lost to the raging river. I know in my heart that nothing that I lost really matters. Joy fills me at the sight of a group of people gathered as they wave at us.

"Praise God, it's Freddy," Hans says. "Stay put!" he yells back and we backtrack to the tunnel that will lead us that way.

Twenty people are there, most of them children from the school. "We were coming to the fight from tunnel fifteen when we heard the explosion," Freddy explains to his father as Hans pulls him into his arms. "We found these wandering about and brought them with us," he says of the children. Freddy is only twelve and tries to show a brave front for his father. He crumples for a moment as Hans hugs him but quickly regains his composure.

Mary kneels among the children. "Where's Sally?" she asks.

"She was behind us when the water came," a little boy says. "She was carrying Sarah because she hurt her ankle."

"We never saw her," Freddy says. Mary nods her head in understanding that her daughter is likely gone. She walks off a few paces and we give her the time she needs.

"You did good, son," Hans says.

"We can't go back the way we came," Freddy says. "It's flooded. What about Ma and the village?"

"It's gone," Hans says quietly so the other children can't hear. "Some got out but I don't know who. We got out through the council chamber. The other way was flooded." Freddy bites his lip to hold back his grief. The little ones look at us with fear showing on their faces. A few of them cry, snuffling silently.

James, Alcide, and Adam move off in different directions to check out the tunnels. Adam goes back to the village. I know he's hoping for a miracle with Peggy. It would have to be a miracle for her to have survived, but I don't blame him for trying, for not giving up hope. We all know our only way out is into the dome, but we don't know what waits for us there. It's certain death in my mind, especially after the disaster that's just happened.

I lean against Pace for the moment, so grateful that we are still together when so many people are lost. Cat comes back to us once more and paws at my knees. I have no answers for him. I don't know what will happen to us. What if we're trapped without access to food or supplies, trapped in between the world that was and the world that hates us? How long will it take us to die?

"Look what we found," Alcide says as he comes back. I look up to see Ghost and the five other ponies that work my shift following along behind him. Their coats are wet; they must have swum but they made it out.

"I can't believe they survived." Ghost comes straight to me and bumps his head against my chest. I put my arms around his neck and tell him how smart he is. How happy I am to see him. The rest of the ponies gather tightly together behind him as they are in unfamiliar territory now. I know the sound of my voice soothes them so I keep talking in low tones to Ghost.

"Good thing you unlocked their stalls." Pace stands close by and rubs one of the ponies. I nod in agreement, overcome with relief that the ponies are safe, but also feel guilty because so many were lost.

"There are more cave-ins." James comes from the opposite direction. "New tunnels have opened up. It looks like the river has changed course."

"It probably has," Hans says.

"What do we do?" Freddy asks.

"I think we should follow the river," I say. "It has to lead somewhere."

Adam returns. His face is solemn and he shakes his head. As Freddy said, that way is flooded.

"We should move on," Mary says. "Put the little ones on the ponies. We don't know how long we'll be walking."

Or where we will wind up . . .

We put the children on the ponies' backs and I show them how to wrap their fingers in their manes to stay on. I lead Ghost by his halter with Cat stalking ahead of me and the rest of the ponies following. Pace, Alcide, Adam, and James take children on their backs and Mary and Hans take the littlest in their arms. The bigger ones, a mix of boys and girls who are around ten years old, walk as James leads us to the new tunnel.

The going is rough and the tunnel slopes downward the farther in we go. The new tunnel is wide but the way is littered with rocks and boulders and I have to lead the ponies around them individually while Cat jumps from one to the next. I bring up the rear. Luckily it isn't a long walk and I soon join the rest in a large cavern with a waterfall. The roar of the water strums against my ears and Ghost lays his ears back at the strange sound.

"I don't think this is new," I practically shout. "I think it's always been here. It's just the progression of the river."

We stand at the bottom of the falls, which pours out from beneath a cave wall. Mist rises around us, quickly soaking our clothes.

"Look!" Alcide says. There is something in the water. Pace follows the line of Alcide's arm with the lamp and we see whatever it is being tossed about in the whirlpools at the bottom of the falls before it shoots out toward the bank. Alcide sets down the child on his back and runs ahead to grab it.

It is part of a chair. The back and legs are broken off, leaving nothing but the seat, which is woven with braided strips of fabric. Pace shines the lamp on it so the faded colors of the fabric show.

"It's from my house," Mary states. "But how?"

"Everything will wind up here eventually," Hans says. "Including the bodies."

"It has to go somewhere," I say.

We move on, walking beside the river until we come to a wide place where sand has gathered. "I'm thirsty," the child on Pace's back says. Cat has already bounded ahead and crouches next to the water to drink.

"We all are," Hans says. We stop and I lift the children from the ponies' backs and ask them to take each one by the halter down to the water to drink.

Pace kneels down with the lamp by his side and I go to join him. He drinks, and then scoops up water in the palm of his hand. He takes Pip from his pocket and sits him in his palm. The little bird dips his beak in the water and drinks. I slake my own thirst by scooping water into my hands and drinking. I take off my kerchief and dip it in the water and wipe my face with it.

Adam stands on a rock up from where we drink. He looks out over the water. More and more things from our village float by, pieces of our lives now as scattered as we are. I know he's looking for Peggy. I dread seeing the first body that shows up. At least now, we have the hope that others might have made it.

I look downriver. I see nothing but darkness. What if I'm wrong? What if it is another dead end and the river just falls farther into the earth? What if we're stuck here without food and the bodies start coming and wash up around us? What if the water rises and we are trapped and eventually drown? These people are here because of me. Because I believed that the river would lead us out. I know out is there. I just have to find it.

"Pip!"

I look at Pace as he calls out after the bright yellow bird. I can see him, flying downstream, a bright yellow patch in the blackness of the cave. Pace shines his light out over the water, swinging it back and forth, trying to find him.

"Come on." I grab Pace's hand and we take off downriver while I try to keep the tiny bird in my sight. We run along the sand and then the going gets rough again with rocks and boulders so we have to slow down. I didn't even realize we'd curved away from the others until the sound of the falls fades from my ears.

"Where did he go?"

"I don't know," I say. "I lost him."

Pace flashes the light around. Cat bounds up after us, jumps up on a rock, turns around and meows, and takes off again.

"Where is he off to?" Pace asks.

"Let's find out." I keep an eye on Cat in hopes that he will lead us to Pip. Cat jumps over rocks and quickly runs on with his tail